NINE NORTH

ART SMUKLER

Published by DIAMOND STREET PUBLISHING, 2022.

NINE NORTH

First edition. November 16, 2022.

Written by ART SMUKLER.

Special thanks to Seth Taras, a brilliant, talented photographer, who allowed me to use his image for my cover.

Many thanks to Ed Caine, Rich Smukler, Neal Koss, and Linda Smukler, whose encouragement and ideas helped to shape the final version of NINE NORTH.

Thank you Michael Banayan, for your many financial insights, not only for NINE NORTH, but through the years.

Thanks to Ira Lesser, MD, whose insights into the current state of hospital psychiatry were so helpful.

And of course, loving thanks to Cindy and Matt who have always supported my writing.

CHAPTER 1

Truth or Fantasy?

• • • •

TWO YEARS AND ONE DAY after Nelson Bennett died, he rose from the dead.

Amidst the hundreds of people strolling down the Third Street Promenade in Santa Monica, California he stood alone, hair dark brown, not prematurely gray like it used to be, and at least thirty pounds lighter.

"Nelson!" Jake yelled. "Nelson!" The man was about fifty feet away – close enough for Jake to clearly make out his features; far enough for Jake to wonder if he was hallucinating. There was no way Jake could ever forget or mistake Nelson's face. It was the face of his older brother, his only brother and only sibling.

The man turned, stared straight at Jake, his blue eyes locking onto Jake's blue eyes. Abruptly, he glanced over his shoulder, a startled look transforming his gaunt, clean-shaven face, and he placed his index finger in front of his lips. Then he pivoted, and like a snowflake landing on a hot windshield, melted away.

"Stop!" Jake hollered, shoving past two young couples walking in front of him, pushing his way through the endless crowd of people toward the spot where Nelson's image had vanished.

There in front of the designer eyeglass store, Jake stretched his six-foot frame and stood on his tiptoes to see over the passing crowd. No sign of Nelson anywhere. How could there be? Nelson's ashes were sitting on a shelf in his closet.

Jake took a deep breath and broke into a run. He knew his behavior was absurd and that Nelson was dead. He also knew what he had just seen.

Jogging and pushing his way down the busy street, Jake's heart slammed wildly inside his chest. Block after block he ran, scanning both sides of the promenade – the Apple Store, the Gap, the soap shop, the perfume store... Drops of perspiration rolled from his forehead into his deep-set eyes, down the sides of his neck, soaking his shirt collar. He pulled off his blue, bulky-knit sweater and tied it around his waist. No one seemed to pay any attention to the lean, twenty-nine-year-old man with dark, shoulder-length hair frantically running down the street – just another LA workout freak.

Jake raced past the AMC Theater, Starbucks, a street vendor selling silver jewelry, a group of people listening to three men with long, dark, wild beards playing Flamenco music. A moment of disorientation took him away from the chase. Why was he running after his dead brother?

Slowing to a walk, he dried his forehead with the back of his hand and glanced at his watch – 2:30. Thirty-minutes before he had to be at the restaurant to set up for the late-afternoon and evening crowd.

Jake reached the location where Nelson had appeared then disappeared, right outside the eyeglass store. The display shelves were filled with Bole, Kawasaki, and Armani glasses – a hi-tech, hi-end store, *definitely* Nelson's kind of place. Nelson loved glasses and had three or four different pairs that he would alternate. Sitting together in the outdoor restaurant in Hong Kong, six months before he died two-and-a-half years ago, Jake remembered him praising the workmanship on his new frameless, Titanium lenses. Look how thin the glass is, how light the frames are. He encouraged Jake to try them on, but since Jake didn't wear glasses, they made him dizzy. Nelson was near blind without his. The man Jake just saw wasn't wearing glasses. He clearly saw his blue eyes, exact replicas of his own eyes. Contact lenses? Lasik surgery?

In Hong Kong, Nelson told Jake that he was involved in an international investment project, and he needed to meet personally with a few of the principals. What type of project? Jake asked numerous times. Nelson was always evasive, changing the subject, making the clichéd joke, 'If I told you, they'd have to kill you'. But it wasn't the least funny. Nelson worked for Coastal VC, a high-end venture capital group. Usually, Nelson loved explaining the ins and outs of his investments. How they picked one company to invest in and why they rejected another. Often, he'd laugh and equate his business to Shark Tank, the popular TV show.

One thing for sure, Nelson really enjoyed the miles of malls, shops and restaurants that connected directly to their hotel, The Mandarin Oriental. The entire jaunt was a corporate expense, Nelson announced, encouraging Jake to just relax and enjoy himself.

Could Nelson have been here in Santa Monica shopping? Jake shook his head in frustration and disbelief. How could a dead man shop? How could a reasonable man even have this crazy discussion with himself? Nelson died in a plane crash travelling from a small, private airport in the Pocono mountains to Philadelphia International. Soon after the Cessna took off, it lost power, exploded, and went down in Lake Wallenpaupack, the third largest lake in Pennsylvania with a fifty-two-mile shoreline. The identification of bodies, there were two, was made using dental records. One was Nelson's; the other was the pilot.

Jake entered the eyeglass store. It was ultra-modern with a glass island in the center, surrounded by dozens of glass-and-chrome display shelves. Classical music, Mozart, played softly from speakers in the ceiling.

A thin, short-statured Asian man wearing a blue smock, stood behind the counter. He was talking to a woman with long dark hair. Jake froze. From the back she looked like Gina, but a little shorter. How many times a week did he still panic when he saw someone who looked like her? Anything more than zero was too many. When would his mind release her image, let him move on? A year had passed. Not a word. Nothing. Why would there be? She was probably happily married.

"Thank you," Jake heard the woman say to the salesman. Then she lapsed into a foreign language. Maybe Chinese?

The woman, an attractive Asian wearing a form-fitting Cashmere sweater, left the counter area, glanced at Jake, and immediately dropped her eyes. She walked quickly out of the store, almost like she was repressing the urge to run.

Jake approached the counter and took a deep breath.

"Can I help you?" the optician asked, his accent belying his British schooling.

"Yes. I'm looking for a pair of sunglasses. Something that might be good for sports...tennis, maybe skiing."

"Prescription?"

"No."

"You'll need impact-resistant plastic, UV protection, and anti-glare."

"Sounds like you're from England," Jake said.

"Actually, Hong Kong." The man smiled, a friendly easy smile that filled his thin face with a sense of merriment and friendship.

"Hong Kong? Really?"

"Why are you surprised?"

"No, no I'm not. I um...was just curious." Jake was surprised, shocked really. He wasn't the kind of person who believed in coincidences. Seeing Nelson, thinking of Hong Kong, now meeting a guy from Hong Kong? Of course, co-incidences could occur, but his take on life was that people often made their own luck or misfortune. He was a great example of turning a lot of good things into garbage. In fact, he had turned that particular quality into an artform. "Do you like it here?" Jake asked.

"Very much."

Jake smiled, took a pair of Bolle` sunglasses off a small rack on the counter and tried them on, looking at himself in the mirror. They fit comfortably, wrapping sleekly around his head – maybe a little like an Italian actor whose name escaped him. "I really like these." He looked at himself again in the mirror.

The optician smiled. One of his front teeth was quite thin, shaped like a needle. "I like them too. Maybe a little like a movie star?"

Jake laughed, glanced at the optician, and back in the mirror.

The optician took out his calculator and tapped in some numbers. "They are ninety dollars, on sale for seventy-five. A bargain."

Jake really did want the glasses. He lost his only pair a few weeks ago. "Okay," he said, taking out his wallet and handing the man a VISA. What's an-other few bucks when he already owed over four thousand? "I was wondering. Was there a man in here about ten maybe fifteen minutes ago? About my height and weight, Caucasian, dark curly hair, wearing a black leather jacket?"

The optician motioned for Jake to insert his credit card and punch in his email address in the electronic processor. "I didn't see anyone of that descrip-tion," he said, his voice totally without inflection; the light-hearted sense of connection and warmth were gone. "Do you want an email or paper receipt?"

"Paper's fine." Jake was mildly confused. Was he imagining the optician's change in attitude? "Would you do me a big favor and ask the other salespeople if they saw him. It's important."

The optician hesitated then nodded. "Of course. Just give me a minute." He walked out from behind the counter and disappeared through a door that led to the back of the store.

Minutes later he returned and shrugged. "Sorry, no one saw the person you described." He methodically cleaned the new glasses with cleaning solution and lens paper, put them in a case, and handed it to Jake.

"Thanks," Jake said, staring hard at the optician. Was he going crazy? One-minute warmth, the next coldness? Imagining an apparition of his dead brother?

The optician nodded, his eyes flickering out toward the promenade, then back at Jake. "Thank you, Mr. Bennett."

"How did you –" Jake cut off his own question in mid-breath. Of course, the optician knew who he was, he just gave him his credit card. He was really losing it!

Jake left the store and walked outside. The sky was still blue, the temperature 75, the promenade still teaming with people. He put on his new sunglasses and took a deep breath. He knew he had to accept the fact that Nelson was gone. Other people suffered losses; they accepted them with a reasonable level of grace and maturity. Why couldn't he? There were a lot of things he just refused to accept.

Maybe if his book got published? For four years he had given up everything to make it happen – a potential good job, a potential wife and life-partner, someone he truly loved – all of it to become a writer. Every day, at least eight hours a day, he worked at his trade. Three failed novels. Now, number four was being read by an agent. Four grueling years of hauling charred ahi, pasta, veal scaloppini and kissing everyone's ass for tips. And what did he have to show for it? A crappy apartment, a broken-down car, thousands of dollars of debt, and a lonely, empty life. Nothing was worth that kind of payoff. Was it?

Turning down a side street to get away from the crowds, Jake stopped, tied back his hair in a ponytail, and tucked in his shirt. It was show time. Time to plaster on a smile. Time to survive another night of his *day* job.

CHAPTER 2

Ciao Ristorante, located a half-block west of the Promenade on Arizona Avenue, sported twenty-foot-high, teak ceilings punctuated by hi-tech spotlights, concrete floors, and four dozen stainless steel tables covered with crisp, black tablecloths and white, linen napkins. Each table was set with Limoges look-alike plates, and wineglasses that begged to be filled with Napa's buttery, oak-barrel finest. Ciao's specialty was making the *beautiful people* feel even more beautiful, condescendingly allowing them to spend a small fortune in the presence of LA's elite. Like Spago's in Beverly Hills, only the connected LA privileged were blessed with a table in the atrium of the restaurant. The unconnected, if deemed worthy after a minimum wait of four weeks, would be seated elsewhere, and brag for weeks about the experience. Jake had gotten lucky last year and because of his good looks, ability to speak Italian, and previous wait-experience, was hired. At least now he made enough money to pay for his apartment, crappy as it was, and enough to eat. Other than that, he was truly the stereotypical, starving writer.

Dressed in black, the wait-staff worked up a nightly sweat worthy of an afternoon at Equinox. Once the shift started, it was run and smile until their feet burned, and their mouths ached from keeping that godawful frozen grin in place.

"Hi, I'm Jake and I'll be your server," Jake announced to the table of six, forcing the required smile, doing his best to push Nelson's image as far from consciousness as it would go. Not an easy task, because since Nelson's death, not a day passed that Jake hadn't thought about him and missed him terribly. He wasn't just an older brother, five years his senior, he was his best friend and the person he always looked up to.

He was there for him when their parents, Leo and Bonnie, were killed in a devastating car crash. They were waiting at a light, just blocks from their home in Lower Merion, Pennsylvania, when a truck skidded on ice and T-boned their Prius. According to the police report, they were killed instantly.

Jake was a senior in high school, already accepted to the U of P. Nelson, who lived in an amazing bachelor pad in center city Philly, immediately moved home. Within months they sold the house, realized enough money for Jake to pay his tuition, get a student apartment, and have enough to cover daily expenses.

Nelson adamantly refused to take a penny from the sale of the house. He resumed his bachelor life, and *always* did everything in his power to be a great brother and friend. He encouraged Jake to follow his dream and to do whatever it took to achieve it. Even if the dream didn't work out, his philosophy was for Jake to still give it his all.

Jake's thoughts drifted to his latest novel, CAIN'S BROTHER, a thriller about two brothers, one a serial killer renegade professor who murdered for the thrill of outsmarting *everyone*, and the protagonist a police detective desperate to find his brother before he murdered again. Jake wondered for the thousandth time whether Danny Gillette liked the manuscript and would represent him. Wasn't it finally time for a break?

After Jake sent The Gillette Agency the first three chapters of CAIN'S BROTHER, Danny requested the whole manuscript, with the proviso that his agency would have exclusive rights until a decision was made. With many best-selling authors currently under Danny's guidance what else could Jake say, but "Thank you, Mr. Gillette, thank you very much."

CAIN'S BROTHER took over 18 months to write. Jake figured that one of Danny's proteges was screening his three-hundred-and-fifty pages. He or she would then give it the thumbs-up or thumbs-down. Then, King Danny would make his pronouncement. Yes, Jake, all your agony and hard work will be rewarded. No, Jake, you will remain a waiter surrounded by yuppies and arrogant narcissists ordering hundred-plus-dollar bottles of wine, complaining that their Chilean seabass is not real Chilean seabass and demanding to switch to veal scaloppini. Then they'll say, after the veal was more than half-eaten, that it was too chewy and will refuse to pay.

"We have four wonderful appetizer specials," Jake announced to the three men and three women dressed in black and gray Armani outfits. The thought raced through his mind that God-forbid someone came in to Ciao dressed in red or bright green, the whole place would go blind with shock. "And three entree specials," Jake heard himself say, the boredom in his voice not at all attractive. He took a deep breath, again forcing a smile. He wondered what would happen if his face muscles just gave out and drooped like the jowls of a

Bloodhound or if he started screaming that they should all shove their designer clothes up their fat asses.

He concentrated on keeping the smile in place. His goal was to do his job, charm everyone, make good tips, and get the hell out of here. After this torture, he would once again check his e-mail and see whether Danny had decided. This was the end of week six and Danny said it would take about a month. Stop obsessing! He admonished himself. Stay positive!

After his shift, he would meet Anna and some friends in Hermosa Beach at The Creole and listen to Jazz. Next week, after Anna's twenty-fifth birthday party, he would tell her the truth, a truth he had practiced dozens of times inside his head but couldn't bring himself to say. His latest version was that the relationship wasn't working. It wasn't her fault; it was his, his problem with commitment, with spending so much time writing he had no time for anything else. She was wonderful and shouldn't take his action as a reflection on herself. Jake hoped that once this was resolved he would finally be able to sleep through the night. It was agony waking up at four in the morning, staring at the ceiling, and listening to the sound of Anna's breathing. He just wanted to be alone. Not once, ever, did that happen with Gina. He had wanted to spend the rest of his life with her. But par for the course, he screwed it up.

"We have chopped Bermuda onions, capers, and gravlax –" As Jake spoke, he noticed the woman at the end of the table staring at him. "Jesus," slipped out of his mouth. It was Gina Carlton. This time it was the *real* Gina Carlton. He blinked his eyes and looked again. Why couldn't it have been her this afternoon? Why now? He caught his breath and instantly felt his heart begin to pound.

"Hi, Jake," Gina said, a big smile on her face, and a big stone on her left ring finger. "It's nice seeing you after all this time." Her eyes didn't look nearly as happy as the smile on her lips. Jake's eyes were filled with shock...and horror, definitely horror. Why did she have to be here, to see him like this?

She was still as beautiful as he remembered – full lips, Caribbean green eyes, dark hair (now chic-punk rather than long like when they lived together), and slim (the kind of muscular-slimness that came from being an avid bike rider and tennis player). Damn it! Why couldn't she have gained fifty pounds? He swallowed. It wouldn't have mattered. He still would have loved her.

"Hi, Gina," Jake said, trying to hold his ground and not abruptly melt into a puddle of shame. Twelve months felt like twelve seconds. The end of their relationship was still a raw wound that often surfaced in the dark hours, the times when his confidence faltered, when he wondered whether she had been right. Was he just another LA writer swimming against a massive riptide, flailing until he sank and drowned in his own inadequacy? They were supposed to get engaged, to marry, to spend the rest of their lives together. The story wasn't supposed to end this way.

Jake would never forget how Gina tried to be reasonable. To the bitter end she was a class act. One evening after work she poured them both a glass of wine and fixed those big green eyes on him. "Jake, will you try and keep an open mind and listen to me?"

Jake took a swallow of the wine.

Gina put down her glass. Her eyes were filled with an intense desperation. "Jake, write in the evening or the weekends. Spend as much time as you need," she said, reaching out and clutching his hand. "I'll be understanding and patient. Please be realistic! You're bright and resourceful and can get a great job plus write as much as you want. Your all-or-nothing approach doesn't seem to be working."

Jake sighed. This conversation was not a new one. It was a well-worn path that always led to a rocky abyss. "Gina, I'm not ready to work for some money management firm or economic think-tank. A dual major in English and economics was a great education, but I'm doing what I truly love." Jake wanted desperately for Gina to change the direction that the discussion was taking, to see it his way.

Twelve months ago, Gina just stared at Jake, her expression turning from desperation to acceptance. Jake was just being Jake. When he made up his mind not much could change it. Nevertheless, she couldn't help but try one last time. "Are you saying you'd rather be a waiter than be with me? I thought we had something pretty special."

"We do. We do have something special. I love you. But writing is what I dream about, what my passion is. Should I just give it up? You sound like my father. In high school I mentioned that I wanted to be a writer. 'Jake, be realistic,' he said. 'How many writers make a living writing? Believe me, son, not many. I'm worried about you.' He'd reiterate and reiterate. My father was a good, kind man. He got stuck working for *his* father as an accountant. Never made much money, always afraid to take a risk. He had the smallest house on a pretty, tree-lined street, and was always worried that there would be a catastrophe, and he'd lose it. He feared that we'd all be out on the street, homeless.

"Gina, I'm not stupid. I know I already have three failed novels. But I'm not about to give up. You've got to trust that I won't be a waiter forever. I'll be successful and take good care of you." He reached out to pull her closer. She stood up and moved a few feet away from him.

"Jake just be realistic. No-matter how good you are, it could take forever to be published. Where does that leave us? California real estate is a fortune. We knew that when we decided to leave Pennsylvania and move here. Cars are a fortune. Should we spend the rest of our lives living in a one-bedroom rental and driving cars that are seconds away from being donated to 'Save a Child'?"

"You don't think I'm good enough to make it, do you? Is that the issue? You said you liked my writing..." Gina's opinion meant a lot to him. She was bright and sensitive and an avid reader. Her years of training as an economics analyst and a mathematics whiz gave her an analytical approach that was refreshing and often helpful. If she didn't like his work, what did that say about what he did, about his chances for success? She was his target audience!

"I do like your work. That's not at all what I'm saying. Jake, life can be very harsh. Sometimes just being good isn't enough. Like they say, 'It's not what you do, but who you know.' You don't know anyone. You spend hours and hours and months and months holed up in front of your computer. You've put years into the effort. Where are you? Still waiting tables and hardly able to make ends meet."

"Gina, you've got to understand, I just can't throw it all away. It's not in my nature."

"Oh, I see. Now it's genetic. You're not really in control of your life. Nature wins over nurture." She shook her head and took a deep breath. "The truth is that you just refuse to compromise. It's Jake's way or no way. Jake, you're an immature, selfish man. Well, man is a stretch. More like a stubborn teenager." Like the wind carrying a leaf far from the mother tree, Gina turned, and silently floated away and out of his life.

It hurt Jake, but it didn't hurt enough for him to go out and get a real job and call her. Not one day passed when he didn't think of finding her, begging for forgiveness, and agreeing that her ideas made sense. He just couldn't do it. Now, another year older and another possible failed novel, nothing had changed. He was still waiting tables and praying hourly for an agent. He was a pathetic excuse for a man.

Taxi, an almost fifty-year-old song by Harry Chapin, a folk singer who died before Jake was born, flitted through his mind. In the song Harry's old girl-friend, now obviously rich, got into his taxi. At the end of the ride, she handed Harry a hundred-dollar bill. Rather than return the money and keep his pride, Harry stashed the hundred in his shirt pocket. Jake heard the song many years ago when he saw a play based on Harry's life. After the show, he bought the CD.

Jake smiled at Gina and took a deep breath. "You look great. I like your hair." Having Gina see him still waiting tables made him cringe. He just wanted to get the hell out of the restaurant and disappear, to crawl deep under his covers, find a warm safe hole, and burrow until the world disappeared.

"Jake, I'd like you to meet Kevin, my fiancé. Kevin, this is Jake, an old friend. A writer." She said it straight, without an ounce of sarcasm. It almost brought tears to Jake's eyes. Since I never made a cent writing how could I possibly consider myself a real writer? Jake thought. If I was anything, I was a cliché, like all LA waiters who were either writers, actors, or models.

Jake swiped at the drops of sweat dripping down his forehead and looked around the table. Gina and her friends looked straight out of Beverly Hills; dazzling jewelry, Rolex watches, clothes almost surely not off the Macy's rack... He flashed back to the time he and Gina were in Macy's and he bought a new sport jacket. At that moment, Nelson had called to chat. Jake told him about the cool jacket he had just purchased. Nelson asked where he bought it, and Jake said they were still in Macy's. Nelson snorted. What? Jake said. Macy's? Nelson answered. I guarantee it can't be cool. Jake retorted. You know Nelson, you're an asshole! Nelson laughed and then Jake laughed with him. He told Gina what Nelson said, and the three of them, Nelson on speaker mode, in the middle of the Men's Department, laughed hysterically. Ever since Gina left, nothing was funny. Ever! Life really sucked.

Jake gritted his teeth and sighed. It could have been him sitting there next to Gina in an Armani cashmere sweater from Saks and a spiky haircut. But he was the smart one, wasn't he? He stuck to his ideals and didn't cave to the whims of society. He was true to his spirit, to his passion. He was a writer!

He had the courage that his poor father never had. Jake's eyes glistened, on the verge of filling with tears. Now he had the very noble task of being Gina's waiter.

He looked at Gina and shrugged, the kind of shrug that said she was right, that he was a fool and a loser. Gina just looked at him, her eyes also filling with tears.

Jake knew that he needed the money as much as Harry Chapin needed the money, but he couldn't do it. He just didn't have the balls to do what was needed.

"I'm sorry, Gina," he said. "I'm sorry for whatever I put you through." With that he turned and walked out of the restaurant.

CHAPTER 3

The early October storm that dumped over three feet of snow in the Sierras, putting the snowboarders and skiers into a state of powder-based nirvana, finally arrived in the southland. The balmy, sunny afternoon was now a chilly, rain-drenched evening. The promenade that was so crowded just a few hours before had thinned to a small core of street people pushing their worldly belongings in food carts, and a smattering of shivering mid-westerners determined to enjoy their few days on the west coast searching for the perfect California trinket.

Jake was three blocks from the restaurant, walking quickly, filled with images of Gina, of jaded memories twisting his gut into a hapless knot of self-doubt. Finally, conscious of the fact that he was headed in the opposite direction from where his car was parked, he shivered, buttoned up his shirt collar, and reversed direction toward fourth street.

Jake couldn't help but reexamine each nuance of what Gina said, each change in expression, the moment that her eyes welled with tears. Was it his imagination that she might still care? He harshly rubbed his face with both hands and walked a little faster. How humiliating! A waiter. He was her freaking waiter! It was no wonder he ran out of Ciao like the place was on fire.

Now what? No money in the bank. One credit card maxed, the other on the verge. Rent due. Living with a woman he didn't love. Hallucinating his brother's return from the dead.

He pulled his cell phone from his pants pocket and called the restaurant.

"Ciao Ristorante."

"Cynthia, it's Jake."

"Jake, where are you? Simone's going nuts."

"I'm on my way to get my car and head for the emergency room. Something I ate for lunch from a street vendor is wreaking havoc with my GI tract. Not a pretty sight. I think I'm bleeding...actually, I am bleeding." Jake sighed. It was only a minor lie. Big red gobs of his self-respect were lying all over Gina's table. Right now, her fiancé and all her friends were probably wondering what was going on, asking her how she could have ever hooked up with such a loser. Probably just an understandable lapse in a young girl's judgement during her slum-

13

ming student days, they would assume, as the new waiter filled their crystal wineglasses with a perfectly balanced and earthy Pinot Noir.

"God, Jake. That's horrible. Are you okay?"

"The ER's not far. Tell Simone I'm sorry, and I'll call in tomorrow when I'm feeling better."

"Okay, Jake. I hope you're alright. Simone's right here. Wanna talk to her?"

"No thanks, Cynthia. I need to get going." Jake passed the storefront that used to house Barnes & Noble bookstore, a tightness gripping his chest. What if Danny didn't like the book? Think positively, he admonished himself. What if the arrogant S.O.B. who's been keeping me waiting for two weeks more than he promised, is enjoying it, maybe even showing it to a few publishers?

Jake turned off the well-lit promenade onto a dark side street. His car was parked at the end of the block, the same deteriorating Alfa Romeo convertible he owned when Gina and he lived together in Philadelphia, when they were juniors at Penn. It was a decade old with over two-hundred-thousand miles, a bashed in passenger side door, and a failing clutch.

Gritting his teeth, Jake felt a renewed sense of determination. For him, waiting tables was simply the means to an end. Right? End of story. He was a writer. A damn good writer! You can't write if you don't eat. It was Gina's loss that she didn't stick around for the next chapter. Her loss entirely. Next time they meet he'd serve her his best-seller on a bed of mixed greens. Wrap the utensils in a New York Times best-seller list.

Reaching the Alfa, he dug in his pocket for the keys and froze. The convertible top was slashed, and the front door unlocked. Contents of the glove compartment were strewn across the driver's seat, soaked by his half-finished container of coffee knocked out of the cup holder and the pouring rain leaking from the cut canvas top.

"Assholes," Jake muttered, glancing all around. The street was empty, no evidence of anyone lurking.

He opened the door, angrily swept everything on to the floor, and sat down heavily behind the wheel. The advantage of being poor was that there was nothing to steal. In fact, if they had taken everything it would have saved him the trouble of having to clean out the mess from this rolling piece of shit.

Jake inserted the ignition key and listened to the engine first putter than roar to life. He put the car in gear and headed south toward the 10 freeway. At the entrance to the freeway, he glanced at the green overhead sign and sighed. From the ridiculous to the fucking ridiculous. First, he saw Nelson's apparition, then the live embodiment of the only woman he ever loved, and lastly his piece-of-shit car was vandalized. He accelerated onto the onramp, the flap of torn canvas fluttering in the wind, and the rain wetting his face. "Go fuck yourself!" he yelled to a God that he didn't believe in, a God who obviously took perverse pleasure in heaping abuse on unbelievers.

• • • •

HE WALKED UP THE CREAKY wooden-stairs to his third-floor apartment, oblivious of the gray paint peeling from the moldy walls and the scent of cooked food that inundated the fifty-year-old, twenty-apartment Hermosa Beach complex. He unlocked the door, turned on the light, and stepped into the small living room. For the twentieth time that day, he pulled his phone from his pocket and glanced at the list of e-mails. "Jesus," he mumbled, his heart quickening.

He clicked open the message from Gillette Literary Associates and stared at the short message. "Sorry, it's not for us. Best of luck, Danny."

Jake's head felt like a fifty-pound cannonball, hanging by neck muscles that lost their will; so heavy it pushed his chin into his chest.

Was this his fate? A Kafkaesque *NO EXIT*, condemned to wait tables until he was an old man. While his peers lived their lives as doctors, lawyers, and stock gurus, he was ordained to recite the daily dinner-specials, an invisible creature who made his living being a servant. Jake picked up an empty glass and threw it against the far wall. It hit a curtain and bounced intact on the carpet – the glass too thick and too cheap to even give him the satisfaction of splintering into a thousand pieces.

Jake stood up, walked across the small living room into the bedroom, and sat down heavily on the unmade bed. When was the last time the sheets were changed? Yesterday? Two Weeks? He didn't remember or care. He got undressed, leaving his clothes in a heap on the floor, and took a shower. Standing under the hot water he decided to push all of this out of his mind. There were other agents. Why let one man's opinion get to him like this? He stood in the shower until the water turned cold and his shivering became uncontrollable.

• • • •

DRESSED IN A PAIR OF jeans, a heavy woolen sweater, a rain jacket and a pair of hiking boots, Jake walked quickly down Hermosa Avenue from his apartment on Seventh Street toward Pier Avenue, six blocks away. The heavy rain, now just a drizzle, kept the usual Friday night crowd indoors; giving the illusion that the community filled with restaurants, bars, and dozens of shops was once again just a sleepy beach town. Jake was determined to not let Danny's decision get him down and was committed to sending out query letters and sample chapters to other agents in the morning.

He glanced in the window of a store specializing in used clothing and remembered the day that he and Gina spent the afternoon laughing while they tried on outfits for a 70's disco party. He pushed the memory out of his mind. Why remember something that can only cause pain? He walked a little faster and for a moment smiled. The way he was going he'd have to block everything from his mind.

In front of the Comedy and Magic Club, a stocky Asian man, wearing a Hawaiian-style, short-sleeve shirt, leaned against the building, protected from the drizzle by the overhead marquis. The man took a deep drag on his cigarette, the smoke catching the reflection of the light then disappearing into the darkened sky. This Sunday, Jay Leno was performing, a *special* benefiting a children's charity. For years Jake had planned to get tickets to see him, but never seemed to find the time...or the money. Besides, just the fact that Leno had dozens and dozens of exclusive, fabulous cars really pissed him off. How much would it cost to have the top on his Alfa repaired? As usual, too much.

At the corner of Hermosa Ave. and Pier Ave., Jake waited for the light to change. A young couple sitting at a window table in a little Italian restaurant caught his attention. The way they looked at each other, the apparent earnestness and intensity of their conversation, tore at him. That was the way he remembered feeling with Gina. They were inseparable, an amalgam of ideas and energy that seemed bound in titanium. He shook his head. Thinking about her was *not* a good idea.

A pair of young skateboarders, oblivious to the drizzle, dressed in baggy T-shirts and oversized shorts, hopped their boards over the curb, and glided across the rain-drenched street. Jake followed them, reaching the end of the intersection that led to a block-long, gray-brick plaza. It was flanked on both sides by restaurants and bars, ending with the strand, a concrete miles-long walkway bordering the beach.

Jake walked through the almost deserted plaza and entered The Creole. He nodded to the humongous bouncer sitting just inside the front door, who barely moved his thick neck in return. A quartet was in the middle of an old Miles Davis piece, and the fifty or so people sitting in the long, narrow bar filled the air with laughter and loud voices.

Heading straight for the bar, Jake ordered a draft of Stella. This is a celebration, he told himself. I'm rededicating myself to my writing, and not letting anything stand in my way. He paid for the drink and gulped down a third of it. Working his way between the tables, he spotted Anna talking with her friend Tilly. Anna saw him and waved, a taut smile on her pretty face, her long, blond hair in a bun. There were no extra chairs at the little table. Jake found one, carried it over and sat down. What struck him, almost taking his breath away, was the fact that he couldn't do this anymore. Not for one more second.

Forcing himself to smile, Jake sat down and joined the two women. Anna smiled back, but the expression on her face was anything but happy.

Tilly stood up. "I'll be back." She leaned forward and kissed Anna on the forehead, and without glancing at Jake, left.

Jake watched as Tilly made her way to the bar. He looked at Anna. "Power outage. They closed the restaurant early," Jake said.

"I know," Anna said. "It's been obvious for months. I just didn't want to face it."

"What?" Jake said. "You know about the power outage?"

"Jake, stop it! Just say what you're really thinking. What you've been thinking and feeling."

Jake was frozen, his heart pounding. Slowly he nodded. She was right.

Anna just sat and stared at him, waiting.

"Anna, I'm sorry. It's nothing you did... You deserve better than me. I'm so obsessed with my writing that I've retreated into a selfish hole. I can't help it."

"Jake, that's probably all true, but there are a few more parts to this tawdry tale."

"What?"

"You don't love me. If you did, all this other stuff could be worked out."

Jake just sat there saying nothing. What could he say?

"The other thing is that you are a dishonest person."

"Dishonest?"

"Many-times you've said that fiction is truer than non-fiction. A great writer shares his soul and emotionally connects with his reader. How can you connect with anyone when you're so cut off from yourself, and you live a lie? You've known for a long time that you didn't want to spend the rest of your life with me. This was all a pretense, a guilt-ridden way to avoid the truth. But it's not all your fault. I just didn't have the courage to stand up for myself."

"I'm sorry, Anna."

Her eyes filled with tears. "Goodbye, Jake. It's over. Did you even notice that I moved all my stuff out of your apartment?"

"No...I didn't."

"Doesn't *that* tell you something?"

"Anna –"

She handed him her keys to the apartment. "Please Jake, just leave."

"I'm sorry. I didn't mean–"

Anna closed her eyes and shook her head.

Jake stood up and left the table. He walked outside and took a deep breath. The rain was coming down harder, and he pulled the hood up on his jacket. If this is what he wanted, why did he feel so sick to his stomach? Nauseous. He was a dishonest piece of shit who made one crappy decision after another. It not only hurt him, but it also hurt others. How could he have not noticed that all her clothes and things were gone? Was she that inconsequential? Was he that oblivious to everyone but himself?

A block later, he caught his breath. The same Asian guy who had been standing in front of the Comedy and Magic Club was across the street and matching his pace. What the hell? Jake started to jog. The guy said something into his phone and cut across the street toward him.

Jake darted into an alley. He ran past the backs of a half-dozen apartment buildings and down another alley. Then he pushed through a large hedge and into the alley behind 7th Street. Halfway down the block, he hauled down a rusty fire escape. After scampering up three stories to the top, he pulled open the unlocked bedroom window, and climbed into his apartment.

Using his iPhone flashlight, he ran over to his desk, opened the small drawer to the left of his laptop, and took out the nine-inch, Italian, out-the-front Stiletto, that he'd owned since he was thirteen years old. When he bought it in a shop in center city Philadelphia, for $30, with money from his Bar Mitzvah, his father spent forever pleading with him to return it, how dangerous it was. Jake agreed and then made sure to do a better job of hiding the knife. He understood that the knife was dangerous; the blade was double-edged and razor sharp, but nevertheless he wanted it. His father was just being a good dad.

Jake made sure the locking mechanism of the knife was in place and slid the weapon into his pocket. Now what? If the Asian guy had been following him, he already knew where he lived. He had to get out of here! He put his laptop, a change of underwear, another sweater, and his travel kit in a backpack. Was that a noise at his front door, someone turning the knob?

Quickly, he backed out the same window that he had entered, and pulled it shut. He scrambled down the fire-escape. When he reached the bottom, he thrust the rusted flight of steps back up to where it belonged. He spun around. The alley was empty.

He readjusted his backpack and ran.

CHAPTER 4

D r. Todd Horowitz, the senior psychiatric resident handling night-time emergencies at New County Medical Center, lay on the narrow bed in the on-call room. Shadows from the cars leaving and entering the emergency room parking lot projected distorted monsters on the ceiling. They brought him back to the time he was a child and consumed with a pervasive fear of death. Back then he was unable to grasp the concept of what life and death really meant. Were things so different now?

It was 1 AM and he was trying to sleep. Maybe there would be a miracle and no one else would show up? He sighed. In the last three and a half years, during his internship and psychiatric training, that had never happened. New County was one of the busiest hospitals and emergency rooms in all of Los Angeles. Most nights were a war zone – Schizophrenia, Bipolar Disorders, suicide attempts, overdoses, family feuds, name a problem and it was here. Over six-thousand psychiatric emergencies a year. Completing his undergraduate and medical school training at the University of Pennsylvania, Todd had his choice of a dozen residency programs. He picked New County because of the diversity and a chance to treat and learn about every psychiatric disorder imaginable. It didn't hurt that he really loved the challenge of helping people with complicated problems. Plus, and it was a big plus, he always had the dream of living in California. That old 1966 song, *California Dreamin'*, by The Mamas and the Papas, still got to him. Philadelphia in the Winter was gray, cold, and dismal. Except for missing his grandmother, his one remaining family member, he never once regretted moving to the west coast.

His mind flashed to the last conversation with his fiancé, Tanya Roth. It wasn't pleasant. In fact, it was quite disturbing. In less than seven months, June 30th, he'd be finished his training and had to decide what to do career-wise. He was friendly with Les Belmont, the head of the mood disorders clinic at The Ronald Reagan Medical Center on the campus at UCLA. Les had mentioned that there might be a clinical position available in July. He was also very clear that he needed Todd's decision by the end of next week. Combining teaching and clinical work was exactly what Todd imagined his future to be. In a few years, he could work his way up the clinical ladder and become a professor.

Everything about academic life – a chance to be around other intellectually oriented physicians, research, teaching, and seeing very challenging patients – appealed to him.

Tanya had other ideas. She thought that the salary, $150,000 per year, was ridiculous and strongly advocated the job at Kaiser Permanente where he could earn twice as much. He explained numerous times that it would be like working in a factory. Psychiatrists at Kaiser only prescribed medication, and all psychotherapy was done by social workers and marriage and family therapists. Each patient was allotted about fifteen minutes of a psychiatrist's time. Three or four patients an hour meant seeing at least twenty-five patients a day. That was over a hundred-and-twenty-five patients a week! No research. No teaching. No psychotherapy. Helping patents uncover the unconscious reasons for their behavior was subtle and nuanced, a psychological chess game. He was one of the few residents even interested in this aspect of psychiatry. A psychotherapy session was forty-five minutes, usually with a break between patients. A psychiatrist who did psychotherapy could see at most, eight or nine patients a day. Obviously, Kaiser needed and employed the most cost-efficient use of personnel. The thought of working for them was horrifying.

To be fair, Tanya came from a whole different world than he was used to. Her father was an investment banker and senior-partner-big-shot in Roth & Associates, a one-hundred-and-fifty-person-firm. Ted Roth pulled in well over a million-and-a-half bucks a year. They lived in a mansion on Beverly Drive in Beverly Hills, one of those houses that looked like it should be on a southern plantation – 15,000 square feet, eight bedrooms, ten bathrooms (great if you had a diarrhea attack), a living room that could host two or three-hundred freeloaders, a movie screening room, and on and on. It was disgustingly impressive. The walk-in closet was bigger than his two-bedroom rental in Redondo Beach. Three-and-a-half years ago, when Todd moved from Philadelphia to LA to start his residency, he was lucky to get the place. It wasn't fancy, but it was two blocks from the beach, near all the restaurants and shops, and suited him. A year and a half ago, when he and Tanya first started dating, she acted like it was fine. Not now. Now she wanted what her parents had. The mansion was probably worth twenty million. If he was able to save twenty thousand a year, he'd be able to afford a Beverly Hills mansion in a thousand years. Maybe he should have explained that to Tanya and she'd have felt better.

The other issue, one that was probably even more difficult, was her constant harping on him about wearing a yarmulke. He wasn't at all religious, in fact he didn't even believe in God, and never went to synagogue. Nevertheless, he felt a strong Jewish connection to his grandparents, especially his grandfather, Papa Bernie Horowitz. Todd's parents died when he was just five years old – his mother from breast cancer and his father from a freak accident, where he slipped in the shower, struck his head, and by the time he was found had succumbed to a massive brain hemorrhage. His father's parents, Bernie and Rivka Horowitz, raised him.

Both were born and raised in Paris. In 1939, six months before Germany invaded France, fourteen-year-old Rivka and her family immigrated to the United States and settled in Philadelphia. Bernie's family wasn't as lucky. Bernie had been playing outside with friends. From a nearby rooftop, he'd watched in horror as German soldiers shot their next-door-neighbor and threw his parents into a truck with a dozen other Jews. They were all sent to Auschwitz and murdered.

After months of living in alleys, eating garbage, and running for his life, Bernie met Phillipe, another desperate sixteen-year-old. Phillipe knew who to see and where to go to join the French underground. Until Germany was defeated, both boys became resistance fighters, risking their lives to save other Jews. In 1944, while trying to blow up the railway tracks used to transport Jews to concentration camps, Phillipe was shot and killed. When Bernie told Todd what happened, his tears and sobs were as raw as if he was right back in that railyard outside of Paris.

Bernie didn't believe in God and wasn't religious, yet he wore a yarmulke. Why? Todd asked when he was ten years old. Because I *never, ever* want to forget who I am, where I came from, and the love and respect I have for all the Jews who were murdered by those Nazi butchers. All this was said in Bernie's heavy, melodic French accent.

Soon after Todd was accepted to medical school, Bernie had a myocardial infarction, and within days died. At his funeral, on a bitter cold December afternoon, Todd wore a yarmulke for the first time. Standing over Papa's grave, his tears dripping on to the casket, he made a personal vow to never take the yarmulke off. Todd was six feet, two inches tall, had long, blond hair, and was president of his class at Overbrook High School. Through the years, uncountable people had asked him why he wore a yarmulke, observing that he didn't look Jewish. Todd would answer, 'What's a Jew supposed to look like'? They would shake their heads, unable to respond. Looking in a mirror and seeing himself wearing a kipah, his grandfather's term for a yarmulke, gave him a sense of belonging. His love for Papa was unshakable. Not a day passed when he didn't miss him. The man had never raised his voice or his hand to him. No question or challenge or request was ever too great or too much trouble. Bernie's love and devotion were beyond question. Todd also loved his grandmother, Rivka, now eighty years old. When he explained to her, and only her, that he wore a kipah to remember Papa Bernie, she sobbed in his arms. She still lived independently in West Philadelphia, in the small row house where he was raised. At least once a week, Todd called and talked to her. For reasons that still escaped him, Todd never told anyone, even Tanya why he really wore the Kipah. He just explained that he preferred to remember his ancestors in this fashion.

Whatever the rational reasons or the unconscious way his mind worked, Todd was beginning to feel that he didn't love Tanya the way Bernie and Rivka loved each other. He needed to end this. When it came right down to it, all the arguing about money, where he should work, and yarmulkes, took away all the love that he once felt toward her. Did he still want to marry her? He didn't know whether he wanted to spend even one more minute with her.

Todd closed his eyes and began to drift off to sleep. As a psychiatrist, didn't he need to fix his own life before he could help fix others? The answer was obvious.

CHAPTER 5

Thirty minutes later, the phone rang.

"Dr. Horowitz," Todd mumbled into the receiver, half-asleep.

"Dr. Horowitz, you have a seventeen-year-old boy who can't move his right arm."

Todd took a deep breath, got out from under the covers and sat on the side of the bed. "Can't move his arm? Really? Are you sure you don't need a neurologist or an orthopod?"

The nurse laughed. "That's what the intern thought. The boy's already seen both and was transferred to the Adolescent ER. It's hot potato and you're it. Dr. Kenyon, your neurology colleague, said you'd really enjoy this one."

Todd groaned. "Everybody's a comedian. Terrific... Okay. Be there in a few."

Todd stood up, walked over to the small sink at the end of the room and washed his face. He smoothed out his blue scrubs and hair, put on his yarmulke, and walked down the long hallway to the emergency room.

Two in the morning and the ER was packed. Most people couldn't afford to miss work or had no medical insurance, so no-matter what the hour, or the tedious wait, they used the ER as their personal concierge service. It didn't hurt that New County was dedicated to helping everyone, rich or poor, and that the attending physicians were often highly respected experts. Over four-hundred resident physicians and fellows in various specialties were captivated by the opportunity to treat all forms of illness and to get a chance to learn from world-famous experts. This year's internship class, the first year before specialty training started, came from Harvard, Yale, Penn, Berkeley, UCLA, University of Chicago, University of Michigan, NYU, among other top-tier institutions.

To Todd, the scent of an emergency room was unmistakable. It was a concoction of detergent, body odor, alcohol, blood, sickness, and fear. What was interesting to him, right from the beginning, was how this smell was not distasteful, but more like a signature-scent underlining how complicated and how important it was to be available to help the sick and needy. Helping to treat their fear and pain wasn't anything that he bragged about. It was just what he did – even in the middle of the night.

He walked quickly through the large waiting room with at least two-dozen patients waiting to be seen, around the corner to the adolescent section, and unlocked the door. Even now, at this time of night, the nursing and clerical area had five staff members sitting at the long desk typing patient-care notes on computers. The notes would be immediately available to any physician. Sally, the charge nurse, a fifty-year-old, five-foot, three-inch, ER-fixture, handed him the chart. What she didn't know about an ER would fill half a teacup. "Dr. Horowitz, your boy is back in Room 3. Like I said on the phone, he's been cleared by both neurology and orthopedics."

"What do you think?" Todd asked, poised to go into the patient area.

"I think you need to put on your thinking cap, and I'm not referring to that yarmulke."

Todd laughed. "Shalom to you too, Nurse Sally."

Sally smiled.

Todd sighed. "At 2 AM, my thinking cap is shrunken and awfully tired."

"Well, in a few more months, that shrunken cap won't have to put up with this anymore." She smiled and picked up an incoming phone call.

"I'll miss you, Sally," Todd said. This wasn't just a throw away. Todd really meant it.

Sally made eye contact with Todd, smiled, and refocused on her phone call.

Olander Jackson was a seventeen-year-old, rail-thin, five-foot, six-inch, very-dark, African American boy, lying face-up on a stretcher in the small examining room. He looked years younger than his stated age. Sitting in a chair next to him, an equally dark, heavy-set woman, held his right hand.

Todd stepped in the room and closed the door. "Hi, I'm Dr. Horowitz, a psychiatrist. I'm here to help you."

"I'm Mizz Jackson, Olander's momma." She stood up and grasped Todd's outstretched hand with both of her hands. Olander lay peacefully on the stretcher, looking at Todd like he didn't have a care in the world. "I'm so worrie 'bout him. One minute he's fine, da nex he paralyze." Tears rolled down Mizz Jackson's cheeks.

"What do you mean paralyze?"

"His arm flopped like it was dead. The other doctors zamine him and said he was fine. How he fine if his arm paralyze?"

"Which arm?"

"The right. The other arm not paralyze."

"What happened before he became paralyzed?"

"What you mean?"

"Was Olander doing anything or saying anything? Was he drinking alcohol or taking any drugs or medicine?" Todd watched as Olander lay peacefully on the bed, seemingly unperturbed by anything that his mother said, or the questions that Todd asked.

"No! He dun use no drugs or no alcohol. He wanned to take the car. I said no, and he came perturbed."

"Perturbed? How?"

"Got loud. Say I selfish. I give dat boy everythin'. How can I be selfish?"

"Did he say anything else?"

"He holler dat I was selfish. A bad motha."

"That must have been upsetting."

"He shouldna talk dat way. I tole him dat."

"And then, that's when his arm became paralyzed?"

"Maybe? He got real upset and when his arm paralyze, I took him here."

"Anything else you can remember?"

She shook her head.

"Thank you, Mizz Jackson. Let me spend some time with Olander, so I can figure out how to help him. If you could just wait in the waiting room, I'll come out and get you as soon as I'm done."

"Thank you, Docta." She picked up her large canvas bag, took a last look at Olander, who didn't look at her, and left the examining room.

"Hi, Olander, I'm Dr. Horowitz. Would you please tell me what happened to your arm."

Olander stared straight ahead, never looking at Todd.

"Olander did you hear me? What's wrong? Why are you here in the hospital?"

"Ma arm stop workin." He held up his left arm and the right arm lay dead on the bed.

"Can I examine you?" Todd asked.

"Yes, suh."

Todd picked up Olander's right arm and let it go. Olander's arm went straight back down on the bed. He lifted it again, this time over Olander's torso, and the arm went straight back down on the bed. By all laws of physics, it should have hit Olander in the stomach. Todd did it a few more times with the same result.

Todd pulled over a chair and sat down next to Olander. "Has this ever happened before, Olander?"

Olander shook his head, no.

"Code Blue! Code Blue! ICU! ICU!" blared from the ceiling speakers. Olander's dark eyes flickered open and shut. "Wats dat? Wats dat mean?"

"A patient's having trouble breathing in the intensive care unit. Doctors are being called to help. It's an emergency." Todd's face showed no evidence of anxiety. The announcement was just a part of being in a hospital.

"Is dat gonna happen to me?" For the first time, Olander made eye-contact with Todd.

"No. You have a different problem. There's nothing wrong with your breathing. There won't be any need for the emergency team."

Olander stared straight ahead.

"Have you ever been paralyzed before?"

"No, suh."

"Good. I'm glad to hear that. Where do you go to school, Olander?"

"Centennial."

"In Compton?"

"Yes, suh."

"Seventeen years old. You must be a Junior. Right?"

"Yes, suh."

"How are you doing?"

"Okay."

"Good grades?"

"Okay, but not so good in math."

"Algebra?"

"That's the hard one."

Todd nodded. "All those equations aren't easy."

Olander nodded. "Ya got dat right."

"So, tonight is, well it actually was, Friday night. So, you wanted the car to go out and celebrate the weekend?"

Olander nodded. "I was meetin frens."

"And your mother refused?

"She had no right. I did everythin she ask."

"What do you mean?"

"I clean my room. Did dishes. Finished homework. She had no right."

"You have a driver's license, right?"

"Yeah! Got it las year. No accidents or nothin. I'm a good driver."

"Why'd she refuse you?"

"I don know!" Olander's right arm twitched.

"You must have been really angry." Todd was now certain what the problem was. The question was how to fix it.

Olander closed his eyes. "I'm real tire. What time's it?"

Todd glanced at his watch. "2:40 in the morning."

"My mamma's a good mamma. I ain't angry." Olander was back staring straight ahead. No sign of any feelings.

"Where's your dad?"

Olander shrugged. "I don know him."

"Ever?"

"No."

"I'm sorry. Any brothers or sisters?"

Olander shook his head, no.

"So, it's just you and your mother. You sure you didn't get angry and want to hit her?"

Olander stared straight ahead, not answering. Finally, he said, "I'm real tire."

Todd nodded. How strange he thought. On almost no sleep, he wasn't tired at all. "Okay Olander, here's the plan. I'm going to give you a shot to relax the arm muscles, so they'll work again. Then, maybe you and your mom can come back to the clinic to talk to me, and we can figure out a way to prevent this from happening again. Okay?"

"Is the shot goin to hurt?"

"A tiny bit, like a pinch. Then it should work right away."

"Why you wear that funny cap on yo head?"

"It's called a yarmulke. It's to remind me to be humble and remember my past."

Olander nodded.

"I'll get your mother, explain the plan to her, and have the nurse give you the shot. Okay? Be back in a few minutes."

Todd went out to the waiting room, repeated exactly what he told Olander to his mother and ushered her back into Olander's room.

He went to the nursing station, asked Jenny, an attractive twenty-three-year-old, to please get a small syringe, draw up a cc of saline, and inject it in Olander's arm.

"What's goin' on, Dr. Horowitz?" she asked with a quizzical expression.

"Olander, the seventeen-year-old boy in Room 3, has a Conversion Disorder. He came into the ER with a paralyzed right arm. Wanted to hit his mother because she wouldn't give him the car, but he also loves her; so, this was his unconscious solution."

"You mean drag her here in the middle of the night?" She laughed. "That's probably worse than getting slugged."

Todd laughed. "Good point."

"How did you make the diagnosis?" Jenny looked intently at Todd. It was the same look that Tanya had when they first started dating, before all the money and yarmulke issues began.

"He showed signs of La Belle Indifference, a French term for not showing any anxiety or caring. Normally, if someone has a paralyzed arm they'd be worried off the charts. Not caring about something that serious makes no sense. That's what gave me the first clue."

"Interesting."

"He also moved his arm a little."

"You play poker?" Jenny asked, a smile on her pretty face.

"Why?"

"You spend your life watching for tells. Maybe you can do the same thing at a poker table?"

"No, I don't. Do you?"

She laughed. "I'm an open book. I'd lose every time." She drew up the saline, got an alcohol swab, and followed Todd into Olander's room. She smiled at Olander, her full lips wide and inviting, her dark eyes sparkling. Todd wondered how anyone could possibly resist her when she turned on that charm. "Hi, Olander," she said. "This will feel just like a tiny, tiny pinch. Ready?"

"Yes, ma'am."

Jenny swabbed the biceps muscle of Olander's right arm and injected the salt solution. When the needle went in, his arm jerked. After the injection, she gently massaged the area below the injection. Less than a minute later, Olander, picked up his right arm.

"How does it feel?" Todd asked.

"Good," Olander said. "It works again." He moved his arm up and down, flexing and extending all his fingers. "You fixed me! Thanks."

"You're welcome."

Olander looked at his mother and then back at Todd. "Can I go home, now?"

Nodding, Todd said, "Yes, but please call the clinic tomorrow and set up an appointment." He handed a card to Olander and another to his mother. "Promise?"

They both nodded and started gathering their belongings.

Todd knew that the chances of Olander coming back for an appointment was miniscule. But he had to try. It's what he did.

Back at the nursing station, Todd said to Jenny, "Maybe just the arm massage would have worked? We could have done away with the injection." He laughed, maybe a little too loudly.

Jenny rolled her eyes, but her smile was as inviting as any Todd had ever seen.

CHAPTER 6

Gina Carlton knew from the moment that Jake Bennett slid into the seat next to her in Experimental Economics, the first day of her third year at the University of Pennsylvania, that she was more than interested. Who knew exactly how pheromones worked? He wasn't drop-dead gorgeous, because his features were a tad off – nose a little too big, chin a little too square, lips somewhat pouty, dark hair way too long, down to his shoulders, over six-feet tall but maybe ten pounds too thin, but the combination gave him a throwback look, like maybe someone who led an underground cell for the French resistance. The black turtleneck sweater and threadbare black jeans also added to the fantasy, as did his four-day stubble.

"What?" he said, as he took out a notepad, getting ready for the class to begin, and looked her squarely in the face, his large blue eyes, not so bad either.

"Huh?" Gina mumbled, not knowing what he was talking about.

"You're staring at me," he said, with a sweet smile and something resembling a twinkle in those deep-set eyes.

"It's the French resistance look. I was hoping someone had the courage to stand up to the Nazis. Finally, we'll be saved from those disgusting monsters."

"What?"

"Seriously, did you plan your outfit? Do all the guys in your secret cell dress the same way?" Her green eyes crinkled with pleasure, her smile backlit by a thousand-watt light source, and a captivating grin that could sink at least a thousand ships. Within seconds, like maybe two, any reservations that Jake might have had disintegrated like dry brush overwhelmed by a raging forest fire.

Jake stared wide-eyed before breaking out in hysterical laughter, loud enough for the other students to turn and look. Both Jake and Gina were laughing, having trouble catching their breath. It didn't matter what the other students or the professor thought. After that moment, nothing mattered to either of them but each other. Within days they were inseparable.

Gina was an aberration. The oldest of three sisters, she took after no one in her family. Her father, a history professor at Temple University, her mother, an intellectual property lawyer at a large center-city Philadelphia law firm, and

her two sisters, were all smart, astute people, but none had any interest or aptitude in mathematics. By the time Gina graduated Lower Merion High School,
on the fabled Main Line in the Philadelphia suburbs, she had completed two
years of advanced calculus and eventually tested out of any required college-
level math courses. Massachusetts Institute of Technology, Caltech in Pasadena
and U C Berkeley department of mathematics all accepted her, but she turned
them down. University of Pennsylvania's Wharton School of Business had exactly what she wanted, a combination of mathematics and business. There was
a lot going on in the world, and she was determined to learn how to navigate
her way through the complicated maelstrom affecting the world-wide stock and
money markets.

When she met Jake, her goals never wavered. He was brilliant and intellectually they were a perfect match. His interest in fiction and how human nature affected the world fit well with her analytic take on the human condition.
In fact, over the next two years, they took six economics courses together and
developed an algorithm to predict market upswings and downswings. It wasn't
perfect, but it was better than anything else out there. After graduating from
Penn, she was accepted into the MBA/PhD program at the UCLA Anderson
School of Business. Jake always had fantasies about living in California, so he
was happy to just be with her and begin following his dream of becoming a novelist. After living in LA for three and a half years, she was about a year or so
away from achieving her PhD in economics. Her plan was to get her PhD and
teach on the college level.

For her, the relationship with Jake was a 100% commitment. She was never
surer about anything before or after she met him. They fit together perfectly –
even her parents and sisters were crazy about him – especially her father. It was
no secret that for him Jake was like having a fourth child, but this time a boy.
The two of them could talk for hours about politics or the history of the world
or just inane sports nonsense. Watching them yell about a miscall or a great play
during a football game never failed to cause all four women in the family to roll
their eyes. But even the eyerolls were filled with affection.

When Gina and Jake decided to move to Los Angeles, everyone in the family was upset, but it was all about loss. No anger, no bitterness, and no real conflict. They understood and promised to visit. Jesse, the middle sister, was a history major at Northwestern and Carrie, the baby, was a sophomore at Lower

Merion High School. Maybe one day they would join them in LA, but obviously it would be a while.

After Gina left Jake, she hoped he'd reconsider his actions and they'd get back together. Finally, she accepted the truth. It was over and she had to move on with her life. Six months later she met Kevin at Kazu Nori, a small sushi restaurant in Westwood Village. He was a law student at UCLA. They found themselves sitting next to each other at the oval-shaped counter and started chatting about the food and eventually about themselves. They started dating, and one month ago Kevin proposed. He was a hardworking, wonderful guy, and she agreed to marry him. Everything seemed fine until her *baby sister* Carrie visited. The evening before Carrie flew home, she went out with friends and just happened to see Jake waiting tables at Ciao Ristorante. Just those few seconds of seeing Jake convinced her that he wasn't happy. She told Gina. So what? Who cares if he's not happy? Gina retorted. Did you know that he's working at Ciao Ristorante on the evening shift? Carrie asked. No! Why should I know? Why should I care? Gina blurted out. Carrie shrugged, a tiny smile flashing across her young face.

That night, Gina told Kevin that she read some excellent reviews about Ciao Ristorante, and how 'bout if they went there for dinner Saturday night? She arranged to have Jake be their server and convinced the scheduler to keep it to herself, that it was a surprise. Gina knew that she wasn't madly in love with Kevin and wanted one last chance to make sure she was making the right decision.

The night that she saw Jake, she knew.

He looked haggard. He'd lost weight and seemed distracted even before he saw her at the table. When he saw her, she was afraid he'd start crying right in front of them. Jake had broken her heart, but it didn't give her any joy to see that his heart looked broken too. God, she missed him. The next morning, she called Carrie. How did you know? She asked her. You're a little seventeen-year-old pipsqueak. Carrie laughed. Gina, we all miss him. If you triple those feelings, I guessed that's how you felt. Gina sighed. You're so annoying. I can only imagine how awesome you'll be when you're my age. Well, you're already beyond awesome. Carrie hesitated, then said, my dream is to find someone just like Jake. You did the right thing to leave him, but maybe now the right thing is to go back and save him from himself. Gina was dumbstruck. Would you please explain how a mere high school student came by all this wisdom? Easy, Carrie said. I have two unbelievable sisters and a great father and a fabulous mom who coached me on how to trust my own instincts. Isn't that what strong, capable women do?

Sunday afternoon, Gina drove to Kevin's apartment. She told him that he was a wonderful man, but that she didn't want to marry him. It was emotionally brutal. She returned the ring, got back in her car, and for the first time in months felt a sense of freedom and relief. Whether she ever got back with Jake or not wasn't really the issue. If she couldn't find someone that she felt as connected to as she felt with Jake, she was determined to live her life as a single person and enjoy the independence and freedom that came with that decision. On the other hand, her plan was to take a few days to think about it.

CHAPTER 7

S till breathing hard after running from his apartment, Jake crouched in the bushes across the street from his car. Was he still being followed? All of this *had* to be related to seeing Nelson. Right? Maybe, he wasn't hallucinating? He needed to think this through, but he was exhausted.

The only thing he was sure about was that he desperately missed Gina. He wanted to call her, to explain or plead or do whatever. If she married that rich guy and he didn't at least try to get her to change her mind, he'd never forgive himself. Life without her had been pure shit. There was absolutely nothing wrong with Anna, but she wasn't Gina. No one was Gina except the real Gina. She was like a Porsche – other cars tried to emulate the way it handled, the way the engine sounded when you accelerated, and how beautifully it was designed, but they all failed. Only a Porsche had it all... Except maybe his piece of shit convertible. He chuckled to himself.

Poised to go across the street and get into his car, he froze. A light went on in a car halfway down the block, a black, full-size Lexus. It looked like the glow from a cell phone. Slowly he moved from a crouch to lying flat and pulled his hood up to cover his head and face. The passenger door of the Lexus opened and a wide, Asian man, wearing a rain jacket and combat boots, got out. He strode down the middle of the street and stopped next to Jake's battered Alfa. He looked inside, bent down on his knees, and reached under the driver's side of the car. Thirty seconds later, he stood up, and brushed his hands off. Then he turned, looked up and down the street, and walked back to his car. A minute later, the Lexus pulled out of the parking spot and disappeared down the street.

After waiting five minutes, Jake crawled out from behind the hedge and jogged to his car. He got down on the wet asphalt and shined his I phone flashlight under the car to where he saw the guy bend down. A small black box, about four inches by two inches, was stuck about a foot under the chassis toward the middle. Jake pulled the box, held by large magnets, off the sheet metal. It was a tracker. You could buy one for less than a hundred bucks, and the magnets could hold an object that weighed thirty pounds. This little box was only a few ounces; so no-matter what the terrain, it wouldn't fall off. Counter intuitively, the best place to put a tracker was on the bottom of a car. The signal from the tower bounced off the street and created a stronger signal than if the device was in the trunk or glove compartment.

While writing his last book, Jake had spent many hours researching how a police department worked, even going on a drive-along with a cop from Hermosa Beach. Cruising the dark streets and confronting suspicious strangers quadrupled his respect for law officers. After the drive-along, he spent hours hanging out at the police station, getting an education as to what really went on behind the scenes.

Jake even checked out a spy store, located in a small strip mall in Redondo Beach, south of Hermosa Beach on Pacific Coast Highway. They sold dozens of spy-tools that could do almost anything that the police, FBI, or the CIA could do. The salesman was friendly and very talkative. In less than an hour, Jake had gotten an education in surreptitious sleuthing – really cool James Bond kind of stuff.

The rain beginning to taper, Jake walked briskly toward Hermosa Ave. An eighteen-wheeler, engine still running, was parked in front of Starbucks. On the street-side of the truck, Jake knelt down, attached the magnetic side of the box to the underside of the truck cabin, then sauntered across the street into the shadows of an alley.

He walked back to his car, got in, and drove away.

Now what?

The guy who set up the tracker was probably working with the guy who followed him. For sure they knew where he lived and obviously what he drove. That meant they knew where he worked and a dozen other things about him. How hard was it to get into a database and find out what credit and debit cards he used? Probably not all that complicated. He had about a hundred bucks in his pocket, thousands in credit card debt, and no other assets except his four-year-old computer. If they had any juice, they could also get into the AT&T main frame and uncover who he called and who called him.

During the drive-along with Officer Gary Milton, they had a detailed discussion about tracking people using sources that were available to everyone. If you knew even the basics of how to use the search engines already on the internet, like safari and google, it wasn't that hard. For just a few bucks more, there were sites that could give you information about almost anyone. And what about the deep web or dark web, or whatever it was called? That was a total mystery to Jake. But, if he was on the run, that's what he'd learn to use. Maybe that's what Nelson used? After all, his brother was, probably still is, a computer genius. Both he and Nelson were off the charts when it came to mathematical aptitude. Jake set his aside when he decided to be a novelist. He recalled a discussion they had before Nelson *died*. It pertained to a search engine that could insinuate itself almost anywhere. You mean like Safari? Jake said. Nelson shook his head. Safari is like using a toy sandbox-shovel to dig a coal mine. What I'm talking about is more like an excavator that can dig a foundation big enough for a fifty-story building. We're talking deep... Huh? Jake responded, not really understanding what Nelson was talking about. Nelson laughed. You have no idea, Bro.

A few blocks from the Redondo Beach Pier, Jake pulled onto a side street, cut the engine, and got out of the car. He needed some fresh air, maybe coffee to wake himself up. There was an all-night diner around the corner.

Halfway down the street, a car screeched around the corner, hi-beams glaring, and pulled right in front of him. Both doors swung open and the same big guy who put the tracking device on his car, and the driver, an even bigger Asian man, jumped from the vehicle and ran toward him. Jake ran in the opposite direction, pulling the stiletto from his pocket. Running as fast as he could, he reached the end of the street and stopped cold. The driver had doubled back and was running toward him. Behind him, he heard pounding footsteps. Seconds later, they were both just a few feet away. "Jake," the driver said, in perfect English, catching his breath. "We just want to talk to you. There's nothing to be alarmed about."

"Who are you?" Jake held the knife handle flat against his leg; his finger poised above the release button. He kept angling toward an alley.

"Just come with us. Get in the car and we'll explain everything," the guy behind him said.

"Stop moving! Explain now!" Jake yelled.

"Just calm down. It's not what you think."

"Bullshit! You have no idea what I think!"

Both men rushed Jake. The driver hit Jake hard in the face, breaking his nose and stunning him. Jake pushed the button on the stiletto and in a split second the blade shot out of the handle. Jake lunged forward and slashed the driver on the side of his neck, blood immediately spurted from his severed carotid artery. The other man slugged Jake in the back of the head with something hard, like metal, almost knocking him out. Off balance, Jake pivoted and punched the knife through the guy's jacket and into his abdomen. The guy groaned and sunk to his knees.

Jake staggered down the alley into the street, swiping at the blood running down his face. He remembered that the police station was just a few blocks away. Keeping as much in the shadows as he could, he headed toward Pier Avenue. When he saw the station, he tossed the knife under some decrepit wooden-steps that led to the front-door of a house, hesitated for a moment, then also tossed his wallet with his driver's license and credit cards in the same place. House # 345. Remember that! he told himself. He reached into his pocket, took his money out, and shoved the wad down the side of his boot.

He pulled out his phone and punched in 911. A woman answered. Jake croaked, "I was mugged. I'm injured and bleeding. Dizzy. About to lose consciousness. I'm outside the Redondo Beach Police Station on Pier Avenue. Half-a-block away... Look out the window. I'm here...on the sidewalk."

CHAPTER 8

"Dr. Horowitz, you have a consult on five west, room 506," Patty Browning said. She was a pleasant, rotund, fifty-year-old woman, who handled all the scheduling and paperwork for the psychiatric outpatient clinic. Her desk was located at the entrance to the psychiatric barracks, one of dozens of wooden structures that had been around for over seventy years and now served as the outpatient treatment facilities for numerous medical specialties. For years, New County was supposed to demolish the barracks and build a more modern facility, but the money never seemed to materialize. Fortunately, the decrepit structures did have updated heating and air conditioning and each psychiatric resident was assigned a 10' by 10' office for their last two years of training.

"What department?"

Patty checked her notes. "Neurology. The patient was brought in by paramedics four days ago and had a complete work-up. Apparently, he won't talk and is acting strangely."

"Thanks, Patty. Please tell them I'll do it around 4:30 when I finish in the clinic."

"Consider it done."

At 4:45, Todd poured himself a cup of coffee, and headed across the sprawling parking lot to the hospital, a modern, 500-bed facility.

On the fifth floor, he picked up a tablet from the nursing station and reviewed all the information and tests that were recorded for the patient in 506. The man still hadn't uttered one word. He had no identification on him and no known next-of-kin or friend that had come forward. The initial physical exam showed a well-developed male, about six-feet tall, one-hundred-and-seventy pounds, with a skull contusion and an eight-inch laceration, a broken nose, and obvious cognitive dysfunction. Before passing out, a block from the Redondo Beach Police Station, he called 911. He reported that he'd been mugged, was bleeding, and about to pass out. Paramedics arrived within minutes, found him lying on the sidewalk and transported him directly to New County. According to the police report, they concurred that it was an apparent mugging. The patient's wallet was missing, but $105.00 in small bills was found inside his boot.

Neurological exam, Cat Scan and MRI of the skull and brain were all normal. According to the neurological notes, he didn't appear psychotic, yet he wasn't acting reasonably. After all blood and lab tests came out within normal limits, the neurology resident requested a psychiatric consult.

Todd looked around the nursing station and located the charge nurse, a guy in his forties with a full beard. "Hey, George, how ya doin?" Todd asked.

"Pretty good. How 'bout you, doc?"

"Same. Thanks. They asked me to see the patient in 506. What's your take?"

"Strange," George said. "I swear, the guy acts like he can't talk, but I think he can. I don't know. Maybe you can figure it out."

Todd nodded. "I'll let you know."

Todd walked down the hall and entered 506, a two-patient-room. The second bed was empty. Patient X lay in the bed, on top of the covers, wearing a blue hospital gown. He was tall, good-looking, lean – like a runner's build, and had about a week's-plus worth of facial scruff.

Holding the chart, Todd approached his bed. "Hi," he said. "I'm Dr. Todd Horowitz. The neurologist asked me to see you. I'm a psychiatrist."

Patient X glanced at Todd, with an almost imperceptible widening of his eyes, like maybe he was surprised, but then the look on his face changed back to a neutral, stoic expression.

Todd's expression didn't change, but he too was surprised. This guy looked familiar! Where had he seen him before? "Do I know you?" Todd asked. Patient X stared at the ceiling. "Look, I'm just here to help. Do you know where you are?" No answer, no eye contact. "What's your name?" Nothing. Todd chatted about stress, PTSD, how everything would be confidential, but the guy just stared at the ceiling.

Back at the nursing station, Todd called the psychiatric unit, and was relieved when he learned that there was a male bed available. He wrote for Patient X to be admitted to Nine North. Every instinct in Todd knew that the guy was voluntarily not speaking and probably not psychotic, even though he couldn't prove it. After three years of psychiatric residency training, Todd had learned to trust his gut feelings.

Theodor Reik, a psychoanalyst, and one Freud's earliest students, wrote a book over seventy years ago, *Listening with the Third Ear*. It emphasized how important and essential it was to allow gut feelings to come to the surface and to use these feelings when trying to understand a patient. It was one of the mainstays of intensive psychotherapy and psychoanalysis. For most psychiatrists it had become a lost art. Among his peers, Todd was an outlier. His colleagues treated patients like an internist would. Evaluate the presenting symptoms, make a diagnosis, and prescribe the proper drug. Depression? Use an antidepressant. Bipolar? Start a mood stabilizer. Crazy? Initiate an antipsychotic. The nuances of the mind – why someone might have gone berserk, how anxiety can be perfectly normal – were all somewhat irrelevant. *But not to Todd…*

Todd also respected the nagging feeling that this guy was familiar. He'd sleep on it. See Patient X tomorrow and figure out who he was and how to deal with him.

Todd went back to the barracks, put on his khaki, army-surplus jacket, grabbed his backpack and walked to the parking lot. He unchained his old Harley Sportster, put on his helmet, and headed toward Western Ave. In ten-minutes he'd be at the end of San Pedro and on Palos Verdes Drive, beginning one of the highlights of his mornings and his evenings and probably of his life, the spectacular drive along the road bordering the Pacific Ocean – through Rancho Palos Verdes, into Lunada Bay, and through Malaga Cove. This evening, the ocean was gray and punctuated with whitecaps, the sun just on the verge of dipping into the cold depths. He couldn't imagine anywhere in the world, except maybe the Amalfi Coast, being more beautiful. Even passing The Trump National Golf Course in Rancho Palos Verdes, didn't dull the experience.

Thirty minutes later, he roared down Palos Verdes Blvd., made a left onto Pacific Coast Highway, a left on Knob Hill, and a right on Catalina. A minute later, after pulling into his garage, he sat perfectly still. Who was Patient X? Why was he so sure he knew him, and why did it bother him so much?

His phone buzzed. It was Tanya. He let the phone go to voicemail and walked upstairs to his townhouse. He changed into a pair of Levi's, a washed-out Harley T-shirt that he'd worn all through college, and slipped on a pair of re-soled, thrashed Birkenstock's. Rummaging through the small freezer, he found a frozen Trader Joe's Tiki-Masala dinner, read the directions, and slid it into the microwave. He popped opened a bottle of Sapporo, took a long swig, and wondered why he was feeling so crappy. Nothing in his life was significantly different, and this morning he was in a good mood, or at least he thought he was.

An hour later Tanya called again. Todd turned off his phone, clicked on CNN, and watched as the president of the United States wriggled and lied and squirmed as the House of Representatives came closer and closer to impeaching him.

That night, Todd awoke at 4 AM with the vague recollection of a dream where he was happy, walking hand-in-hand with a dark-haired woman in Fairmount Park, by the Schuylkill River. Before he could analyze the meaning, he fell back to sleep.

In the morning, a bright sunny day, blue sky, blue Pacific, and a clear run all along the coast, flashes of the dream kept nagging at him. Just after making the turn onto Western Avenue, he pulled over to the side of the road, took off his goggles, and dried the tears dripping down his cheeks. He knew what the dream was all about, and he knew who Patient X was.

CHAPTER 9

As Professor Ju Chen finished her morning economics lecture, a comparison of technological investment practices between China and the United States, Gina joined the dozens of fellow grad-students filing out of the large auditorium in the UCLA Anderson School of Management. Hours ago, sitting at the small kitchen table in her apartment, sipping a cup of coffee, she made the decision to see Jake. The plan was to just show up at his doorstep. Calling seemed too awkward, and she wanted to personally view his reaction when she arrived unannounced. Strictly speaking, she was half-owner of that dumpy rental since they cosigned the lease. As far as she knew, he never renegotiated the lease or had her removed from it. Also, the possibility of Jake ever hurting her financially or in any other way was never a consideration. He just wouldn't and couldn't take advantage of her. Maybe that was a crazy, naïve way of thinking, but nevertheless, she 100% believed it.

She left the building and cut across the upper campus through the sculpture garden, an idyllic, five-acre area, with over seventy mainly bronze and steel sculptures, surrounding a reflective fountain. In the middle of the fountain was a statue called Obos 69 – square, weird-looking, avant-garde. What it symbolized totally escaped her.

Ten minutes later, she got off the elevator on the fourth floor of her apartment building and entered her small one-bedroom. She washed her face, brushed her hair, making the spikes look a little spikier, and grabbed an old U of P sweatshirt. Often it was a lot cooler at the beach than here in Westwood. She walked to the front door, hesitated, turned around and went back in the kitchen. Rummaging through her junk drawer, she found the old set of keys to Jake's apartment and put them in her purse. She took the elevator down to the parking garage and walked directly to her one-year-old, white Prius, a for-no-particular-reason gift from her parents.

At eleven, on a Wednesday morning, the fifteen-mile trip down Lincoln Boulevard and Pacific Coast Highway to Hermosa Beach took about forty-five minutes. She knew the area and Jake's apartment well; since they lived there together for a year and a half. After she moved out, she considered staying at the beach, but opted to be closer to campus and avoid the daily commute that was getting more and more odious.

When she reached Seventh Street, she started looking for a parking spot. A miracle! Just ahead, an SUV pulled out. That was one of the negatives of living at the beach, the parking was impossible unless your building had a garage. Their building had no garage. Every night was another search for the right spot. Somehow though, they managed, and after a while it didn't seem like a big deal. When they were together, nothing seemed like a big deal except when they weren't together. Had he changed? Would he consider getting a real job and do his writing in the evening or weekends? What if he was still adamant about continuing to wait tables so he could devote more time to writing? She honestly didn't know what she would do if that were the case, but she desperately wanted to see him and talk to him. Of course, she wanted a home, a family, and all the things that she grew up taking for granted. But, not having Jake as her partner was like imagining a rainbow without the colors.

She entered Jake's apartment building, walked up the familiar three-flights of steps, and knocked on the door. No answer. She knocked again and after waiting a few minutes tried to open the door. As expected, it was locked. She turned to go, then changed her mind, and took the set of keys from her purse.

When she opened the door, she gasped. The sofa lay on its side, the bottom ripped open, dining-room table and chairs turned over, bookshelves empty, books and knick-knacks strewn everywhere, walls discolored where paintings used to hang, desk drawers open, pens, paper and supplies scattered everywhere, dishes and silverware all over the floor in the kitchen, and even food from the cupboard and the refrigerator haphazardly tossed. In the bedroom, the mattress was ripped open, and Jake's clothes and shoes covered the floor. Whoever was here went through *all* of Jake's belongings. Panic-stricken, Gina turned, and ran from the apartment.

Where was Jake? Was he hurt? Worse?

Gina ran to her car and immediately punched in Jake's phone number. It went directly to Voice Mail. Hands shaking, beads of sweat dotting her forehead, she started the Prius and headed toward the Hermosa Beach police station.

CHAPTER 10

Lying on his back, propped up by two pillows under his head, Jake slowly regained consciousness. Colors – orange, yellow, flashes of white and blue – moved in a kaleidoscope of twisted shapes until the ceiling fluorescent lights and the curtain surrounding him finally registered. Above him, an IV pouch filled with clear fluid swayed gently on a stainless-steel pole. The fluid dripped slowly through a long plastic tube, buried under a swath of gauze below his right wrist. Groaning, as he tried to sit up, he could only move his arms, legs, and shoulders. Help! He almost screamed, until realizing that a wide restraining belt encircled his waist and bound him to the stretcher.

Gauze was wrapped tightly around the top of his head, and packing filled both of his nostrils. A wave of claustrophobia made him gasp and strain against the restraint until he accepted the fact that breathing through his mouth wasn't as terrible as he first thought. Pain flowed from his head down the front of his face and back up again to his head, a circle of agony. Nevertheless, he sighed in relief. He was in a hospital! They didn't get him!

A middle-aged woman with short, dark hair and a pleasant smile, wearing blue scrubs and a stethoscope draped around her neck, came closer and stood next to Jake. "Oh good. You're finally awake. Hi, I'm Jane Clay, your nurse."

Jake looked at her and was about to answer when another thought came to mind. He just swallowed and stared at the ceiling.

"Do you know where you are?"

No answer.

After a few moments Jane said, "You're here in the emergency room at New County Medical Center. Do you know what happened to you?"

Jake continued to stare at the ceiling, the vague idea that he had before passing out, took a more concrete form. It was an idea that sounded crazy, but what was crazier than his brother emerging from the afterlife and two strangers, maybe three strangers, trying to kill him? Well, after all, he was the heir to a battered Alfa and thousands of dollars of debt. Silly me. They were after the Alfa's parts. Maybe they wanted the canvas convertible top too?

"What's your name?" Jane asked.

Jake said nothing. He needed time to think, to figure this out, to come up with a more definitive plan to survive. Right now, all he could think of was to be anonymous. Whoever was after him had the power of the internet and unlimited access to search engines. How hard would it be to log onto the county hospital server and look up the names of recent admissions?

Jane patted Jake on the shoulder. "Just relax. I'll have your doctor, Dr. Manus, come over and talk to you. Okay? It'll just be a few minutes." She walked away.

Sometime later, Jake thought he might have dozed off, Dr. Manus, a tall, skinny guy, with a huge Adam's-apple, also wearing blue scrubs, materialized. "I'm Dr. Manus," he said. "I've been taking care of you for the last eight hours, since the paramedics brought you in."

Jake's rough calculation was that it was now 10 AM.

"Jane, the nurse who's also been taking care of you, asked you a few questions, but you didn't answer. What's wrong?"

Jake looked at the doctor with no change in expression.

"Don't you understand?"

Jake closed his eyes.

"I'm assuming, maybe incorrectly, that you can hear me and understand me. Last night, while you were unconscious, the neurology resident, Dr. Reilly, was called in for a consultation and ordered a Cat Scan and an MRI of your brain. Both are normal – no skull fractures or any evidence of a subdural or epidural bleeding. That would have required brain surgery. What you had was an eight-inch scalp laceration on the back of your head that we sutured. Also, your nose was broken, so we reduced the fracture and packed it. That's why you're breathing through your mouth. We also started you on an antibiotic to make sure you don't get an infection. Now that you've regained consciousness, Dr. Reilly will come back and finish his evaluation. Okay?"

Jake didn't change his expression. He had no idea whether his plan made sense. He had no plan B; so, he decided to stick with A.

A few hours later, Dr. Reilly finished testing Jake with a rubber percussion hammer, poking him with needles, looking into his eyes, and squeezing different parts of his body. Whatever he told Jake to do, like raise his arms or legs, blink his eyes, turn his head, or squeeze his hand, Jake just pretended he didn't hear or understand. Do what acting coaches all over the world encouraged actors to do. Stay in character – brain damaged, stressed, out of it, a basket case.

After the exam, Jake was placed in a wheelchair, wheeled down the brightly lit hallway, and up the elevator to a double room on the fifth floor of the hospital.

The next morning, Dr. Kim, Susan Kim, the resident in charge, told Jake that she hoped he'd be able to talk after some time passed, maybe a few days, hours? He was obviously traumatized and sometimes the best healer was time. She said he was probably suffering from PTSD, Post Traumatic Stress Disorder. Jake did his staring routine, wondering how long he could act this way before they kicked him out of the hospital. Then where would he go? Who would he call? Where were his clothes, keys, phone, his paltry stash of crumpled bills?

It struck him how isolated he had become. Since Gina left, the only social life he had was with Anna and her friends. Now he had no one. What happened to him? Isolative. Brooding. Depressed. When Nelson was alive, or before he feigned his death, they saw and talked to each other all the time. Even when he and Gina moved to California and Nelson continued to work and live in Philly, they talked almost every day. Was it all bullshit? It couldn't be. They were close, very close. Nelson must have had an extraordinarily good reason to do what he did – a life or death reason.

Back in college Jake had friends – especially Craig and James. They went out at least once a week for beers or a movie or coffee. After he moved to LA they lost touch. If he was being really honest with himself, when he was with Gina he made no effort at all to reach out to anyone. She wasn't only the love of his life; she was his best friend. Why was he so isolated? Gina had friends. Anna had friends. Why did he become such a loner?

Jake lay in bed, ate his meals, tried to ignore his headache and nose pain, and attempted futilely to figure out the enigma of his screwed-up life and what he could do to make sure he stayed alive. After breakfast, on the second day, the one where he was supposed to miraculously start talking, two police officers, LA County Sheriffs, came into the room – a bald, hydrant-shaped guy and a muscular woman with a butch haircut. After a few minutes of questions, like, did you see who did it? What time did it happen? Was there a car involved? The officers looked at each other, shrugged, and left.

Later, in the early evening, as he was chewing a piece of dried chicken and staring at spinach that looked like twisted grass, a tall, lanky, blond guy, wearing a yarmulke, came in. He announced that he was a psychiatrist and here to help him. Jake put the plastic lid over his meal and almost gasped out loud. He knew that guy! Shit! Where did he see him before? He looked so familiar. At the beach? Somewhere in LA? He couldn't place him. Like every other doctor, the shrink had a dozen questions. As he blabbered on, Jake took a deep breath and tuned him out.

After the guy left, Jake was transferred up to Nine North, the psychiatric ward.

CHAPTER 11

Todd scored a narrow space in the hospital parking lot, in between a vintage Jeep Wrangler and a ten-year-old BMW 318. He gave the Harley a few revs just to hear that throaty roar, locked her up with a heavy-duty, case-hardened steel chain that cost him over eighty bucks, and walked up the rickety wooden steps into the barracks. He went directly to his office, and put his jacket, helmet, and backpack out of sight next to his desk. The office was so small that there was no room for a closet, just enough space for a desk, desk chair and a patient chair. Family and couple sessions were held in the larger conference rooms.

Todd hurried down the hall to the restroom, washed his face, took a quick look in the mirror, and straightened his yarmulke. Along with remembering who Patient X was, he also remembered his ex-fiancé Bonnie, and how devasted he was when she broke off the engagement. He sighed. Her rejection came out of left field. Obviously, it still hurt.

He was running just a few minutes late. Mulling over a vague idea about how he'd deal with the insight he just had roaring along the ocean, he pulled himself together and walked briskly to the waiting room to get his first patient of the day.

Carly, twenty-one-years-old, skinny, disheveled dark-hair hanging down to her waist, wearing a creased-dress that covered her ankles, and flip-flops on her mud-stained feet, sat hunched-over staring at the dark-wood floor.

"Hey, Carly," Todd said, standing a few feet away from her. "Good morning. Sorry, I'm a few minutes late."

With her head down, eyes on the floor, she stood up and followed Todd into his office. Todd closed the door and they both sat down.

"How are things?" Todd asked.

After a long hesitation, Carly answered. "Same."

"Fill me in. What exactly did you do in the last month since we met?" Todd took a deep breath and wondered what it was really like to be inside Carly's head. By history, she was a normal eighteen-year-old until her freshman year at Long Beach State University, when she had her first psychotic break. The campus police found her wandering around campus at 2 AM, totally naked. She reported that a man raped her. When she was examined by a physician at Long Beach Memorial Hospital, there was no evidence of any injury or rape, but no one could say for certain that it didn't happen. Two days later, Carly's parents brought her to New County where she was admitted to the psychiatric unit. She became Todd's first-ever inpatient. When he did his initial consultation, she was unable to give any details and in fact stated that nothing happened. When he asked her why she was walking around campus at 2 AM naked, she said that she was hot. That night, the temperature ranged between forty-five and fifty degrees.

After three weeks in the hospital, Todd stabilized her on an antipsychotic medication called Abilify, and she was able to return home. But no-matter what he said or suggested, she was never able to get re-engaged in life. All she did was garden and take care of the two, family dogs. With the advice of supervisors, Todd tried a few other antipsychotic medications, but with no noticeable improvement. A year ago, on the advice of another supervisor, he stopped all the meds just to see if by any chance the meds might be making her worse. Three weeks after being free of all medication, she was brought to the ER at 4 AM in full restraints. After screaming obscenities, smashing her mother in the face, and smearing feces on her bedroom walls, the police were called. Todd hospitalized her and immediately re-started her medication. It took over three months for her to improve enough to return home. Even though she never admitted to hearing voices or any obvious delusions, her diagnosis was Schizophrenia. Now, just like when she was first admitted to the hospital, after over three years, she still described events in her life in that same flat, affectless manner.

Today, sitting with Todd in the office, Carly's gaze never moved away from the floor.

"Carly, you're quiet today. Tell me what happened last month."

After moments of hesitation, she mumbled, "I gardened and walked the dogs."

"Did you leave the yard and walk them around the block like we talked about last session?"

"No. I don't like to leave the yard."

"Remember we talked about how important it is for you to try new things? Not to stay so isolated."

"Yes."

"I know how frightened you become, but can you try a little harder?"

"Okay." All this time, Carly never looked up.

"How about that group I've been mentioning, the one where you can talk to people and get better at having conversations?"

"No, thank you."

"It would really help, Carly."

"No, thank you."

"Carly, how can I help you if you won't do anything that I recommend?"

"Please, Dr. Horowitz, I'm trying. Don't be angry at me." For the first time Carly looked up, her eyes filling with tears.

Todd sighed and leaned forward in his chair. It was heartbreaking to watch how helpless Carly was against this terrible illness. Schizophrenia was devastating. "I'm not angry, Carly. I just get worried."

Carly nodded.

Todd spent the next thirty-five minutes trying to encourage Carly to talk about herself, but as usual the results were minimal.

The next patient was Rocky Tablitski, a dockworker from San Pedro with a bipolar disorder and alcoholism, who did well if he took his Lithium and didn't drink. When he drank, the chances of him not taking his medication were high. The last time he went on a binge, voices told him to jump off the Vincent Thomas Bridge. This month, Rocky was taking his Lithium and going to AA meetings. He had lots of praise for Todd. You're the best, Doc. I'm telling all my buds about you. Todd knew that next month, or the month after, Rocky would have a few beers, then a few more, and the praise could just as easily turn into verbal attacks. You're a sorry excuse for a doctor. You're an asshole! Why would you try and poison someone with that Lithium shit? Last year, Rocky's wife and two sons dragged him back to the hospital where amidst all the cursing and threats Todd put him on a 72-hour-hold which then turned into a 14-day hold. Hospitalized against his will, Rocky was "dried out" and his Lithium restarted. Now he was back to being Todd's greatest fan, at best a dubious distinction.

At 10:45, Todd walked over to the hospital.

On the ninth floor, he took out his keys, unlocked the door to the closed unit, and went in. The gray tile floors, bare walls, and harsh fluorescent lighting looked like a prison. Nine North, like most locked psychiatric units, was by necessity furnished in a minimalistic manner. The fact that so many of the patients were psychotic, depressed, suicidal, homicidal, and out of control was the main reason. If there weren't pieces of furniture or paintings hanging on the walls, there wasn't anything to throw or use as a weapon.

Being a senior resident had its advantages. One was that the first year and second year residents took care of most of the patients on the inpatient unit. The senior residents were assigned outpatient and consultation work. Yesterday, Todd had the option of transferring the care of Patient X to a more junior resident or caring for him himself. He chose the latter. Now that he remembered who Patient X was, he felt confident that he had made the right decision.

Through the eight-foot by ten-foot, plate glass window, Todd could see what was going on in the group therapy room. Patient X, a gauze bandage still wrapped around his head, and his nose packed, sat in a circle of nine patients. A woman was speaking, but Patient X didn't look at her or for that matter look at anyone. Todd glanced at his watch. Social Therapy would be over in just a few minutes. He walked down the hall to the nursing station, sat down, and reviewed Patient X's information. He was cooperative, ate his meals, showed no evidence of bizarre behavior, no evidence of hostility, and followed all the rules. He still hadn't uttered a single word.

As Patient X, dressed in blue scrubs, followed the other patients out of the group room, Todd walked up beside him.

"Hi," Todd said. "Let's talk."

With a blank expression, Patient X followed Todd and waited quietly while Todd unlocked a door at the end of the hall. The consultation room, furnished with a leather sofa and four heavy leather chairs, bare walls, a tile floor, and one window that looked back into the hallway, was as stark and utilitarian as the rest of the unit. Todd motioned for his patient to sit wherever he wanted. He chose the sofa and Todd sat down across from him in one of the leather chairs. "Would you like some water or coffee?" No response, just a blank stare that succeeded in never making eye contact. "Okay... I just spoke to the head nurse who told me that you've been cooperative but still haven't said anything." Patient X made no motion indicating that he understood, but as Todd looked at him, his gut reaction was that he understood *everything*. Why he was behaving this way was the question. Exactly how much Todd should divulge about what he remembered was the conundrum. Confront him and get it all out in the open?

Be patient? There were reasons why X was behaving this way, and maybe the best approach was to let things evolve a little more. Get some clarity.

Todd asked a few questions, but within minutes realized that this approach was fruitless. From a physical and psychiatric point of view, X could be discharged in the next 24 hours and be followed as an outpatient. Physical exam and lab studies were normal. He wasn't suicidal, homicidal, or gravely impaired. There were no imperative reasons for him to be hospitalized, but since Todd knew for a fact that Patient X was bright, articulate, and intuitive, and wouldn't be acting this way without a good reason, he wanted to help him. That was his job, right? Why he chose to be a doctor.

CHAPTER 12

Gina left the Hermosa Beach police station in a state of shock and power-lessness – her mind spinning in disbelief. It felt as if her lungs collapsed, and she couldn't inhale enough oxygen. Calm down she admonished herself. This is not the time to have a panic attack! Relax. Think this through.

We have a lot of break-ins in the beach cities, Sgt. Chambers, a tall, mus-cular man wearing a blue uniform, told her. We'll investigate your complaint as soon as possible. When will that be? As soon as we can. What about the fact that Jake Bennett didn't answer his phone, that he's disappeared? Yes. We understand. You put all this info on the form, right? Phone number, address, date of birth? Of course, I did. Sgt., you don't seem that concerned. Chambers glanced out the window at the ocean, then back at Gina. We're very concerned and take your concerns and all our citizens' concerns very seriously. We have your phone number, right? Yes! It's on the form, Gina snapped back. Good. We'll be getting back to you with our findings, the unperturbed Sgt. responded. You are an absolute jerk! Gina wanted to scream. She nodded, gritted her teeth, and left.

Back in her apartment, Gina scrambled two eggs, swallowed a forkful, and tossed the rest down the garbage disposal. The last time she was this upset was when she left Jake. This was worse! At least back then she believed he would come to his senses. What if he was injured or...worse? She remembered read-ing about a college secretary who was found dismembered in Mexico, her body parts decaying in the trunk of her car. Stop it! She cautioned herself. Stop over-reacting. Break-ins are common. Probably thousands every day, all over the world. People are hungry. Desperate. They need money. She called Jake's cell phone. Again, it went immediately to voice mail. "This is Jake. Leave your num-ber and I'll call back." It was the same message he had when she first met him in college.

That evening, her cell phone rang.

She answered on the first ring, thinking it might be the police. "Hello!"

"Gina? Gina Carlton."

"Yes?"

"This is Todd Horowitz, a voice from the past."

"Todd? Oh my God. It's been what, four or five years?"

"Something like that. It's been a long time. For whatever reason, I never deleted your cell number."

"This is a surprise."

"I'm sure it is. Are you in Los Angeles? Wasn't that where you were headed?"

"I am. Westwood. We, Jake and I, moved out here about four, four and a half years ago. Then things got a bit complicated. Where are you calling from, Todd?"

"Redondo Beach."

"Wow. So, you're out here too. I had no idea."

"I'm at New County, finishing my residency in psychiatry."

"Psychiatry. That makes sense. Do you like it?"

"Very much. Listen Gina, what I'm going to tell you is going to sound crazy. It's also not exactly following the rules, but I'm doing what I think is best."

"Okay?"

"Are you and Jake still together? Maybe married?"

"No. But a very scary thing just happened. After not seeing him for a year, I went to his apartment. It was trashed. *Everything* was strewn about. Even the pictures were ripped off the wall. I've called his cellphone a dozen times and it goes straight to voice mail."

"You mean, Jake destroyed his own apartment?"

"No! Jake would never do that. Someone broke in and now he's missing."

"I was afraid of something like that. Gina, can you meet me? There's a Starbucks on Crenshaw Boulevard near the intersection with Torrance Boulevard."

"Yes. This time of night, the 405 shouldn't have too much traffic. It'll take about thirty or forty minutes. Why?"

"It's complicated. I'd rather tell you in person."

"Oh no! Is it Jake? Is he alright?"

"He's fine, but I want to explain things."

Gina glanced at her watch. "I can be there by nine. Is that okay?"

"Yes. See you then."

Gina grabbed her keys and took the elevator down to the parking structure. For the first time since moving into her apartment, she was scared. What if the people who trashed Jake's apartment saw her? She had a can of Mace in the glove compartment of her car. Great, she thought. That does me a lot of good.

The parking structure looked like it always did. Quiet. Cars parked in their usual places. No one around. She took out her keys, ran to her car, got in, and immediately locked the door.

Heading for the freeway, it felt like she was in a time warp. Her past enveloping the present. As she drove, she kept her eyes riveted on the rear-view mirror. When she reached the 405 South, she accelerated into the carpool lane, a perk from owning a Prius. After a mile or so she edged back into a middle lane, then another mile, and she zipped back in the carpool lane. All the while, she kept her eyes riveted on the rear-view mirror. She'd seen enough TV thrillers to watch for a car three or four car-lengths behind, weaving in and out of traffic as she changed lanes. As far as she could tell, no one was following her. She put on a soft jazz station and tried to relax.

Gina hadn't thought about Todd in years, but hearing his voice brought back a slew of memories. At Penn, she lived in a remodeled brownstone with four apartments. Todd lived in the apartment above her. One day when her car broke down, he stayed with her until AAA showed up and then he took her on his motorcycle back to the apartment. Often, they chatted, and half a dozen times had coffee. He was easy to talk to, and she always felt comfortable around him. She remembered that he was dating another medical student, and in fact was on the verge of asking her to marry him. Did he? Was he still wearing his yarmulke?

Gina exited the freeway at Crenshaw Blvd., drove about three miles, and saw the Starbucks sign off to the left. She pulled into the parking spot next to Todd's old Harley and went into the coffee shop. When Todd saw her, he immediately got up, came over, and hugged her.

"You look terrific," he said, "just like back in college."

"You too." He did look good – lean, blond hair long, almost to his neck, and of course his signature black yarmulke. But he looked stressed, his smile somewhat forced, and a few wrinkles around his eyes that weren't there back in Philly. Maybe just getting older? Maybe not... Definitely not. He was worried.

"Coffee?" he asked.

"Decaf. Are you having any?"

"Yeah. I'll get it. Cream? Sugar?"

"Just cream."

Filled with anxiety, she waited until Todd sat down and put the two coffees on the table. She took hers. "Thanks, Todd. What's going on?"

Todd took a sip of coffee and a deep breath. "Two days ago, I was asked to do a consult on a man who had been brought to the emergency room unconscious with a deep scalp laceration and a broken nose. CAT scan, MRI, lab studies and a physical exam were all normal. They sutured the laceration and set his nose. Other than the head trauma, there was nothing amiss."

"Why were you called? You know, a psychiatrist?"

"He wouldn't talk. Won't talk. He's perfectly cooperative but refuses to say a word. When I saw him, it took a while, but I remembered the two of you. It's Jake. I think he knows who I am, but I can't be sure."

"So, why's Jake doing this?" Gina asked.

"I don't know, but I hesitate to have him discharged because my hunch is that he has a good reason to do what he's doing."

"You mean emotionally ill?"

"No. Nothing like that. If you saw the unit, you'd readily agree that no rational person would want to spend any time at all there. Why he wants to stay on the unit is a mystery, but he won't utter a word. Will you talk to him?"

"When?"

"Now."

"Now? Aren't there visiting hours?"

"It'll be fine."

"Okay. Let's go."

CHAPTER 13

Jake lay face-down in bed with the sheet pulled over his head. At least the packing was finally out of his nose, and he could breathe more easily. One of his roommates was pacing around the room assuming various karate poses. The other roommate was mumbling about monsters who were out to get him. Maybe they were the same monsters he was running from?

He felt someone touch his shoulder and froze. What now? "It's Dr. Horowitz. Please get up. We need to talk."

Jake slowly pulled the sheet off his face, and in the shadows saw Todd standing beside the bed. Can't this fucking wait? he wanted to say. But since he was in a self-imposed vow of silence, he kept his mouth shut.

Jake swung his legs over the side of the bed, slipped his feet into the New County flimsy cotton excuse for slippers, and stood up. The damn things just wouldn't stay on his feet, for that matter, on anyone's feet. That was why most patients shuffled around the ward. If you tried to walk like a normal person, the slippers would slide off.

He followed Todd down the hall to the room where they had talked this morning. A light was on, but a shade covered the large glass window. Todd unlocked the door, stepped aside, and Jake entered the room. Immediately, Todd closed the door and locked it.

"What the hell!" Jake blurted out, stopping cold when he saw Gina – tearful, teeth clenched, sitting on the sofa.

"Please sit down, Jake," Todd said, and took a seat across from Gina.

Jake turned and looked toward the door.

"Please, Jake. We're here to help you. I know that you're not mentally ill, but I don't know why you're behaving this way. I also know that you know me and remember me from Penn. Just like I remember you. I promise that I won't do anything to hurt you or do anything that you don't want me to do. You know that Gina and I lived in the same apartment building and became friends. I had no idea that she lived in LA, but when I recognized you, I called her. This was all my idea to find out what was going on and not make your life worse by kicking you out of the hospital. Refusing to talk is not a psychiatric illness. You'll be medically and mentally cleared tomorrow, to be discharged. I just heard you talk, so obviously you can. What's happening?"

Jake sat down on the sofa and stared silently at the floor.

No one said a word.

"Jake, what's wrong? Please talk to us," Todd said.

After a long silence, Jake looked up at Gina and then at Todd. He said, "Todd, is it okay if I call you that?"

"Of course."

Jake sighed, glanced at Gina, then looked away, then glanced again, like a strange new-age eye dance. Finally, he said, "Todd, I'm sorry I was so difficult. I recognized you right away, but by then I was into my silent routine. So, I kept playing out the role."

Gina sat frozen, tears coursing down her cheeks.

"Gina, I've been so stupid. Ever since you left me, I've been miserable."

"Is that why you're here?" Gina said with a sob.

"God no! It has nothing to do with you. I've never stopped loving you. I need you to give me another chance. Being in here is a whole different story."

Gina kept swiping at the tears rolling down her cheeks and shaking her head.

Todd leaned forward in his chair. "Jake, let's start off by you telling us what's going on? Okay?"

"What will you do with the information?"

"Whatever you want me to do with it."

"Do I have your word that whatever I say, including and especially my name, stays with the three of us?"

"Yes."

"I'll continue to be Patient X, like I heard the staff refer to me, or whatever new name I create?"

"Yes."

Jake looked at Gina. "I'm so sorry I got you involved in this."

Todd interrupted. "I got her involved to help you! She had no idea where you were."

"I know you did, but she's here and what's happening is dangerous, beyond dangerous. Gina, I think it's a good idea that you leave before you're any more involved."

"I'm not going anywhere!"

"This could jeopardize your life. Your future. You're engaged to be married."
Jake swallowed and tears filled his eyes. "I hate that you have a new life and a future without me, but what else could you do? I was so stubborn and immature."

"Jake, I'm here. I'm not leaving." She sighed. "Also, I'm no longer engaged."

"Really?"

"Really."

Jake stood up, crossed the small space that separated them, and sat down next to Gina. He put his arms around her, and they both began to cry. He snuggled closer to Gina, tears streaming down his face, vowing to never, ever let her go again. No-matter what happened, no-matter what she wanted him to do, he'd do it. Nothing else seemed important.

Todd took a deep breath and almost started to cry with them. He waited until they both composed themselves then said, "Okay, Jake. Time for the details."

With his arm around Gina, Jake sat up and looked directly at Todd. "Todd, no matter what happens, or what you think, I can never thank you enough for what you did tonight. Most doctors would have just kicked me out of here or punished me. You know, forced me to take drugs. Thank you."

Todd nodded. "You're welcome."

"This whole thing is going to sound like I'm nuts, a hallucinating, delusional crazy person. I assure you that I'm not." Jake took a deep breath. "Last Saturday afternoon, right before I went to work, I was walking on the Third Street Promenade, and I saw my brother."

"What?" Gina blurted out. "Nelson's dead."

"That's obviously what I thought. You were there when I received his ashes. So, I saw this guy who looked exactly like my brother, less fifty pounds, his hair dark instead of prematurely gray, and I yelled out to him. He looked at me, put a finger up to his lips, like don't say anything, and melted into the crowd." Jake put his finger up to his lips just like Nelson did. "I ran after him, but he was gone."

"How sure are you that it was Nelson?" Todd asked.

"You mean was I hallucinating?"

"Well, I am a psychiatrist," Todd said with a laugh.

"That's what I thought too, that I was going crazy. So, I went into this eye-glass store, right where I saw Nelson disappear. I asked the owner, an Asian guy, if someone matching Nelson's description had just come in? Immediately, he became guarded."

Gina had a confused look.

"That alone was nothing, I mean the guy's reaction. I blew it off and went to work." Jake turned to Gina. "That's when I saw you and your friends...and your fiancé. It was overwhelming. Beyond overwhelming."

Gina moved closer to Jake.

Jake took a deep breath and continued, "After I saw you, I bailed, and ran out of the restaurant. And this is part two of the craziness. When I got to my car, the top was slashed. Someone had obviously broken into it. I chalked it up to another pauper looking for something to sell so he could eat."

"Is that the same fine ride you had back in Philly?" Todd asked, barely hiding a grin.

Jake laughed. "That wasn't very psychiatric, Todd. You know, I may take back all those nice things I just said about you." Todd and Gina laughed with him.

"I drove my excellent vehicle with the floppy top and flawed clutch to my apartment, changed, and walked to a bar in Hermosa. On the way there, an Asian man was standing in front of The Comedy and Magic Club talking on the phone. No big deal, right? An hour or so later, on my way back to the apartment, he started running after me."

Gina interjected. "Oh my God. Jake, were you aware that your apartment was broken into? Yesterday, I went there to talk to you—"

"No! It was fine. You know, as fine as that place can be. How bad was it?"

"Trashed. Everything was all over the floor. Even the pictures were off the wall."

"Jesus. Someone thinks I have something they want. What the hell are they looking for?"

"It all started after you saw your brother," Todd said. "What happened?" He pointed to Jake's head. "Was it the Asian guy?"

"No. The plot thickens, as failed novelists say." Jake rolled his eyes. "After seeing the Asian guy, I ran back to my place and packed. Minutes later, I heard someone at the front door. I climbed out the window and went down the fire escape."

"That rusty, rickety just-waiting-to-fall-down fire escape?" Gina said.

"Same one. Anyway, back on the street, I hid behind a hedge and watched my car. I wanted to make sure the guy who was running after me wasn't lying in wait. Five minutes later, a different Asian guy, big, way over six feet, got out of a black Lexus. I saw him put something under the Alfa. After they left, I checked under the chassis. A small box, a GPS tracker, was attached by magnets to the underside."

"How'd you know what it was?" Todd asked.

"I did some research, for my last novel, in a spy store. They sell covert operations paraphernalia. Anyway, I removed the unit, but it's possible there were two units; or they were somewhere still watching me. After I parked on a different street, to get some coffee, they found me. One smashed me in the head, using maybe something like brass knuckles. I had this switchblade, that I've had since I was a kid, and cut them both. I got away. Just before passing out, I called 911. Now I'm here."

"Why wouldn't you say anything?" Todd asked.

"If I talked, the hospital would have wanted to know my name, insurance, all the identifying details. Also, I didn't know where to go. They knew where I lived, what I drove, plus," he glanced over at Gina, "I didn't have much money and my credit cards were maxed."

Gina squeezed his hand.

"It has to be related to Nelson," Jake said. "We were really close. Not only brothers, but best friends. He would do anything for me. My theory is that he did what he had to...to protect me. I know it."

"Okay," Todd said. "Let's get some sleep. Tomorrow, we'll figure out a plan." Todd stood up. "Jake don't say a word to anyone. Keep up the silent routine."

"Okay, I will. Gina, you're not safe. When you went to my apartment, there's a possibility that they saw you and put a GPS tracker on your car."

"What should I do? Take Uber? Not go back to my apartment?"

"Gina won't use her car until it's checked out, and she won't go home tonight. I'll make sure that she's safe," Todd said.

As Jake and Gina embraced, Todd unlocked the door. He looked up and down the hallway and motioned for Gina to follow him. "Jake, I'll see you tomorrow, probably late afternoon."

Todd unlocked the Nine North security door and he left with Gina.

CHAPTER 14

Gina followed Todd down the dimly lit back stairs of the hospital. Speaking just above a whisper Todd said, "Gina, the safest thing is for you to stay at my place."

Gina nodded, her face a frozen mask.

When they reached the ground floor, Todd opened the door slowly and peered out – just a well lit parking lot with half-a-dozen randomly parked vehicles. Staying in the shadows and walking close to the building, he led Gina around to the front of the hospital and pointed to the barracks. "Please stay here. I'll get my stuff, drive away, then circle back. If anyone follows, call me on my cell."

Huddling in the dark, close to the wall, she nodded. She took out her cell phone and scrolled to recent calls. Her finger poised to immediately call Todd, if need be.

Todd jogged to the door leading to the back stairs, unlocked it, and walked quickly through the hospital – through the lobby and out the front door. He wanted it to appear that he was alone, just a tired doctor finishing a long day. Five minutes later, the sound of the cycle reverberated through the parking lot, and then out to the street. No one followed and no car lights went on. Todd circled back to the hospital, picked up Gina, and they left.

He took the short route, away from the ocean and down Pacific Coast Highway. When they arrived at his townhouse, he clicked open the garage door, pulled in, and waited the extra few seconds until the door completely closed. They both got off the cycle and Todd led Gina up the stairs. He turned on the living room lights just as his cell phone buzzed.

"Hello," Todd answered, expecting it might be the hospital.

"Todd, what's going on?" Tanya's strident tone left no doubt how she was feeling.

"What are you talking about?" Todd answered. He got Gina's attention and mouthed, "Sorry".

"You don't answer my calls and now you're with another woman! That's what I'm talking about. What do you think I'm talking about?"

"It's not what you think."

"Fine! Why don't you tell me what I think, and better yet, tell me what *you* think! I'm sitting outside in my car."

"You were waiting for me?"

"Yes! I want to know what's going on. I can't believe you're treating me this way." She started to cry. "I thought you loved me. Now you're with someone else?"

"I'll be right out. Give me a minute." He clicked off.

"Everything okay?" Gina asked.

Todd sighed. "My girlfriend wants to know why you're here...and why I've been sort of ignoring her. Please take my bedroom and I'll sleep on the sofa. It's a pull-out and comfortable."

"Absolutely not! Don't argue or I'll leave!"

"Argue about what?"

"Just give me some sheets and a towel, maybe an extra toothbrush if you have one, and a sweatshirt or a bathrobe. I'm sleeping on the sofa. Period!"

Todd shook his head. "I'm surrounded by feminists. I apologize for trying to be a gentleman."

Gina laughed and took Todd's hand. "You're a good guy and a gentleman. Whoever she is, she's lucky to have you."

Todd smiled. "Tanya. She's Tanya."

As Todd left, a sick feeling washed over him. Was he that unstable? Until just a few days ago, he thought he was in love and would marry Tanya. Now he was thinking of ER nurses and everyone but her. Tanya enraged him! The thought of kissing her and making love to her was the last thing he wanted to do. Her grand plan for how he should live his life, a mini-daddy surrogate, was disgusting. Money, money, and more money. Was he just a prop? How could he have fallen for such a self-centered, greedy narcissist and stayed with her for a year-and-a-half?

He opened the front door and looked to the right and left. Tanya's Audi was parked across the street under a streetlamp. How was it possible for him to know if he was being watched? Nothing appeared to be out of the ordinary. He crossed the street, opened the Audi's door, and slid onto the front seat.

Tanya's face was mottled with tears and her eyes were swollen. She stared down at her lap, her hands gripping the steering wheel like she was about to fall off a cliff.

Todd took a deep breath. "First, the woman who's in my apartment is Gina Carlton, a friend from Philly. We both lived in the same apartment building. It's a convoluted story, but she's in a committed relationship with a man I'm treating at the hospital. He was pretending to be psychiatrically ill because he was violently attacked on the street and wasn't sure what to do next, kind of hiding out in the hospital. It's likely that whoever attacked him also knows about Gina. She's staying with me tonight until we figure out where they can go. He's still in the hospital; not really my patient, but a friend, someone I want to help."

Tanya turned toward Todd, her eyes wide with rage. "You actually expect me to believe this...this story? Do you think I'm stupid? Or naïve? Or what? Are you writing a second-rate screenplay?"

"Actually, I don't give a shit whether you believe me or not, because there's a second part to all this."

"A second part? You mean like a tawdry Act 2?"

"No, for your information, Act 1. Even before Jake, that's Gina's boyfriend, was admitted to the hospital, I was avoiding you."

"No kidding!"

"I'm sick of buying into your self-absorbed master plan for our future. To be accurate, *your* future. Not mine! You were determined that I should work for Kaiser and make a lot of money. I've told you countless times what I love about being a psychiatrist, and how Kaiser would have turned me into a robot, a pill-pusher. None of that mattered to you. You want a house like your parents, cars like your parents, and a lifestyle like your parents. I don't blame you. There's nothing intrinsically wrong with money, but I have no interest in living in a freaking mansion and spending my time impressing people. You can't accept that, and I was on the verge of telling you that it was over, but I was avoiding the confrontation. I'm not proud of being so passive and weak. That's over!" Todd glared at her.

Tanya started to sob and hyperventilate. "Don't do this, Todd. Why are you doing this? I love you."

"How much can you love me when you expend so much energy trying to change me? I'm not interested in changing!" As the truth flowed out of him, like steam bursting out of a boiler, Todd felt an enormous sense of relief.

Amidst her sobs, Tanya said, "What if I didn't want to change you? What if I accept what you want? What then?"

"That's not the only problem!"

"What do you mean?"

"How many times have you whined about me wearing a yarmulke? How it's silly. How I'm not even religious. How it makes no sense. Well, I accept some responsibility for your confusion, because I never told you exactly why I wear a kipah, my grandfather's term for it."

Tanya nodded and swiped at the tears running down her cheeks.

"Bernie was my grandfather, and he and Rivkah, my grandmother, raised me after my parents died. Bernie was just a teenager in Paris when his family was murdered by the Nazis. At a young age, he became a French resistance fighter and was, and in my mind remains, the most important person in my life. This kipah," Todd took it off and waved it, "is my tribute and my determination to always be true to myself and be there to help people, to be the kind of psychiatrist I believe in. To be the kind of person that my grandfather was and raised me to be. You can take your mansion and your designer bullshit and shove them!" Todd yelled, his face red and his fists clenched.

Sobbing, her body rocking, her face in her hands with tears dripping through her fingers, Tanya was startled. She never heard Todd yell like this.

"I'm not doing this anymore!" Todd took a deep breath and said in a more controlled tone of voice, "I'm sorry, but you'll be happier with someone else, and so will I."

He turned to open the car door and Tanya grabbed him around the shoulders and clung to him. "Please. Please just give me a moment. Please let me say," she sobbed, unable to get out the words. "Please don't leave. Let me say something, please."

Todd took a deep breath and let go of the car handle.

Tanya released him and sat up straighter, her sobs diminishing. "So, tell me this. If your grandfather was so important, and it's clear he was an unbelievable person, and an essential part of your life, why didn't you say something? Why did you let me keep harping about an issue that I now understand is non-negotiable? It doesn't make any sense."

Taking a deep breath and shaking his head, Todd's eyes welled-up with tears. He covered his face with both of his hands and quietly sobbed. Tanya sat frozen, not saying a word. Softly he said, "After my parents died, he and Rivkah gave me a chance to have a life. No one could have loved me more than they did, and Rivkah still does. Bernie never failed me. Not once. Never. It's so painful to think that he's gone. I was afraid to bring it up because I knew I would fall apart."

"Todd, you're not falling apart. Crying is *not* a weakness. Bernie succeeded in helping you become the wonderful person you are, the person I want to spend the rest of my life with."

Todd looked up and stared at Tanya.

"Todd, I knew you weren't happy with me. For months I felt you drifting away." Tanya took a deep breath. "Honestly Todd, I don't know why I behaved the way I did. Up until a few months ago, I imagined what life would be like with you being a professor at UCLA and doing everything you worked so hard to accomplish. I thought it would be wonderful. I guess the truth is that I don't know what to do with my own life. I love my mother, but she spends her time buying artwork, clothes, taking care of the house, vacations, and who knows what else. It works for her. I don't like my job. It's so different than what I dreamed about when I was a girl. You love your job. I feel trapped and powerless in mine."

Todd just looked at her.

"You know I went to NYU drama school. To get accepted was beyond challenging. I got all As, an almost perfect score in my English SATs, a 788, and I got a 5, the highest grade, in AP English. As a junior at NYU, I wrote a screenplay and was halfway through a second one. Also, I loved helping orchestrate all the behind-the-scenes work, especially set design. I loved it all! Then, my father flew out to spend a weekend with me and have a heart-to-heart. How will you make a living and be independent? he asked. Be realistic, honey. Thousands try to support themselves in "The Biz" but they fail. Will you spend the rest of your life working as a waitress trying to get a part in a show or sell your screenplay? He convinced me to change my major. That's how I wound up getting a teaching certificate. He meant well, but it was *very* bad advice. I wasn't strong enough or mature enough to reject it.

"Dealing with middle school kids, who have no other goal except to defy authority, is torture. Two years of that has not been pleasant. If anything, it convinced me that I must make a change, a dramatic change."

"Okay, that makes sense. But setting the yarmulke aside, why have you been so overbearing about *my* life? What I should do. Where I should work."

Tanya shrugged. "Maybe I thought that by having more money, I could be like my mother."

"Like your mother? When did you aspire to be more like her? I like your mother, and I like spending time with her, but you never said anything about wanting to be just like her. I guess I missed all that."

"You didn't miss anything. I know it makes no sense because I've always wanted a career of my own. To be independent and not need my parents to support me. Having a mansion and millions of extra dollars wouldn't be bad, but believe it or not, that was *never* my dream. After I met you, my dream was to spend my life with *you*, have a family, but also to have my own career."

"What are you saying, Tanya?"

"Don't leave me. I love you. I know you're right. I was obnoxious and pushy and appeared to only care about money. I need time to figure this out. It can't be that complicated. I'm not poor, and I'm not stupid. Being a trust fund brat also means that I have choices. I can go back to school and follow another path. Or not go back to school. I'm going to follow *my* dream, and starting right this second, I *will not* interfere with yours. Todd, I can do this. I just got scared and lost. Being with you is the best thing that ever happened to me. You don't bully me or push me or do any of the things that I've been doing to you. Please. I know I sound desperate, but I'm not a weak person. I'm not! I know that we've been happy together, that I make you happy, and you make me happy."

Todd just stared at her, thinking how crazy the mind is. A few minutes ago, he was prepared to never speak to Tanya again. Absolutely 100% happy that it was finally over, that he was a free man. Now he wasn't so sure. In fact, where did all that rage go? When they got along, she really did make him happy – smart, funny, insightful, creative.

He remembered what would happen between Bernie and Rivkah. How at times they would glare at each other – clipped words, clenched fists, angry. Then something would happen, an apology, an explanation, something, and boom, they were okay again; laughing, teasing, whatever issue that caused the problem, gone, pfft. Smoke in the wind.

"I know you're not a weak person," Todd said. "I should have talked to you about all of this sooner. Neither of us is capable of reading minds."

"You did try, but I wouldn't listen."

"I didn't try hard enough."

Tanya reached out and took Todd's hand in hers. "Let's be together tonight, okay? If I do this again, this toxic behavior, you have every right to get me out of your life."

Todd nodded. They got out of the car, and holding hands, crossed the street.

Before unlocking his door, Todd looked up and down the street. Nothing moving. No irregularities.

CHAPTER 15

G ina lay under the blanket fully awake, her mind ricocheting – childhood dreams, adult aspirations, her mother, father, sisters, her connection to Jake – when they first met, the passion, the rage, the disappointment. In just one day, her life went in a direction she never suspected. On some level she always believed that she and Jake would be together, but how this all happened was shocking. Now what? What about grad school? Her apartment? Did she have to put everything on hold? Nelson alive? Men trying to kill, Jake? Trying to kill her? Todd tracking her down to help Jake.

She heard the front door open.

"Gina, it's me. I'm coming up with Tanya. Sorry if I woke you."

"I'm up, Todd. It's okay to turn the light on."

Tanya, sexy, curvy, about 5'10", long blond hair, followed Todd up the stairs. Her face was blotched and puffy, like she'd been crying.

Gina got out of bed, stood up, and shook Tanya's hand. Tanya's grip was firm and her hand warm. She had a kind and vulnerable smile. "I'm sorry to intrude," Gina said. "Todd was kind enough to help Jake and me. Right now, everything's a little crazy."

"No. I'm sorry," Tanya said. "It's late, and I obviously woke you. "We..." She looked at Todd, "had a lot to discuss."

"You didn't wake me. I couldn't sleep. I assume Todd filled you in on what's going on."

Tanya nodded. "It's horrible." She re-grasped Gina's hand between both of her hands. "I'm sorry. Let's talk tomorrow morning. I'll do whatever I can to help."

"Thank you."

Todd turned out the lights, and he and Tanya went upstairs to the bedroom.

Gina walked over to the window, pulled back the drape a few inches, and peered out. Cars were parked on both sides of the empty street. No car lights on. No glow from any smart phones.

She got back in bed, her mind doing what it always did when under stress; look for a solution. What would her mother do in this situation? Her father?

No one she knew was ever involved in such overt violence. Her father's interest in civilization's evolution and his subsequent doctorate in history certainly made him a student of all forms of violence, but mainly it was the violence that evolved from nations at war and the men and women who were the leaders of those nations. Personal violence? None that she knew of. Her mother did intellectual battle in the courtroom. That was it. Never any personal physical violence.

She closed her eyes and tried again to fall asleep. It was impossible. Jake hiding out in a hospital on a psychiatric unit was beyond any logic that she could have imagined. She smiled. Leave it to Jake. He was a smart guy. Who would think to look for him there? In-plain-sight but invisible... Maybe that was the answer? Stick with in-plain-sight but invisible. But how? There had to be an answer. Her mind wandered to family dinners at her Noni's house. A dozen-plus, loud, gesticulating Italians, drinking vino, eating pasta, arguing about a hundred different topics, just like in millions of Italian families all over the world. Even her left-leaning parents blended in with the energy, taking whatever side pleased them, knocking back glasses of red, their voices blending in with the cacophony that was the music and foundation of her family. Electrician, plumber, accountant, lawyer, professor...no one could tell who-was-who by looking or listening. Individuals disappeared into the fabric of the family.

She and Jake had never been religious and had never discussed religion as something that they needed to address. Her Italian heritage and his Jewish heritage were never an issue. Did God exist? A higher power? The big bang theory? All interesting, but the answer didn't seem relevant. Even though billions of people believed in a God, they didn't.

She wondered what kind of religious background Todd had. Why he always wore a yarmulke. He was a bright, very intellectual guy, who despite the yarmulke, didn't seem at all religious. He ate everything. Didn't observe the usual holidays that other Jews observed. There must be a good reason. Maybe one day she'd ask him?

She sighed, closed her eyes, and pictured holding Jake's hand and walking along the beach together. When Jake left the hospital, where would he live? He couldn't go back to his apartment. If she had him live with her, how long would it take for *them* to discover that they were together? A minute? A week? A few weeks? Not too long... There had to be a solution she thought, as she finally drifted off to sleep.

At 6 AM she heard someone rustling around in the small kitchen area. She smoothed out the large UCLA sweatshirt that Todd had loaned her and got out of bed.

"Good morning," she said, and walked barefoot into the kitchen. Todd was looking in one of the cabinets.

"Ah, Good morning. I was trying to be quiet and find the granola bars. Sorry I woke you. I think I'm out of them."

"How about I make us some coffee? If you have any."

"I do. I just bought a new Keurig from Costco last week and I have a box of Peet's." He glanced at his watch. "I've got to leave by 6:30. I also have some, relatively, fresh bagels."

Tanya, yawning and somewhat bleary-eyed, padded downstairs. She was wearing another of Todd's sweatshirts, U of P. "Morning," she said with another yawn.

Minutes later, they were seated at the tiny kitchen table with mugs of coffee, and slathering cream cheese on toasted bagels.

Gina kept staring at Todd's yarmulka and the solution came to her. She pointed to Todd's yarmulke. "Whoever is trying to kill Jake knows where he lives, probably where he works, and can easily find him or for that matter me. For years, Jake and I were all over Facebook. Anyone trying to find him would have no trouble linking the two of us together. If any of us are seen with him, we're vulnerable. Right?"

Both Todd and Tanya nodded.

"What if Jake and I disappeared in plain sight?"

"You borrow Harry Potter's wand?" Tanya said, but without a hint of humor or rancor.

"I wish. A few weeks ago, I met some friends at Canter's Deli, on Fairfax. It was like being in another world. One minute it was 2019, the next I was back in the 18th century surrounded by Hasidic men wearing black suits, high black hats, fringes hanging from under their jackets, and long beards. And the women, wearing long, dark dresses and scarves covering their hair, were just as ancient appearing. Even the young boys were dressed in little dark suits and the girls in mini-mommy dresses."

Todd and Tanya were silent.

"So, what if Jake and I become Hasidic Jews?" She shrugged. "At least until we sort all this out. We need to have some kind of life."

"What do you know about Hasidic Jews?" Tanya asked.

"Absolutely nothing, except that they dress so strangely. I never really looked at any of them. I was too busy feeling a bit shocked and in awe that people in the 21st century dressed that way. If Jake and I melded into the Hassidic community, we'd disappear, in plain sight."

Todd sipped his coffee with an expression that seemed very far away.

"Todd, what do you think?" Gina asked. "Is this a crazy idea?"

He shook his head. "No. It's the same kind of idea that Jake had when he *hid out* on Nine North. The two of you have a similar way of approaching a problem. Unique. Impressive."

"What do you think, Tanya?" Gina asked.

"How about something simpler, like going to the police?"

"After going to the Hermosa Beach Police Department, I'm not a big fan of doing that. The Sgt. I spoke to, was an arrogant, obnoxious know-it-all who couldn't care less. Besides, can the police really protect us? It isn't like we have the option to go into Witness Protection."

Tanya nodded, taking it all in. "I think you're right, Gina. What happened to Jake was horrifying. Who knows how long it'll take to figure this out? Cops are overworked and underpaid. Who knows if we can trust them to be discreet? The only people we can trust is us." Her expression was intense and focused.

"You'll help?" Gina asked.

"Yes! I'm tired of always doing the practical and logical thing, and I'm ready to do the right thing. Whatever it takes. It's one of the main issues that got in the way of my relationship with Todd."

Todd reached across the table and took Tanya's hand.

"Thank you. Thank you both." Gina's eyes welled up with tears.

"Gina, we'll figure this out." Todd glanced at his watch. "I've got to leave. Later, I'll make some phone calls. My grandfather knew a man, a Hasidic man, who lives in Los Angeles. He must be in his eighties. I'll call my grandmother, get his information, and see if he can help. He was in the French Resistance with my grandfather and a very close friend."

CHAPTER 16

That evening, Todd and Jake sat alone in the hospital consultation room. "Jake, this morning, Gina had an interesting idea. She suggested that the two of you hide in-plain-sight as part of the Hassidic Jewish community."

"The what?"

"The ultra-religious Jews, who dress in black and look like they're out of the 17th century."

"Was she stoned? Drunk?"

"Cold sober, my friend."

"That's ridiculous," Jake blurted out. "Gina's not Jewish, and I'm at best a cultural Jew. I enjoy a good bagel and lox sandwich and occasionally a potato knish."

Both men laughed.

With a smile, Todd said, "I know. But it's not about becoming more religious. It's about dressing like a Hassid and playing a role until we unravel what's going on. If you're both careful, who would ever think to look for you in that community?"

"I don't know," Jake said softly. "It makes sense. Gina's *very* smart. But we know nothing about ultra-orthodox Jews. Their lifestyle. How we'd relate to them. Where we'd live? How we'd behave? The only Hebrew word I know is Shalom."

"That's it?" Todd smiled again.

"I dropped out of Hebrew school the day after I was bar mitzvah. Wait! I do know one more thing. The teacher would scream, Shekit b'vakasha! Quiet in the classroom." Jake laughed. "So, I'll go up to a fellow Hassid and say, Shalom. Shekit b'vakasha!"

Todd rolled his eyes. "C'mon Jake. Do you have a better idea?"

Jake sighed. "Not really. I can't go back to my apartment. If I lived with Gina at UCLA, she'd be in danger. For that matter, wherever we go, we'd be in danger. Even if we left the state. I'm assuming whoever's doing this can track us on the internet. This is a total mess."

"Okay then. I'll follow through with Gina's idea. I'm waiting to talk to my grandmother's friend, who can possibly help. It might take a while. He has medical issues, but his wife promised she'd have him call back ASAP."

"How long's a while?"

"He's post-surgery and still in the hospital. Any day."

"So, I have to stay here until you speak to him?"

"Not really... Where else do you suggest you hide out?"

"Damn it, Todd. This place is a looney bin."

"True. But so far, it's been a haven."

Jake reluctantly nodded.

"Okay, Jake. Here's the plan. Slowly, very slowly, start to talk. Come up with an alias. Don't divulge that you were attacked. Ever! Just say that you have no idea what happened. No memory how you wound up here. No idea why you're crying at night and waking up at 4 AM, unable to fall back to sleep. No idea why you keep having thoughts that you want to hurt yourself. Voices that call you, 'A piece of shit! Worthless! A loser'!"

"Are you kidding me? Why would I do that?"

"I've got to make a case that you're psychiatrically ill and need to stay hospitalized. In today's world, the object is to get patients out of the hospital. Especially in public institutions, where the bed situation is always critical."

"Okay... Why those symptoms?"

"So, I can justify that you have a Major Depression with psychotic features, and that you're a danger to yourself. Discharging you under those conditions isn't acceptable. The chief of inpatient services won't question my decision.

"Remember Jake, do it slowly. Tomorrow, remember your name. But elaborate that you don't remember how you got here. In two days, act weird like you're hearing things." Todd stared at the ceiling and shook his head like he wanted the voices he was hearing to stop. Then he put his hands over his ears. "See what I mean?"

Jake nodded.

"When anyone asks what's wrong, be vague. Don't answer. Or say you don't remember. Later, you can finally admit that voices are calling you names but then refuse to say what the names are. Eventually, you'll be more specific. We'll talk every day and review what you should do. Hopefully, by the end of the week, we'll have a more concrete plan in place."

• • • •

THE NEXT MORNING IN the cafeteria, Jake sat at a four-top silently debating whether to eat the runny scrambled eggs and over-burnt toast. To his left was his paranoid roommate, Reggie, who thought that the CIA was trying to kill him. Across from him was Larry, a skinny black guy, about thirty, whose face kept contorting, his tongue sticking in and out, his eyes and mouth opening and closing, and saliva dripping down the side of his neck.

"Stop moving your face at me!" Reggie screamed, abruptly standing up, holding his plastic spoon like he was going to stab Larry.

"Hey man," Jake said. "Calm down. No one's trying to hurt you."

"Fuck you, too!" Reggie screamed launching himself across the table at Larry.

Jake leaped out of his seat, wrapped his arms around Reggie's torso and dragged him away from the table.

Within seconds, two male staff were there, each man grasping an arm, and hauling Reggie out of the cafeteria.

Jake sat back down at the table.

"Thank you," Larry said, wiping saliva from his chin.

Jake looked at him, the contortions hard to look at without wincing. He kept his face as neutral as he could. "Did he hurt you?"

"No. You stopped him."

"I'm glad I helped."

"Most people wouldn't do anything. They can't look at me without disgust plastered across their faces."

"That must be tough. What's wrong?"

Larry sighed. "A few years ago, I got really depressed. I went to a clinic in south central, near where I lived, and saw a psychiatrist. He put me on an antidepressant. That didn't work, so a few months later he tried another one. When that didn't work, he added an older medication called Haldol. He said that the newer antipsychotics, the ones that were used in conjunction with antidepressants to treat depression, were too expensive. I wanted to move closer to work, but apartments in the South Bay were exorbitant, so saving money seemed like a good idea. At first Haldol helped, but six months later," he pointed to his face, "this happened."

"What is it?"

"They call it tardive dyskinesia."

"Can they fix it?"

"I've been here two weeks. They were afraid that if they abruptly stopped all the medication, I might become extremely depressed. So, they tapered it. Sometime this week I'm seeing a neurosurgeon."

"Why?"

"They can do brain surgery and hopefully give me my life back."

"I sure hope they can," Jake said.

"I'm Larry Girard," he said, holding out his hand as his face contorted.

"I'm Jerry," Jake said, and shook his hand.

"Jerry, how come you're in here?"

"Had a black out. Couldn't remember anything and couldn't talk. Really confused."

In between facial and tongue spasms, Larry looked perplexed. "Shouldn't you be seeing a neurologist?"

"The doctors told me I already saw one. The neurologist referred me to a psychiatrist." Jake shrugged and changed the subject. "What kind of work do you do, Larry?"

"Computer programming. The company I worked for had a government contract. Ever hear of Tor?"

"No."

"Black web?"

"Sounds like science fiction."

Larry nodded, his face and mouth continually contorting. "It does sound that way and in some ways it's other-worldly. Believe it or not, the government monitors Tor."

A female nurse entered the room and announced, "Okay, time for social group in ten. Finish breakfast and let's go."

• • • •

LATER THAT MORNING, a brawny, Hispanic guy, sat down next to Jake in the patient lounge. "Hi," he said.

Jake nodded.

"I noticed that you were talking to Larry this morning."

Jake nodded again.

"I'm Raoul. A psych tech on the unit. Feeling better?"

"Still kinda spacey."

"What's your name?"

"Jerry...Jerry Kent." Clark Kent's brother. Trapped in a looney bin.

"Do you remember what happened, Jerry? Why you're here?"

"I don't know." Jake screwed up his face and shrugged.

"You were mugged. The cops found you passed out in front of the Redondo Beach police station. Whoever did it bashed you in the head and you needed stitches."

"I don't remember anything."

"Amnesia can happen with head trauma. Maybe your memory will come back?"

"Hope so."

"What do ya do, Jerry?"

"...I'm sorry. I gotta real bad headache. Is it okay if I go back to my room and lay down?"

"Sure, Jerry. Need any help?"

Jake looked around and shrugged his shoulders. "It's that way, right?" He pointed toward the door.

"Yeah. After you leave the lounge, go down the hall to your right. You're in the second room on the left."

"Thanks. I'm sorry. What's your name again?"

"Raoul."

"Sorry. My mind..."

"No problem, Jerry. You're doing better than yesterday. It's moving in the right direction."

Jake left the lounge. As he turned toward his room, a young woman with a shaved head wearing a hospital gown shuffled toward him. As she approached, she pulled up her gown and exposed her vagina and large breasts. "Want some of this?" she screamed, her expression a mixture of lewd and deranged.

Jake quickly stepped away from her and walked quickly to his room.

• • • •

AT 6 PM, JAKE MET WITH Todd.

"Jake, it's not safe for you to stay here on the unit." Todd's expression was dead serious.

"Okay... What happened?"

"Dr. Binette, the chief of inpatient services, said he wanted to talk to me about you. We have a meeting set up for tomorrow at 9 AM."

"Why?"

"He was vague, but something about the Chinese embassy requesting more information."

"Shit. That's not good."

"I know. You need to leave tonight." He handed Jake a key. "The best time is during shift change, 11 PM. Get out of bed and head to the restroom. When you're sure no one's looking, unlock the unit door and leave. Make sure to re-lock the door. It's a dead bolt. Go to the end of the hallway and make a right.

Then go down the back stairs to the 4th floor. They're remodeling that floor, so the door's unlocked. I'll leave a bag with clothes, some of my stuff that I think will fit you, right inside. Change and go all the way down the stairs and out to the parking lot. Tanya, my girlfriend, will pick you up. 11:10 sharp. She'll be waiting by the stairwell exit."

CHAPTER 17

Wearing an LA Dodgers cap, dark glasses, black jeans, and a black pullover jersey, Jake opened the door and stepped outside into the parking lot. Tanya was waiting at the back entrance in her Audi. Jake got in.

"Hi Jake, I'm Tanya. Gina's back at Todd's apartment."

Jake reached over and shook Tanya's hand. "Thank you. I'm sorry that I've involved you."

"You're welcome. Don't be sorry, Jake. I'm happy to help."

Jake took a deep breath. Todd and Tanya were risking their lives to help him. It made him wonder again, what motivated Nelson to fake his own death, and why whoever was after Nelson were now after him.

Tanya exited the parking lot and made a left on Carson. Five minutes later, as they crossed Crenshaw Blvd., Jake asked, "Where does Todd live?"

"Redondo Beach."

"Tanya, would you please stop on the way to Todd's? It's about a half block from the Redondo Beach Police Station, house number 345. I'll know the street when I see it."

"Sure."

"Right before I passed out, I tossed my knife and wallet under the steps of a random house. I figured if the police or an ambulance picked me up with an ID and a knife, it would make things a lot more complicated."

"How'd you know to do that?"

Jake shrugged.

"Hmm. You have an impressively devious mind." She laughed.

"I'm not sure that's a complement."

Smiling, Tanya turned north on Hawthorne Blvd. "Gina said you're a writer. Maybe that explains it."

"She's being kind. I work hard at trying to be a writer, but so far haven't hit pay-dirt. Only dirt. Dirt without a trace of any valuable minerals. It's beyond frustrating, also humiliating."

"You know, Jake. I spend my life teaching bratty, middle-school kids. It's also frustrating and for me unrewarding. For others it's a dream job. The fact that you followed your dream is impressive."

"Gina told you about me?"

"Not everything." She laughed. "But enough to know how much she loves you."

"I was so damn stubborn."

"The opposite of me. I followed all the dots and gave up on my dream."

"What dream?"

Gina made a few turns and then headed north on PCH. "Really, anything having to do with the creative arts. I wrote a screenplay. I love all aspects of staging, directing, and acting." She laughed. "I was Peter Pan in my middle school play."

Jake smiled. "Where did you go to college?"

"NYU."

"One of the best drama and creative schools in the country. I went too far with my dream; you didn't go far enough."

In Redondo Beach, Tanya saw the police station and slowed down. "Which way?"

"Straight. At the next street make a left. Okay. Please stop here. Can I borrow your iPhone? I need the flashlight."

Tanya flipped it on and handed it to him.

Jake got out of the car and looked around. The street was deserted. He crawled under the steps. Seconds later he was back in the car.

"Get it?"

"Yep. Let's go to Todd's."

• • • •

"GINA, TODD TOLD ME in the hospital that you suggested that we become Hasidic Jews. Is that right?" Jake sat at Todd's small table, with Gina, Tanya, and Todd.

"Jake, you're over-dramatizing my idea. Living in an area where Hasidic Jews live and dressing like them is *not* becoming one of them. I don't want either of us to be killed."

Todd laughed.

"What's so funny, Todd?" Jake couldn't believe that all three of them thought that this was a good idea. It was ludicrous. What educated person

could ever believe in an almighty God, the master of the universe? In synagogue, if you carefully read the English translation in the prayer books it was
horrifying. God this and God that and how God was so powerful and all-know-
ing blah blah. To Jake it sounded like the rantings of a demented narcissist.
Whoever wrote all that drivel should have toned it down. Especially the story about God demanding that Abraham sacrifice his son Isaac as proof that he
idolized God. Nonsense! Destructive! No reasonable man would ever contem-
plate doing such a thing to his son. The prisons were filled with crazies who did
stuff like that.

"Just the expression on your face. You act like Gina asked you to jump off a
cliff," Todd replied. "Luckily, my grandfather's friend called, and now we have a
legitimate contact."

"Fine. Are you religious? Do you believe any of this ancient nonsense? Destructive nonsense." Jake pointed to Todd's yarmulke.

"No. I don't."

"If you don't, why do you wear a yarmulke?"

"It's a long story." Todd glanced over at Tanya and took a deep breath. "And
a fair question... Let me give you the abbreviated version." He restated what
he'd just told Tanya the night before, how much he loved his grandfather and
grandmother, and how this was a tribute to his grandfather and to the collec-
tive past.

Jake closed his eyes and nodded. "You had a lot of pain in your life, but
you also had two people who had no agenda except to cherish you. To love you
deeply and without reservation."

Todd sighed. "Jake, you're a poet and a philosopher."

"Poets and philosophers are on the same pay scale as unpublished authors."
Jake shrugged.

Gina leaned forward and kissed Jake softly on the lips.

Jake kissed her back and then turned toward Todd. "Okay, I get it. Since I
can't come up with a better alternative plan, I'll do it. We'll do it. Whatever it
takes. Do you know enough about Judaism to help us? Can you also help me
squelch the negative feelings I have about religion in general?"

Todd said, "I don't know much about Judaism, and I'm not a believer. But
the man you're going to meet is a believer. He's the grandson of my grandfather's friend, probably in his early thirties. Avrum Goldstein is one of the rabbis

at the Chabad in Westwood. I already called him and explained everything. He offered to help."

"In Westwood, on campus?" Gina broke in. "Where?"

"On Gayley."

"On the weekends, I've often seen religious Jews wearing black suits and black hats and women with head scarfs and long dresses. I had no idea that there was a Chabad so close by."

Todd turned to Jake. "In my opinion, Gina's idea makes sense. It'll take time to figure out why your brother had to fake his own death. This will give you a cover while we unravel the mystery. The rabbi will meet you at 10 AM tomorrow morning. He said to park in back.

Rabbi Goldstein explained that by helping you he'd be performing a mitzvah, a blessing. He called it tzedakah. It's a Hebrew term for doing the righteous thing, a sense of fairness and justice. I heard of tzedakah from my grandfather, but it never registered till now. It feels exactly right, and why I personally want to help you. I get the feeling that if I were in trouble, you'd help me."

Jake nodded. "I would. I will. You can count on it."

"I'm Jewish and never heard of tzedakah," Tanya said. "But I also want to do the right thing. Just don't make me wear all that Hassidic stuff. Although, I think wearing a scarf on one of those days when my hair's a disaster isn't such a bad idea."

They laughed and Jake raised his wine glass. "To my friends, who I will never abandon and will always cherish."

CHAPTER 18

At 2 AM, Todd drove Jake back to the hospital on his Harley. Together, using flashlights, they crawled under Gina's Prius and searched for any GPS units. When they were sure that nothing looked amiss, Jake followed Todd to the underground parking garage at Roth & Associates, Tanya's father's investment firm in Century City.

Jake used the access card that Tanya had given him, and parked Gina's car where Tanya had advised. The garage was almost empty, just a few high-end vehicles in reserved parking spots. Jake sighed, accepting for maybe the first time in his life how nice it would be to have more money. He really was tired of worrying if the Alfa would start in the morning, or how much it would cost for the shoemaker to replace the soles on his boots. The most important thing in his life was Gina. Thinking about her almost made him forget the threat to his life. How incredibly fortunate he felt to be getting a second chance. He locked the car, turned a full 360 degrees to make sure no one was following him, and jogged up the steps to the exit. Todd was waiting. He got on the back of the cycle, put on the helmet, and they roared away.

Early the next morning, using a Roth & Associates credit card, Tanya went to a local Avis car rental agency and leased a gray Toyota Corolla.

At 9:50 AM, Jake and Gina pulled into the Westwood Chabad parking lot. They got out of the rented Toyota and walked directly to the back door. It was unlocked.

Once inside, they passed through a small kitchen and entered a large sanctuary. There were a dozen men with long beards, wearing dark suits, yarmulkes, and tallit, sitting on wooden chairs facing a stage. Two younger men with dark full beards, and an old man with a long, gray beard, read from the Torah. One of the younger men, thin, six feet tall, in his thirties, backed away from the others and walked down the steps toward Jake and Gina. He motioned with his hand for them to follow.

They entered a spacious office – no windows, three desks, floor to ceiling bookshelves bursting with prayer books, scholarly texts, and cardboard boxes filled with yarmulkes and handouts. The man motioned for his two guests to stand beside him, and he handed Jake what looked like a tree branch. Jake took it, having no clue what it was.

"I'm Rabbi Avrum Goldstein. Shalom, Jake and Gina." He turned and solemnly shook hands with each. "I just handed you a lulov, a palm branch joined together with myrtle and willow branches. Today is the first day of Sukkot. Welcome to our sanctuary on this important holiday."

Both Jake and Gina nodded respectfully as the rabbi spoke.

"I'm one of the three rabbis here at Chabad, and the one who spoke to your good friend Dr. Horowitz. Before we talk more, I'd like you to pray with me, to celebrate Succoth. The festival began on the eve of the 15th of Tishri, that was last night, and commemorates the final harvest of the year and the shelter of the Israelites during their 40 years in the wilderness."

Jake and Gina nodded.

"Are you Jewish?"

Jake nodded yes, and Gina said, "No, Rabbi."

"It's no matter. All are welcome. Please Jake, repeat after me. Ba-ruch A-taw Ado-nai E-lo-he-nu Me-lech ha-olam," and he continued as Jake repeated each word after the rabbi. "Blessed art thou, Lord our God, King of the Universe, who has sanctified us with his Commandments, and commanded us to dwell in the Sukkah." He turned to Jake. "Are you a practicing Jew?"

"I was Bar Mitzvah," Jake said, "but haven't participated in any formal religion since I was thirteen."

The rabbi nodded and pointed to the three branches of the lulov. "All Jews and non-Jews are welcome. The spirit of Chabad is never clearer than during Succoth, seven days of coming together to eat, pray and discuss all important intellectual and spiritual issues. We do this in the Succah, a structure built like one that our ancestors lived in during the forty years in the wilderness. Deeply religious Jews, Jews who are more spiritual than religious, and Jews who are non-sectarian are all welcome. All are invited to partake." He looked at Gina. "You are sincerely, welcome too. I hope you will share this sacred time with us." He took the lulov, placed it on a desk, and motioned for Jake and Gina to sit down. Noticing the office door was open, he closed it, then sat down across from them. "Please, tell me how I can help. Dr. Horowitz shared some of the issues, but I'd like to hear what you both think."

"Thank you, Rabbi Goldstein. It's a long story. Do you have time now, with the service going on?"

"Yes."

Jake started at the beginning – seeing Nelson on the promenade in Santa Monica, escaping from the man following him, how he was attacked and then fought back, and how he hid out on the psych unit. "Rabbi, I have no idea why any of this is happening. What I do know is that I'm in mortal danger and anyone associated with me is also in danger. It frightens me to place anyone else at risk. You, your congregants, anyone who associates with me is in danger. I can't use any credit cards or my real name, because whoever is doing this can employ electronic sources to trace my actions and my location."

The rabbi nodded thoughtfully, pulling a bit on his scraggly beard. "Whoever is doing this knows what you look like?"

"Yes."

"Did you have a beard when you were first attacked?"

"No. I just shaved that morning, around ten days ago. He ran his hand over his scraggly facial hair. Why do you ask?"

"Do you wear glasses?"

"You mean corrective lenses?"

"Yes."

"No. Only sunglasses."

"Please stand up." Jake stood and the rabbi stood next to him. He looked at Gina. "We're around the same size and build, right?"

"Yes."

"Gina, will you be staying with Jake?"

She nodded.

"Okay. Gina, would you please stand up?" Gina stood – slim, five feet, seven inches tall, short dark hair, wearing a pair of washed-out jeans, a gray UCLA sweatshirt, and a University of Pennsylvania baseball cap. The rabbi looked at her and shrugged, like he was stumped.

"What's wrong?" Gina asked. "I know I'm not dressed appropriately for a house of worship. I hope this doesn't offend you."

"No. No. Please, you don't offend me. You look very fine. It's just that I'm not so good at estimating clothing, size and so on. The last time I bought my wife an outfit it took her a long time to stop laughing." He chuckled. "Would you mind if she met you?" He glanced at his watch. "She should be here any minute with my children. It's for the holiday. Many young families eat together outside in the Sukkah. Say prayers, talk, share the meal."

"That's fine. Of course, I'll meet her."

Minutes later, a four-year-old boy, dressed in a tiny dark suit, burst into the room. He ran up to the rabbi and hugged him around the knees. A petit woman wearing an ankle-length dress, a head scarf, and carrying an infant, followed behind. The rabbi swept the little boy up in his arms and kissed his face. "Ah, bubalah. Shalom, my handsome little one. What a joy!" The boy squirmed out of the rabbi's arms and ran back to his mother, snuggling in the folds of her long dress.

The rabbi walked over to his wife, lifted her hand in both of his and kissed it. Leaning in close, he whispered in her ear. She nodded a few times, walked over to Gina, and shook her hand. "I'm Rebecca Goldstein. Very pleased to meet you."

"Hi Rebecca, I'm Gina Carlton. I'm very pleased to meet you too."

Rebecca stepped back from Gina, looked at her carefully, and nodded. She turned to her husband. "Leila is about the same size. It won't be a problem." She turned back to Gina and to Jake. "My husband is very smart and very kind. I know he will do everything to help you and so will I. Please excuse me, I need to prepare lunch in the Sukkah. May God bless you both and keep you safe."

After Rebecca and the children left, the rabbi again closed the door, and sat down close to Jake and Gina. In a soft voice he said, "I understand that you both are in mortal danger, and I have decided to do everything I can to help you. Staying here, so close to the university campus, would be too dangerous. Our congregation is small, and our manner of dress and our customs stick out like a sore thumb. It's a bad analogy but you know what I mean. I have a cousin, Mordecai Toland, who is a history professor on sabbatical from USC. He lives in an area of the city where the customs of Hasidic Jews are part of the neighborhood. He gave me permission last night to let you live in his home, two months of free rent, then two thousand a month. He is doing this as a mitzvah. Homes in the area rent for $4000 a month. Also, I have a good friend who lives right in the neighborhood. He can show you around. Get you both acclimated." He looked at Jake. "You're a writer?"

"Yes, but I also have a degree in economics."

The rabbi looked at Gina. "What is your background, if I may ask?"

"Also, economics. I'm in the PhD program at UCLA."

"Excellent. Morrie, Morris Weisberg is my friend. I'll give him the information. Sometimes God works in mysterious ways," the rabbi said with an enigmatic smile.

Jake leaned forward in his chair, closer to the rabbi. "Rabbi Goldstein, you know how dangerous this all is. Are you sure it's, okay?" Jake took a deep breath. "I feel so conflicted accepting your help."

The rabbi closed his eyes for a few moments then looked directly at Jake. "Not for one second do I doubt my decision to help you and Gina. It's a long story, but Bernie Horowitz, Todd's grandfather, saved my grandfather's life. They were both young boys in Nazi run Paris. Bernie shot and killed three German soldiers who were kicking and clubbing my grandfather, almost to death. He carried my grandfather Jorge to a safe place, got him medical care, and fought alongside him until the Americans invaded Normandy and freed the French from Nazi rule. Jorge told me this story when I was ten years old, and I have longed to be the kind of man Jorge and Bernie were. It is my honor to help you. In this time of great danger and the need for courage, may I bless you both?"

They glanced at each other and nodded.

The rabbi stood, walked behind Jake and Gina, and placed his hands on the top of their heads.

Jake closed his eyes as the rabbi gently touched his head. Memories of when he was a little boy raced through his mind. There was a time when he felt so connected and close to his parents. He remembered his father taking him to a Phillies game, eating hotdogs, wearing a brand-new Phillies baseball cap, holding his father's hand. Losing them was devastating. When he believed that Nelson had died, it was heart-wrenching. Now there was hope. He would do everything in his power to find and help his brother.

The rabbi chanted, "Ba-ruch A-taw Ado-nai E-lo-he-nu Me-lech ha-olam... May god bless Jake Bennett and Gina Carlson in their time of need, and may He, in all his strength and wisdom, help them overcome any transgressors. Amen." After a short period of silence, he said, "Please stay here for the next few hours. Rebecca will bring you some delicious food to eat, and soon I'll bring you the kind of clothes you'll need and a key to Mordecai's house. I'm sure you'll be comfortable there until this dangerous issue is resolved. My friend Morrie will come by tomorrow morning and show you around the neighborhood."

"Thank you again, Rabbi," Jake said. "Can I ask you a quick question before we go?"

"Of course."

"Why did you smile and say that sometimes God works in mysterious ways, after we mentioned that we had degrees in economics?"

"Morrie works for one of the biggest brokerages in the city. He's a senior vice president."

CHAPTER 19

J ake parked the Toyota on Sycamore Street, two blocks past La Brea Ave. It was an area populated with lovely single-family-homes, townhouses, apartment buildings, a Jewish educational center, a kosher food market, restaurants, coffee shops, and furniture stores.

A man in a black suit wearing a black yarmulke walked out of the market carrying a shopping bag, as two men dressed the same way entered. Two women in long dresses and head scarves, walking side by side, chatted as they pushed baby strollers. Across the street, three men wearing dark suits and high black hats, stood in the middle of the sidewalk talking and gesticulating wildly.

Jake looked at Gina, shook his head, and grinned.

"What?" she said, grinning back. Gina wore an ankle-length, gray dress with long sleeves that covered her wrists, a gray and black head scarf, and no make-up. Jake looked like he stepped out of the middle-ages – black-suit, white long-sleeve dress shirt, medium-height black hat, and tzitzit, a woolen vest-like piece of clothing with fringes hanging from each of its four corners that hung below the bottom of his jacket.

"Shalom," he said, and kissed her. "I've never seen anyone as beautiful as you. You look like the movie-star version of the biblical Ruth."

"Shalom back to you, my Rebbe." She grazed her fingers softly over his scraggly beard and kissed him.

Laughing, they got out of the car, popped the trunk, and took out four large shopping bags filled with food and clothing. Rebecca insisted they needed it all and wouldn't take no for an answer. No arguments. Period! That woman was a five-foot-one-inch tigress.

Filled with more love than he ever thought possible, Jake held Gina's hand, and they walked up the steps to the front door. His failed novel, credit card debt, sense of alienation, humiliation at being a waiter, all seemed so inconsequential. He unlocked the door, and they went inside.

Gina looked around and smiled. "Jake, this is a really nice place. I like it. In fact, I love it. Do you?" The living area, dining area, and kitchen were all situated in one spacious room. Sunlight filtered through a half-dozen tall windows and filled the space with a bright yellow glow. Steps led upstairs to three bed-rooms.

"I love being here with you. I was such a stupid jerk."

"All true, my Rebbe. But I was referring to the architecture."

Jake leaned down and kissed Gina. "You want to try out our new bedroom? See if the bedroom architecture is up to your standards?"

"Are you sure a Rebbe is supposed to act this way?" she said, with a lascivi-ous grin.

"Yes. It's written in the Torah. It's a bracha. A blessing."

"Hmm. That sounds serious. I wouldn't want to break any holy brachas, Rebbe Bennett." She took Jake's hand, and he followed her up the stairs.

• • • •

THE NEXT MORNING AT 8 AM, the doorbell rang. Dressed in his black suit, white shirt, and wearing a black yarmulka, Jake opened the door.

Standing on the stoop was a man shaped like a fireplug – 5 feet, 6 inches tall and very wide. He had a long salt and pepper beard, wore a black suit and a black fedora, pinched in the front. "Good morning," the man said, and thrust his hand out. "I'm Morrie Weisberg, Rabbi Goldstein's friend."

Jake reached out and shook Morrie's hand. "Pleased to meet you, Morrie. I'm Jake Bennett." At that moment, Gina walked down the stairs, dressed in a long dress and headscarf, and approached the door. Jake turned, took Gina's hand, and said, "This is Gina Carlton. Gina, this is Morrie Weisberg, Rabbi Goldstein's friend."

Gina smiled and reached out her hand. "Pleased to meet you, Mr. Weis-berg."

"Likewise," Morrie said, and shook her hand. "Please Gina, call me Morrie. Have you had breakfast yet?"

"No," both Jake and Gina answered.

"Good," Morrie said. "Come, we'll have breakfast and coffee, and I'll help get you situated."

A few blocks away, at La Brea Bakery, they were seated in the spacious, French-modern, dining room. The place was bustling with men and women in

Hassidic dress and just as many in casual secular attire. No one looked out of place.

"They have terrific omelets and coffee. My treat," Morrie stated, as they settled into their chairs.

"No, please, Morrie. My treat," Jake said. Todd had given him a hundred and twenty dollars in small bills. He said he'd get the money back from hospital storage. It was the money that Jake had shoved into his boot.

"Next time it's on you." Morrie smiled and shook his stubby finger. "No argument, boychick."

"Thank you," Jake and Gina said, almost in unison.

"My pleasure."

The waitress, an older woman wearing a long-sleeve blouse, a skirt that covered her ankles, and a curly brown wig, took their orders.

When she left the table, Morrie said, "Avrum told me all about what's going on, how you need to live here until you're out of danger. He mentioned that you both have degrees in economics from the University of Pennsylvania. A fine school. Are you interested in work?"

"Yes," Jake answered, and looked at Gina.

She nodded in agreement. Her thought was that she'd call Professor Givens, the chairman of her department, and explain that she had a family emergency. Hopefully she'd let her continue to work on her PhD thesis.

"I'm with IBC, Imperial Bank of Canada. A financial advisor, senior vice president," Morrie said with a mote of pride.

"Oh," Jake responded, keeping a poker face. He was up until 4 AM, reviewing economic theory. It was amazing how much he had forgotten and how much came back after he started to review the economists that he studied in college.

Morrie smiled. "Never heard of it, huh?

"Heard of what, Morrie?" For a moment his mind had wandered.

"IBC."

"I haven't been that involved in economics for the last few years," Jake responded.

"It's the largest investment bank in Canada," Gina chimed in. "On the same par as Merrill Lynch, Morgan Stanley, and RBC. It has a great reputation."

Morrie nodded. "Do either of you have your Series 7 and Series 63 licenses?" Morrie asked.

Jake nodded. "I do. Just renewed both in July."

"What?" Gina said, obviously shocked. "You never told me."

Jake shrugged. "I got my Series 7 back in Philly before we graduated. Remember, I was working part time at Fidelity? They sponsored me. When we moved to California, I added the Series 63."

Gina just stared at Jake wide-eyed.

"I know. Too busy studying to get yours," Jake said kindly. He looked at Morrie. "Gina is on the last leg of getting her doctorate in economics at UCLA. She's brilliant. The smartest person I know."

The waitress brought their meals and filled the coffee cups.

When they were finished eating, Morrie took a sip of coffee and looked directly at Jake. "What would you consider your basic economic or investment philosophy to be?" He was all business.

Jake thought for a moment and then said, "I'm a bit old fashioned. I know that Warren Buffet's approach is basically applying the Firm Foundation Theory. You know, buy securities below their intrinsic value, and then sell when they are temporarily too high. He also acquires a commanding percentage of a company, so he's in control. Plus, he's a long-term investor and believes that given enough time his choices will pan out and make money."

Morrie nodded, listening carefully.

"I agree with all that," Jake added, "but I'd also lace my investments with a strong dose of John Maynard Keyes, the Castle in the Air Theory. He came up with this philosophy in 1936, but I believe that he should still be taken very seriously."

Gina stared raptly at Jake; an expression of awe written all over her face.

Without missing a beat, Jake continued, "His idea to estimate how a crowd of investors will behave and then to beat them by investing first is a solid idea. Even after sixty years, it's still absolutely viable." Jake laughed. "You can also call it, 'The Greater Fool Theory'. It's brilliant. If you invest soon enough, there will always be a slew of followers that'll make you a great deal of profit. But keep it too long, and it becomes a bust...like The Tulip Mania, in the Netherlands, in the 1600s."

Morrie's expression was deadpan, a world class poker expression. He turned to Gina. "What's your philosophy, Gina?"

"I've been doing a lot of work analyzing Harry Markowitz, who won the Nobel Prize in economics in 1990. In fact, my PhD thesis is based on his initial work...with some of my own permutations. His idea, that I'm sure you're familiar with, is that a portfolio of risky stocks can be put together in such a way that the portfolio, as a whole, is less risky than the individual stocks in the portfolio. I'm working on a theory to simplify how covariance can be applied to MPT, Modern Portfolio Theory."

Gina took a sip of coffee and continued, "Covariance has too long been totally in the realm of theoretical economists. My goal is to simplify and strengthen how it can be applied for the average investor."

Morrie nodded with a pensive expression. He finished his coffee and motioned to the waitress for the check. "I've got to get to the office. Gina, Jake, let me think about some things. Will you be available to talk this evening?"

"I'll be somewhat busy trimming my beard, but I could squeeze you in. How 'bout you, Gina?" Jake answered with a smile.

"Scriptures... I'll be analyzing the uh...Midrash, but for you Morrie, I'll take a break."

They all laughed.

Still looking quite thoughtful, Morrie left money for the check, opened his briefcase, and handed Jake a phone and Gina a phone. "Burners. We'll use them not more than twice, then replace. If it's okay, I'll be at your house tonight at 7." Without waiting for an answer, Morrie got up and left the table.

CHAPTER 20

A t 7 PM sharp, there was a knock at the front door.
Jake, dressed casually in a washed-out U of P T-shirt and Levi's, opened the door. Morrie, still wearing the same black suit and fedora, stood at the entrance. Jake shook his hand and ushered him in.

"Hi Morrie. Like some tea or coffee?" Gina asked, as she walked out of the kitchen, wearing jeans and a powder-blue UCLA sweatshirt.

"That would be great... Coffee, please. A little cream. No sugar. Thanks, Gina."

Minutes later, the three of them sat around the kitchen table, sipping their drinks. Morrie leaned forward and said with a serious expression, "God works in wondrous and mysterious ways. For months, before I ever met either of you, I'd been looking to expand my business. I examined all aspects of how to reasonably grow and have been interviewing potential candidates. The two of you are by far the best I've seen. Full disclosure. I did extensive background checks on both of you. I know pretty much what you've been doing over the past three years and..." He shrugged. "It all works out for me." He took another sip of coffee and focused on Jake. "In spite of not doing anything in finance over the last few years, obviously pursuing other interests, you are still *very* impressive. Phi Beta Kappa from Penn, having your series 7 and 63, and a solid grasp of investment strategies are major selling points. If you want the job, you can be my new associate. You'll deal directly with clients under my license." He turned to Gina. "My current manager is getting married and moving to the east coast. Two weeks ago, was her last day. I need someone to run my office. As soon as you get your Series 7 and 63, you can start dealing directly with clients." He made eye contact with both. "Please, think it over. Sleep on it. Let me know tomorrow morning if you're interested."

"No need to think," Jake said immediately. "I accept."

"I also accept," Gina said.

Morrie took a deep breath and smiled. "That makes me very happy. Given your current situation, it's best that you both use an alias. Take the weekend to get organized. On Monday, when you come in for work, you'll tell me your new names. I'll set up accounts for both of you. At the end of the fiscal year, we'll square things with your authentic Social Security numbers." He shrugged. "We'll figure it out. For now, no worries. God willing, in a few months, there will be no more need for subterfuge."

"You're amazing," Jake said, flabbergasted that this absolute stranger was being so kind.

"I'm just a man doing a mitzvah. It's what Chabad Hassidism is all about," Morrie responded, a sincere expression on his face.

Tears filled Gina's eyes. "Thank you, Morrie. You're helping to save our lives."

"I'm also gaining. Two University of Pennsylvania graduates in economics on my staff. I'm a blessed man," he said proudly.

"Morrie, there's something that we need help with..." Jake took a deep breath. "What do you recommend we do about who we are? As you know, I'm Jewish and Gina is Italian. Neither of us is religious."

Morrie just looked at them, saying nothing.

"So how does this work? We live in an area with a large percentage of Hassidic Jews."

"Are you both good people?" Morrie asked.

"Yes. Absolutely," Gina answered.

"Kind people?"

Both Jake and Gina nodded.

"Then it's no problem. Be yourselves. You have new names. No one here knows you. Probably, the rabbi thought that you'd both fit in better wearing religious clothing, but on reflection, that might cause more issues than necessary." Morrie thought for a few moments then said, "I'm assuming that you're not interested in going to synagogue and participating in prayer services and religious holidays. Right?"

"Right," Jake said.

"Luckily, the area is a mixture of all types of people." He pointed to Gina. "Italians," Then pointed to Jake. "Secular Jews." He pointed to himself. "Hassidic Jews. And just look around tomorrow. Every race and religion are represented in the dozen or so blocks of this neighborhood. You saw what it looked like in the restaurant where we had breakfast. Like I said, my recommendation is to just be yourselves. If anyone asks you anything about religion, Jake, just say that you are a secular Jew and enjoy living in such a diverse neighborhood. Gina, just be you."

Gina stood up, crossed the room, and gave Morris a kiss on his forehead. "You are a kind and a wise man, Morrie."

"Thank you," Morrie said, a deep blush covering his face.

Gina immediately backed up. "Did I do something wrong?"

Morrie sighed. "Not in my world."

• • • •

TODD SAT FROZEN IN his office. What the hell! How, could this be happening? He glanced out the window at the parking lot, almost empty in the gathering dusk. This morning's meeting with Dr. Binette, the head of the inpatient unit, was a shocker. "Tell me about Jerry Kent," he demanded. "I need all the details." Binette elaborated that he was questioned extensively by the state department, who in turn was being pressured by the Chinese consulate.

Todd responded that he had no further information on Jerry Kent or why he ran away. How he got out of the locked unit was also a mystery. Todd's working hypothesis was that the man was suffering from PTSD or possibly acute paranoia associated with a Major Depression.

Binette frowned, obviously not happy with Todd's lack of specificity.

"Dr. Binette, why is the Chinese embassy so interested in him?" Todd asked.

"I can't say. The state department attaché was clear that this was something he didn't want discussed."

"Not even a hint? This is all so cloak and dagger."

"Sorry, Todd. That's just not possible."

"Whatever," Todd answered, getting up to leave.

"What did he look like?" Binette asked.

"Caucasian. Maybe 5 feet, eight inches tall. Scrawny. Unattractive. Clean shaven. Late-thirties. Looked like a burned-out coke addict." Todd repressed a smile. Jake would just love to hear how he described him. "Oh yeah. He had a scar over his left eye. Looked like the wound was never treated properly." Todd pretended to have a very thoughtful expression. Then added, "He walked kind of hunched over. Almost never stood up straight." Anything, to keep prying eyes away from the Hassidic enclave and away from the Chinese finding Jake and Gina.

"Thanks." Binette took some notes and nodded. "Please keep this conversation just between us."

Shocked, Todd took the elevator down to the main level and hurried back to his office.

· · · ·

AT 9 PM, AFTER TRAVERSING up and down a few streets to make sure he wasn't being followed, Todd locked his cycle in front of a CVS drug store. Minutes later, he roared out of the parking lot and headed toward La Cienega.

Thirty minutes later, he pulled his cycle in the alley behind Jake and Gina's new residence. Keeping in the shadows, he walked around the empty block and rang their doorbell.

Jake peered through the spyhole and let him in.

"Todd. What's up?" He double locked the door and hooked the chain. "Hey, Gina. C'mon down. Todd's here."

They sat in the living room and Todd related his conversation with Binette.

"A scrawny, mid-thirties, unattractive, burned-out, cocaine addict? Thanks a lot, Todd," Jake said with a laugh. "Clean shaven was a good idea." He ran his hand through his rough beard.

"I hope the scrawny addict part throws them off. If I said you looked like a rock star, they'd find you immediately."

Both men laughed.

Gina sat quietly, a thoughtful expression on her face.

"What, Gina?" Todd asked.

"They're looking for Nelson. Jake, the two guys who attacked you were Asian, right?"

Jake nodded. "I think I've said this before, but maybe not. Six months before Nelson *died*, he took me on a trip to Hong Kong. We stayed in a five-star hotel, ate at the best restaurants, and Nelson spent money like it was water. Nothing was too much for my rich brother."

"Was he rich?" Todd asked.

"Not really. He had a good job in Philly with a VC firm. Made between one-fifty and two-hundred thousand a year. Had a cool bachelor pad near Rittenhouse Square. But I know for a fact that he wanted to purchase his own home. If he had the money, he would've."

"Did he meet anyone in particular in Hong Kong?" Gina asked.

"He was vague and never included me in the meetings. He used the term, potential investors."

"Names? Places?" Todd asked.

"On one occasion he met with an Asian man and a younger woman. I only saw them from a distance. Like I mentioned before, I think it was the same woman I saw in the optical store, on the promenade. She was leaving, just as I entered."

Todd leaned forward in his chair. "Are you sure it was her?"

"Not 100%. I just saw her for a few seconds, but I could swear I saw her before."

"You saw her right after you saw, Nelson?"

"Ten minutes later. I told you how the optician was warm one minute, then ice cold. He changed right after I asked him if he saw a man that kind of looked like me."

"Why did Nelson want to go to Hong Kong?" Gina asked.

"He said, 'it was a business opportunity', but he was vague about it. In hindsight, Nelson's lack of specificity was uncharacteristic. We always enjoyed discussing marketing strategy. Why one stock in a sector would be a winner and another, same sector, would be a loser. For him to not say anything was off-putting."

Todd stood up to leave, reached in his pocket, and handed Jake a bag. "I just bought two burner phones. I'll stay in touch and try and get more info. Jake, whatever your brother did or didn't do has unleashed an international hornet's nest."

CHAPTER 21

"Jake, it's 4 AM! What are you doing?" Wearing an all-white, oversized Tee, that she just bought yesterday, Gina padded down the stairs and stood behind Jake. He was sitting at the breakfast table staring blankly at his laptop screen.

He sighed. "I went on Facebook, Linked In, Twitter, Yahoo, and Google trying to track what Nelson might have done or said before he disappeared. Nada. Somehow, his entire web presence has been scrubbed clean. It's like he never existed."

"Was Nelson a techy? Did he know how to do all that himself?"

"Yes. He was amazing. Knew all about the Dark Web. I was just on the verge of downloading Tor, but figured who knows what I'd stumble across or who'd stumble across me? Maybe I'd make everything worse?"

"Tor?"

"It's an anonymizing browser."

"Seriously?" Gina rolled her eyes.

"I know. I just learned about it two minutes before you came downstairs. It has special software that acts as a gateway to the Dark Web and promotes total anonymity. The problem is that 90% of the Dark Web is not only dark, but dangerous. You can buy guns, pre-loaded credit cards for 10% on the dollar, sex, hire a hitman. You name it."

"Okay. But once you get on, Tor, then what? What was your plan?"

Jake shrugged.

"Jake. Please come back to bed. We'll rest for an hour and then meet with Morrie. Whatever we do, we need to earn money. Right?"

"How can someone be so smart *and* so beautiful?"

Gina rolled her eyes. "Thank you. Now come upstairs."

• • • •

AT 6 AM, JAKE AND GINA parked in the half-full IBC underground garage. Over the weekend, they each bought a few articles of clothing at Macy's. Jake wore a pair of gray slacks, a button-down shirt, and a blue blazer. Gina wore a skirt that covered her knees and a long-sleeve blouse. They took the elevator to the 3rd floor and headed toward the receptionist's desk.

A thirtyish, clean-shaven, African American man, wearing a dark suit and tie, looked up from the computer screen. "Can I help you?"

'Yes. We have an appointment with Morrie Weisberg."

"Names, please."

"Gabriella and Jackson Wolfe."

The man gestured to a couch and chairs, facing a large TV screen showing how stocks were faring in the minutes before the market opened. "I'll let him know you're here."

A minute later, the receptionist called from his desk. "Mr. Weisberg's expecting you. His office is down the hall, third on the left."

Morrie's office was small, about ten by twelve. He had two monitors on his desk, one wall of floor-to-ceiling bookshelves jammed with books, and a small window overlooking Wilshire Blvd.

Morrie stood up, smiled, and shook their hands. "Coffee?"

"Yes," Jake and Gina said in unison.

"Please sit," he said, motioning to the two chairs in front of his desk, and left the office. He returned five minutes later with two mugs of coffee. "I made it fresh." He pointed to a container on the desk with pods of cream and packets of sugar, "Please, help yourself."

After Morrie settled in behind his desk, Jake said, "Morrie, I'm not sure how you're going to engineer the details, but we came up with a new identity. We're a happily married couple, Gabriella, and Jackson Wolfe."

Morrie jotted down their names. "No worries. I'll take care of it." He looked up and smiled. "I like how you both look. Professional. Very good." He pointed down the hallway. "I have another office that my receptionist and former associate used. That'll be for both of you.

"Gina, I mean Gabriella, there's a stack of notes that I made, mainly letters that need to be sent to clients and bills to be paid. Also, a half-dozen potential clients who are waiting for appointments. You'll figure it out. Jackson, stay here with me. I have a cold-call pitch that I'd like to show you, and a list of hundreds of potential clients."

Gina got up to go to the other office.

"Wait," Morrie called, glancing at his watch. "Let's have lunch at 1PM when the market closes. We'll talk about compensation."

• • • •

"WHAT'S WRONG, JAKE?" Gina asked, as they sat in their home finishing dinner. "You're so quiet."

"I'm worried about Nelson."

"I know."

"Another thing, Morrie's a gem. My salary of 80 K, plus bonuses for new clients, and a percentage of how their portfolios perform is more than fair. Soon, you'll make the same. In the meantime, you making 60 K is fine. But, and it's a big but, we're essentially prisoners. Being free to wander, see your family, is too dangerous. The Chinese probably know that you're involved. If you contact your family, there's a good chance that you're putting them at risk."

"What do you suggest, Jake?"

"I have an idea how to find Nelson, but we need to understand why he had to go on the run."

"How?"

"I've got to do a little more research."

"What about Morrie?"

"We go to work, do everything we can to make Morrie and us a lot of money, and keep our heads down. How 'bout you start studying for your Series 7 and 63? They'll always come in handy. In the meantime, I'll figure out how to find Nelson without getting us murdered."

CHAPTER 22

Todd took the elevator up to Nine North, but instead of heading toward the psych unit, he casually walked past Dr. Binette's office. As expected, his office door was wide open. Manuel, a skinny Hispanic guy, was working his way up and down the hall buffing the tile floor.

Todd turned around and walked back to the unit. After unlocking the door, he went directly to the nursing station. He filled a large paper cup with coffee, lots of creamer and sugar, waved to Willa, the charge nurse, and left the unit. Around the corner from the elevators, he poured the coffee on the floor in front of a locked closet, making sure the coffee went under the door, stepped in the wet puddle, and tracked the wet mess down the hallway.

He walked quickly back toward Binette's office and found Manuel.

"Hey, Manuel, how are you?" Todd said.

"Pretty good, doc. How 'bout you?"

"Tired. Too tired. I'm a walking danger." He shook his head, feigning frustration. "I slipped and spilled a big cup of coffee. It's a mess. Tracked it all over the floor. I'm sorry to cause you any more work."

"No problem, doc. Where?"

"Maybe grab a bucket? I'll show you."

Manuel walked across the hall and picked up a bucket filled with soap and water and a mop.

Todd pointed and together the men walked toward the spill.

Manuel saw the brown liquid and footprints. He waved his hand. "Get some sleep, Dr. Todd. No problemo. The people with the real problems are behind that locked door." He pointed to the psych unit.

"You're right, but I'm still really sorry."

Manuel held up his hands. "It happens." He dunked the mop in the bucket and got to work.

Todd left. When he turned the corner, he hustled over to Binette's office, went inside, and headed directly for the large desk piled with papers and books. As he rifled through everything the thought crossed his mind that if he were caught, he was done. Would they fire him? Call the police? His life as a physician and a psychiatrist might be over. In the middle of the pile of papers was a narrow sheath of documents from the US embassy. Todd took out his phone, rapidly took shots of the three pages, and left.

Forty minutes later, he was back home and printing it out.

His iPhone rang. It was Tanya.

"Hi," he said.

"I'm outside and just parked. This whole thing is freaking me out. Can you open the door and I'll run in?"

"Of course. I'm walking down the stairs right now."

He opened the door and seconds later Tanya was in his arms. "I'm so glad you're here," he said, and kissed her. After they walked up the stairs, he said, "You gotta see this." He took the papers out of the printer, and together they read them.

It was an official document from the office of Alex Padilla, the California Secretary of State. At the request of the Chinese government, Padilla directed Dr. Binette to forward all information he had regarding a patient, Jerry Kent, to his office. Padilla stated that the request was time sensitive, and that the Chinese were treating this as a national emergency.

"Todd, where'd you get these?"

"After Dr. Binette left for the night, I went into his office. It was right on his desk. I took pictures."

Tanya sighed. "How'd you get in?"

"The door was open."

She gave him a skeptical look. "Now what?"

"Warn Jake." He took out the burner and speed-dialed him.

Jake picked up on the first ring. "Todd, what's up?"

"About an hour ago, I copied the letter that the State Department sent to Dr. Binette, the head of psychiatric inpatient services. I'll read it to you."

When he was finished, Jake said, "A national fucking-emergency? What the hell did Nelson get himself into?"

"I hear you. Any ideas?"

"None that I can think of."

Tanya tapped Todd on the shoulder and made a motion that she wanted to talk. "Jake, Tanya's with me. I'm putting her on speaker."

"Jake, my father's friendly with a man who used to work for the State Department. The ambassador to Italy. He's retired and plays golf with my dad."

"Do you trust him?"

"I hardly know him."

"The question I'd want to ask him is, 'How often does Beijing reach out to the US State Department regarding a total stranger and call it a national emergency?' Remember? I just made up the name, Jerry Kent, a few days ago."

Todd interjected, "Jake, since Jerry Kent doesn't exist, there's no way that the Chinese got your name legally. They must have hacked into the hospital database."

"They probably have access to every hospital database in LA, or for that matter, in the country," Gina added.

"This is beyond scary," Tanya piped in. "I can't risk talking to my father's friend and giving him some half-baked story. He might very well call a colleague, who calls someone else, and before you know it, we're surrounded by Chinese hitmen."

"I agree," Todd said. "The question is what to do next."

"Let's sleep on it," Jake said. "In the meantime, Gina and I will go to work and try our best to blend into our new community. Thanks, Todd. I really appreciate it." Jake clicked off.

After a few moments of silence, Gina said, "Jake, what do we do about our apartments? Keep paying rent? That's like throwing away thousands of dollars every month. And what do I do about my family? They've called half-a-dozen times. If I don't reach out, they'll notify the police that I'm missing."

"Good point. If the Chinese hacked into the hospital database, we assume that they're monitoring our phones and your family's phones. Maybe, call your dad at work tomorrow morning? The message will go through the university's phone system. Wait! Have you used your iPhone at all?"

"No. It's been off since we talked at the hospital."

Jake sighed in relief. "Let's buy a few more burners and destroy our iPhones. If we turn them on, we can be tracked."

"Okay. What shall I tell my dad? I think that the truth is too dangerous."

"How 'bout telling him that you're taking a sabbatical from school? It's all approved by your chairman, and you'll continue to work on your thesis. A group of friends rented an RV, and you're all taking a road trip."

Gina laughed. "Maybe the Chinese will spend their time researching trailer parks and campsites? I'll tell my dad that I'll touch base in about three or four weeks... Not to worry. My friends are all very responsible."

"Also, don't mention me. That way, there's no obvious connection. As far as your apartment, is there anything of real value that you need to get?"

"My books. Some cheap jewelry. Clothes. Luckily, my laptop was in the car when I met with you and Todd. Sneaking back and getting the rest of my stuff might be too dangerous."

"Is anything irreplaceable?"

"Nothing. The apartment came furnished, so the furniture isn't mine."

"How 'bout you text your landlord that you left school. Tell him or her to keep the deposit. Are you comfortable just walking away from everything? Within a few months, we should have enough money to replace whatever you need."

"What about your place, Jake?"

"If I pay my rent, the Chinese will know that I'm still around. If I don't, all I lose is my credit rating which is already a mess. Whatever we do, we can't let anyone know where we are."

CHAPTER 23

Jake sat in his IBC office scouring the Wall Street Journal, Barron's, and the internet. Before he reached out to Morrie's clients, he wanted to come up with something unique. Morrie had given him a week to do research and develop a new plan, or to simply follow what Morrie had been successfully doing. He had three days left.

The problem, and it was a big one, was that he had no ideas. Right from the beginning, years ago, when he first studied the stock market as a freshman at Penn, it was clear that there was no sure way to predict anything. Even the giant companies were subject to market fluctuations and sometimes catastrophic losses. Enron, Kodac, and GE were just a few examples.

Jake's mind wandered. He remembered reading about Peter Lynch, a well-known stock analyst in the seventies and eighties, 'Invest in what you know' was one of his mantras.

But Jake wasn't in Peter Lynch's strata. How could he possibly know anything about sophisticated investing when he spent most of his time writing and waiting tables and feeling like a loser? A degree in business didn't automatically give him, or anyone for that matter, any great insights into what stocks to buy or sell.

Jake remembered when Amazon purchased Whole Foods for 13.7 billion dollars in 2017, another brilliant move by Jeff Bezos. Now, Amazon was even more powerful. Its tentacles reached almost everywhere influencing how the whole world purchased goods and did business – Amazon Prime, an on-line presence with an infrastructure that could deliver almost anything within days and sometimes in hours, easy returns of goods, and on-and-on. Then there was Apple and Google and Facebook and of course Netflix. FAANG was a gargantuan powerhouse. But these were all high betas – high risk and in return a very high reward. But what about investors who wanted more safety? He needed to come up with a package that also attracted those folks.

He motioned to Gina who was sitting across from him. Stacks of folders sat on her desk as she carefully went through them, collating and inputting information. "Gina, what companies consistently produce an income stream and would be appropriate for conservative investors?"

She thought for a few moments and then said, "Proctor & Gamble, Kraft, Johnson and Johnson, Pfizer, Coca Cola, Duke Power, IBM…"

"I like them. They cover Consumer Services, Healthcare and Energy sectors. We still need Financials and Real Estate."

"Okay. How 'bout B of A? Maybe Home Depot? I think it has a yield of 2%, a lot of growth potential and of course brand awareness. I'd personally stay away from REITS. Too much lability even though they often have a healthy yield."

"Thanks. That helps."

"How's your pitch coming?"

"Better. I'm trying to think more like an investment advisor than a waiter."

Gina rolled her eyes.

"Seriously!"

"Jake! Get over it. You were only waiting tables so you could write. Because you're focusing on investing, doesn't mean you can't write anymore. Why are you so all or nothing?" She stood up, walked over to Jake's desk, leaned down, and kissed

him. "Whatever happens, my love, we'll be together."

Jake closed his eyes and sighed. He was a lucky man…very lucky.

• • • •

IT WAS MONDAY MORNING, and Morrie sat behind his desk, all business. "Okay, Jake." Morrie hesitated, then asked, "Is it okay if I call you, Jake, when we're alone?"

"Probably not, Morrie. Safer if I'm now, Jackson. Believe me, it's taking a lot of getting used to."

"Sure. No problem. Did you come up with a plan, Jackson?"

Jake nodded, stroking his almost full beard. "Morrie, here's my thinking. Gina, I mean Gabby, and I set things up so there will be an appeal to both risk takers and conservative investors. We tried very hard to make the choices easy and intuitive. Using Peter Lynch's philosophy, from back in the seventies and eighties, 'buy what you know and combine intuition with strategic logic', I'm extrapolating here a bit, but here it goes…

"The big players haven't lost their attractiveness. FAANG – Facebook, Amazon, Apple, Netflix and Google are still the leaders in their field. In my opinion, they have a very long way to go before they max out. But, as you know, nothing is a sure thing. Even Proctor & Gamble, Kraft, Johnson and Johnson, Pfizer, Coca Cola, Duke Power, IBM, Bank of America, VISA, Disney, Mastercard, Paypal, Berkshire Hathaway, Nike and Home Depot aren't sure things. Every company has its ups and downs. *But* and this is an important differentiation, other than the FAANG companies, the other companies that we came up with have decent yields. Whether they go up or down, investors will still get an income stream. Not as high as one would get with REITS, energy investments or high yield bonds, but very respectable." He handed Morrie a computer printout with the breakdown of the different investment possibilities.

Morrie looked carefully at the page.

"Morrie, you can see that it's broken down into three units. Unit one is for the investors who don't mind more of a risk, unit two is a balance of both conservative and risky investments, and unit three is for the risk adverse. It'll be a play that can go side-by-side with the other investments that you've recommended to your clients. It's like a mutual fund, but the investor owns every share and it's all here at IBC. All under the same umbrella as every other instrument that the investor owns. The difference is that the individual investor will not have an input as to which stocks to buy, sell, or keep. They can do that with their other investments, but it won't be a part of *this* investment. All three units will contain stocks that Gina and I, and of course you, choose."

Morrie nodded.

"Unit one is two-thirds FAANG and other high betas, and one-third big caps. Unit two is fifty-fifty. Unit three is one-third FAANG and other high betas, and two-thirds big cap. Gabby and I both think it's an excellent plan. We even came up with a proprietary name for the system, *West Coast Investment Trust 20.*"

Morrie looked lost in thought, staring hard at the information that Jake had given him. Finally, he looked up. "Jackson, this looks very interesting. Let me think about it. Let's meet later this afternoon when the market closes. Please have Gabby join us."

• • • •

AT 1:30 THAT AFTERNOON, Morrie, Jake, and Gina sat in Morrie's office with full cups of coffee. Morrie asked, "Jackson, how do you imagine the trust being managed?"

Jake looked over at Gina. "This part was mainly Gabby's idea. Let me have her explain."

Gina sat forward in her chair, took a sip of coffee, and said, "Each portfolio is limited to twenty stocks. If we decide to sell one, it will be replaced when the numbers work. Every week, or whatever time-period you think is appropriate, the three of us will meet and decide what action to take. Jackson and I will do the research, so our decisions will be fact based. Not just subject to feelings or hunches."

Jake chimed in. "We'll also focus on what's happening world-wide and how that might affect each individual stock – embargoes, war, whatever. Even the FAANG stocks are subject to replacement. But this portfolio will, for the most part, be relatively stable. Some stocks may be included for years, others just months. It'll all depend on what's happening in the world and in the market-place. Hopefully we can stay ahead of the curve and lead the way."

Gina looked at her notes. "We researched the fees on this type of investment and came up with a graded fee structure. It starts at 2 ½% for the minimum investment, which is $100,000, and the fee structure is stepwise reduced as the investment amount increases. For example, the rate would be 1 ¼% when the investment reaches $500,000 and above. One million and higher is a flat rate of 1%."

Morrie sighed. "I love it! Every aspect of it. The two of you are amazing. Just one request. Gabby, please get your series 7
and 63 ASAP. I want you both fully on board and working on this. Let's start next Monday. I'll compile a list of my clients who will be good candidates."

Jake smiled, happy that Morrie liked the plan, but the smile was forced. He had an idea how to find Nelson, but he knew it was risky.

CHAPTER 24

J ake crouched behind a large dumpster in the alley behind the Third Street Promenade in Santa Monica. It was almost 10 PM, and with his full beard, black jeans, black sweatshirt, and a black baseball cap, he was almost invisible. He tensed and stretched his neck. The stores on the Promenade closed in just a few minutes. He'd been hiding since 9:40.

Ten minutes later, the back door of the optician's store opened. Two men came out. The first man was the guy he saw standing outside the Comedy and Magic Store who chased him! The second was the optician. They walked together toward Arizona Avenue.

Jake waited till they made the turn out of the alley and then followed. The guy from the Comedy and Magic Store, turned south. The optician went east. Two blocks later, on Fifth Street, the optician entered a parking structure. Jake started to follow and then decided against it. He remained standing in the shadows at the exit and took out his iPhone. A week ago, he bought it from a private party on Craig's List. The seller was a techy who swore that he had disabled any connection to Apple or to any server. The phone, according to him, was untraceable.

A few minutes later, a late-model, white, Ford Fairlane, came slowly down the ramp. The optician was driving. Jake snapped a picture of the rear license plate. Across the street, an elderly lady was walking her miniature poodle. As the poodle squatted on a small patch of grass, a homeless man, mumbling to himself, walked down the middle of the street.

Jake backed out of the shadows and jogged the remaining two blocks to his car. He opened the passenger side door and slid in.

"Was he there?" Gina asked, as she pulled onto Wilshire Blvd., and headed home.

"Yeah. I took a picture of his license plate. How hard can it be to find out more about him online?" Jake took a deep breath. "One surprising wrinkle. The optician was with the same guy who ran after me before I wound up in the hospital."

"One of the men who beat you up?"

"No. He never got the chance. Maybe he was the lookout for the two who attacked me?"

"So, the optician is associated with the attackers?"

Jake shrugged. "I have no idea. But hopefully he can lead us to Nelson."

"Jake, you keep forgetting one obvious fact. Nelson doesn't want to be found. The more you stir this up, the more of a chance that the Chinese will find him."

"So, you never want to see your family again? Tell me that and I'll stop. I'll never do anything to risk losing you again."

Gina sighed. "You're right."

Thirty minutes later they were home and on their computers. An hour later, they looked at each other and shrugged. Jake said, "We need a cop or a PI to get into the right database. It's not so easy tracking down a license plate."

"Jake, maybe Todd knows someone?"

Jake speed dialed him. A few minutes later, he clicked off and sighed. Todd and Tanya don't know anyone either. Then on impulse, Jake called Todd back. "Todd, do you remember a guy, Larry Girard, on the closed unit. He was making horrific facial contortions."

"Yes, I do. He had Tardive Dyskinesia. Why?"

"He's a computer whiz. Did it for a living. He knew all about Tor and the black web. Any idea what happened to him?"

"Last week a fellow resident presented him at Grand Rounds. He had a miracle response to ablative surgery. Not perfect, but the horrendous facial and tongue movements are almost gone."

"I'm really glad to hear that," Jake said. "He's a nice guy who was going through hell. I know you can't give me his phone number, but can you give his doctor *my* number? The number of the burner I just called you on. I liked Larry. Maybe he can help? I'll reimburse him for whatever he charges."

"Can't promise anything, but I'll call his doctor now."

"Thanks, Todd. One more thing. Larry knows me as Jerry Kent."

An hour later Jake's phone rang. "Hello," Jake answered.

"Jerry Kent?"

"Yes, that's me."

"It's Larry from the hospital. My doctor, Dr. Jensen, said you were trying to reach me. You, okay?"

"It's a long story, but I'm fine. How 'bout you?"

"Much, much better. I'm almost human again."

"I'm so happy to hear that. What a nightmare you had to endure."

"Tell me about it."

"Larry, it's a long story, but I'd like to ask a favor. Do you know how to track down a license plate, find out who owns the car and where the person lives?"

"I've never done it, but it couldn't be that hard."

"Will you do it for me?"

"Sure."

"Also, and this is very important, you need to do it in a way that nobody knows you're doing it. It could be dangerous if anyone finds out who you are and what you're after. It's one of the reasons I wound up in the hospital."

"Someone was trying to hurt you?"

"More than trying. They smashed me in the head and gave me a concussion and broke my nose. Luckily, I got away before they could do any more damage."

"I understand. I know how to do it safely."

"Thank you very much, Larry. And whatever you charge, I'll take care of it."

"I'm glad to help. Absolutely no charge. I'll call or text you anything I find regarding the license plate. It might take a bit."

The next afternoon, just as the stock market closed for the day, Jake's cell phone buzzed.

"Hello."

"Jerry?"

"Yeah. Larry?"

"Yes. I got the info."

"Thank you, man. That was quick."

"Okay. The owner of the car is Hi Tech Optical, Inc. The address is The Promenade, 1407 Third Street, Santa Monica, California."

"Any more specifics? The name of the owner? Other addresses?"

"Nah. That's it..."

Jake sighed in frustration. "Larry, thank you. What do I owe you?"

"Like I said, nothing. It was no big deal."

"I really appreciate this."

"I'm glad I could help."

"I owe you one. Now that your medical condition is improved, are you going back to work?"

"Next week. Finally, some semblance of normality."

"You're a good guy, Larry. Stay well." Jake cut the connection and stared out the window at the traffic flowing along Wilshire Blvd. He glanced at his watch. Tonight, he'd resort to Plan B.

• • • •

JAKE PATTED HIS STOMACH. "Hmm. Gina, when did you learn how to make potato latkes?"

"Yesterday. Our neighbor, Rebecca, and I started to chat. She went on and on about her new latke recipe and gave me a copy. Glad you like it." Gina laughed. "When we were chatting, I controlled myself and didn't ask, 'What are latkes?' Now I know."

"Did she ask anything about you being Jewish?"

"I told her that I was Italian and married to a secular Jew. That we both loved the area. She wondered if I knew how to make kosher meatballs. I said that I knew how to make the best meatballs outside of Italy, and that I'd research how to make them properly kosher."

Jake laughed. "You're amazing. Already making friends." Jake sighed. "I have another idea how to learn more about the optician."

Gina put down her fork and gave Jake her full attention.

"Since I know his car, I swung by the promenade on the way home, picked up a tracker, and stuck it underneath his car chassis. Tonight, I want to follow him. See where he lives. The tracker relays all its info, for at least seven days, to an app on my iPhone. I can stay a few blocks behind his car and not lose him."

Gina nodded. "We," she said.

"Huh?"

"*We* can stay a few blocks behind his car."

Jake was about to protest, saw Gina's determined expression, and nodded. "*We* need to leave by 9."

"No problem. As they say, an army travels on its stomach. Interested in some chocolate mint ice cream?"

"Of course. Sit. I'll get it."

"It's kosher. Bought it at the market around the corner."

Jake laughed. "A real balibusta."

"What?"

"That's Yiddish. My grandmother used the term to refer to women who were terrific homemakers. She said, 'Jakey, make sure you find yourself a real balibusta. She'll make you *very* happy'."

Gina beamed, "Nice. Thank you, Rebbe."

• • • •

ON 4th Street, a block from the optical store, Jake and Gina sat in the car staring at his iPhone. When the car image in the app moved, Jake started the engine. The image hesitated, then crossed 4th Street. Minutes later, Jake took the entrance to the 10 Freeway and followed the image onto the 405 South. Ten minutes later, they exited at Venice Blvd. and followed the image west. The image turned left on Abbot Kinney, the main shopping street in the heart of Venice – filled with restaurants, cannabis stores, coffee shops, and clothing stores. All home-grown entrepreneurs. Chain-stores were generally frowned upon.

The image wound around another three or four blocks, made a right on Washington Blvd. and another right on Wilson Ave. Jake sped up, and they watched as the Asian man parked and locked his car on the street. He ran toward a small cottage surrounded by a white picket fence. On one side of the cottage was a three-story ultra-modern home that must have cost millions, and on the other side a two-story teardown, with mottled siding, paint peeling, and a front yard overrun with weeds, garbage cans, and rotting wood. All typical Venice. The rich, the poor, the homeless – all mixed together in an area that refused to give up its hippy roots.

Jake parked at the end of the block, across from a row of five glass-and-steel townhouses. He looked at Gina. "Ready?"

Gina nodded, opened her door, and they stepped outside.

They were both dressed in jeans and dark sweatshirts. Jake pulled up his hood and Gina adjusted her baseball cap.

Holding hands they walked down the street, just two lovers out for an evening stroll. The lights in the optician's cottage went on. They walked to the end of the street, turned around and retraced their steps. After doing this twice, they got back in the Camry.

"Now what?" Gina said, staring at the cottage. "Is there a prayer you can conjure up as to what we do next?"

"Why was he in such a hurry?" Jake asked, more to himself than to Gina.

The cottage door abruptly opened, and the optician ran across the street pulling a suitcase behind him. He heaved the suitcase in the trunk, got into the Fairlane, and accelerated down Wilson. Seconds later the car disappeared around the corner.

"What the hell?" Gina mumbled. "That was some prayer."

Jake started the engine and followed. On Washington Blvd., he accelerated, passed three cars, and spotted the Fairlane.

"Jake, we should call the police!" Gina said, staring wide-eyed out the windshield.

"What? And tell them that we're following an absolute stranger who I think will lead us to my dead brother?"

CHAPTER 25

As the Fairlane veered off Washington Blvd. and onto Washington Place, Jake speed-dialed Todd on the burner.

"Hello."

"It's me."

"Okay..." Todd answered tentatively.

"Where are you?"

"Home."

"Gina and I followed the optician to his house in Venice. We were sitting outside in our car when he ran like hell to his car, dragging a suitcase. He headed east on Washington. Wait! He just turned onto the 405 North. I wanted to let you know in case... I don't know."

"Jake, I'm ten minutes from the 405. I'll go north and keep my Bluetooth buds in."

"No! I just wanted you to –"

"Relax, buddy. We're in the same foxhole. Give me ten minutes and let me know where you are. I'm on my way." He cut off the connection.

Staying as far behind as he dared, Gina stared at the app. The optician kept up a steady 65 miles-an-hour.

"Well," Gina said. "Now, I feel a lot better. A writer slash waiter slash money manager, a psychiatrist slash academic and a scared-shitless slash economics major are on their way to who slash knows slash where."

"One more thing, Gina. Full disclosure... Look in the glove compartment."

She opened the compartment. "A gun?"

"Excellent! You guessed it on the first try."

"Very funny, Jake. So, how'd you get it?"

"Morrie knew someone who knew someone."

"Seriously?"

"A PI, private investigator."

"Do you even know how to shoot it?"

"The PI lives up the hill in a canyon in Malibu. He has a gun range, or whatever you call it, right in his backyard. He gave me a one-hour-lesson. I know how to shoot it. Be careful, it's loaded."

"You'd actually shoot someone?"

"To protect Nelson, yes. To protect you, yes. No question." Jake said with determination.

"You sure you won't call the police?"

"Gina, that would take hours to explain. Would they even believe us? Maybe the guys who tried to kill me are hooked up with law enforcement? They're certainly hooked up with our state department. Given the ineptness of the FBI and CIA, I don't trust anyone...except you and Todd and Tanya."

"Jake, he's getting off the freeway. The Skirball Center / Mulholland exit."

"Okay." Jake followed the Ford up the ramp and across Skirball Center Drive. He hung back about six car-lengths, made the right onto Mulholland Drive, and speed-dialed Todd.

"On my way," Todd said. The sound of his cycle reverberated in the background.

"He got off at the Skirball / Mulholland exit. I'm on Mulholland going east. That's a right turn onto Mulholland."

"I'm at the Sunset exit. Just a few minutes behind."

"Wait! He made a right at the first light. There's a sign for the American Jewish University."

"I know where that is. It's a development of nice homes. Just up the hill is the Stephen Wise Temple. I've been there a few times."

"Okay... He just turned into a cul-de-sac and flashed his lights. Now a garage door is opening. He drove in. I'll circle back and park at the American Jewish University. How 'bout you meet me in the parking lot?"

"Will do."

Five minutes later, Todd pulled into the parking lot next to Jake and Gina. He locked up the cycle and got in the back seat.

Jake drove to the end of the cul-de-sac and pointed to the two-story Spanish style home – white stucco, black window frames, and a red-tile roof. Splashes of light peeked out of the edges of the drapes on the first floor. The second floor was dark. "He's in there." Jake's thoughts went back to that grim time when their parents were killed in the car crash. Nelson never once did anything that was self-serving. He *always* took Jake's well-being into consideration. When they sold mom and dad's home, Nelson gave him *all* the proceeds to pay for college. In addition, every month, Nelson deposited four hundred dollars in his bank account. When Jake tried to reason with Nelson about getting a part-time job, Nelson went batshit. 'Your job, Jake, is to excel in school! Period! *That* is what I want! *That* is what our parents would have wanted. Don't give me a hard time. Study! Do whatever it takes to be successful. *That* will more than pay me back.' 100%, Nelson faked his death to protect him. 90%, the optician was Jake's friend. No proof, but a strong sense of intuition. The way the optician behaved after he realized that Jake saw Nelson was him trying to protect Nelson. For some reason they're about to go on the run. Why else would the optician have packed a suitcase and hurried back to his car? This might be the last time that he'd have a chance to talk to his brother. Who knows where he'd go next? And why? What is he running from?

Jake said, "I think the best thing to do is for me to just knock on the door. I have this strong feeling that Nelson's in there. I don't think the man from the eyeglass store is our enemy. My hunch is that he's an ally."

"What if you're wrong, Jake?" Gina said, never taking her eyes off the house.

"It's possible, but I don't think so."

"What if I go with you?" Todd said.

"Maybe I'm wrong, but I'd feel better if you both stay here. Then if I'm in trouble, you can call 911."

Todd shook his head. "It takes forever for the cops to respond to an emergency. Okay, how 'bout this? Jake, I'll call you now. Keep your phone on so we can hear what's going on."

Gina reached across the seat and embraced Jake. "I love you," she said, tears running down her cheeks.

"I love you, too."

Jake clicked the phone on when Todd called and put it in his jacket pocket. Before he left the car, he took the loaded gun out of the glove compartment, and slid it inside his belt, at the small of his back.

"Jake. What the hell are you doing?" Todd said.

"Just being safe."

"Safe? If that gun goes off, you'll be a eunoch."

"It won't." Jake left the car. He crossed the street, walked up the stairs to the house, and pushed the doorbell. A buzzer sounded.

No answer.

He buzzed again.

Still no answer.

He remembered something that Nelson taught him when he was eight years old. Dot-dot-dot. Dash-dash-dash. Dot-dot-dot. SOS. 'It's the universal code for an emergency,' Nelson said. Jake emulated the sound with the buzzer. Three short rings, hesitate, three long rings, hesitate, three short rings hesitate.

No answer.

SOS again.

Then again.

Finally, a male voice called from behind the door, "Who is it?"

"It's Jake, Nelson. Please open the door. It's just me."

Slowly the door opened, and the dead man from the promenade stood in the doorway. For what seemed like the longest time, but was just seconds, the brothers stared at each other. Then, they tightly embraced.

Finally, Jake stepped back and glared at Nelson. "Nelson, would you please explain what the fuck is going on?"

CHAPTER 26

"**I**t's a long story," Nelson said, and then raised his voice. "Chen, Lila. Please come out." The optician and the Asian woman that Jake saw leaving the eyeglass store walked in the room. "Jake, I'd like you to meet my wife, Lila, and my father-in-law, Chen Wang."

Chen approached Jake and held out his hand. Jake shook it. Lila did the same. Then, Jake embraced her. "Welcome to the family, Lila."

Lila's eyes filled with tears. "Thank you, Jake. Nelson told me all about you."

"I'm so pleased to meet you both," Jake said. He looked at Nelson. "Gina, who you know, and our good friend Todd, who probably saved my life, are waiting outside. Can I have them join us?"

Nelson nodded.

Jake took the phone out of his pocket. "Todd, can you hear me?"

"We're on our way, Jake."

A minute later there was a knock at the door and Nelson let them both in. "Hi Gina," Nelson said, and warmly hugged her. "I'd have bet anything that you two would be married by now."

"Well, we had a bit of a detour. But we're back on track," Gina said with a smile.

Nelson shook Todd's hand. "Thank you for helping Jake. It means everything to me... How 'bout we sit down. I'll open a few bottles of wine, get some cheese and crackers, and I'll do my best to explain what's been happening."

Ten minutes later, everyone seated in the living room sipping chardonnay, Nelson said, "It's been a harrowing, dangerous few years." He looked directly at Jake. "The only reason I didn't tell you what was going on was because I love you too much to risk your life." He took a deep breath. "I'm sure you remember our trip to Hong Kong."

Jake nodded.

"It all started out, just as I told you, with a meeting of investment bankers and high-worth investors. The object was for them to use their influence with Chinese contacts, and for me to use my influence with US contacts. The result would be an international fiduciary liaison. One of the potential investors was Lila's brother, Bingwen."

Lila looked down at the floor, tears welling up in her eyes.

Nelson put his arm around her. "Bingwen held the first meeting at Chen's home in Hong Kong. That's where I met Lila." He kissed her softly on the forehead. "But that's another story. The main problem, which I didn't know at the time, was that Bingwen was very active in Occupy Central, one of the largest protest movements in Hong Kong. He was also on the faculty of HKU, Hong Kong University, and like many faculty members, pro-democratic. Any of you hear of the Umbrella Movement?"

Jake, Gina, and Todd all shook their heads, no.

"In 2014, umbrellas were used as a tool for passive resistance. Two examples. One, faces could be hidden from the Hong Kong police and the thousands of cameras located all over the city. And two, they could protect protesters from pepper spray that was used to disperse the crowds. Simply put, the people wanted to keep the freedoms that they enjoyed before Beijing took over from the United Kingdom. Once Beijing took over in 1997, freedom as they knew it, was gradually withdrawn. If you spoke out against the Chinese regime, you were risking your life and the lives of your family. It was a nightmare." Nelson took a sip of wine. "So, back to our first meeting. It was quite successful. Everyone was on board to line up major corporate investors. Then it got complicated. OCLP, Occupy Central with Love and Peace, had grown to over 800,000 people. They were pushing for Beijing to back off and go back to the way it was under English control. By the way, OCLP didn't believe in violence.

"Anyway, Beijing didn't play by the same rules as OCLP. They escalated the conflict. They brought in 14K, a violent and powerful Hong Kong Triad. 14K is a worldwide operation with connections in Europe, Asia, Cambodia, the US and has at least 20,000 members. It was Beijing's way of doing what they wanted to do but with deniability for their violent actions."

"14K!" Jake exclaimed. "Two of them attacked me!" He pointed to his neck. "I saw the tattoo. It's how I wound up in the hospital."

"Jake, you were lucky. Members of 14K do whatever they're told. If Beijing wanted you dead. You'd be dead."

Jake sighed. "They wanted me dead. No question."

"But first, they would have tortured you to find out what you knew about me. Since you knew nothing, you were expendable," Nelson said grimly.

"Nelson, why'd you need to go into hiding?" Gina asked.

"Obviously, it was a lot more than hiding. I needed to no longer exist. Hiding wouldn't have worked. With the Chinese, there's no place to hide. They control so much more than we ever suspected. Whatever you post on the web, they'll find it. And they'll find whoever posted it. Not even the black web is safe. They are brilliant and relentless."

"So that's why you never told me what was going on," Jake said.

"Like I said, they'd use you to get to me. Then they'd kill both of us. Imagine an enemy with no ethics or boundaries. The only rule that matters is strict obedience."

"So, why were they after you, Nelson?" Gina asked again.

"Money. I owe them 10 million dollars. If I had anywhere near that amount, you can be sure that I'd have given it to them. I faked my death and went off grid. Then," he pointed to Jake. "I lowered my guard and Jake saw me. By the way, after you saw me, how did you find me?"

Jake started at the beginning and told the whole story, leaving nothing out.

Nelson smiled. "Pretty clever. So, now you and Gina live amongst the Hassidic Jews."

"Yes. We're comfortable and we're together; so that's all good. But we're still in hiding. Any ideas how we can get back to normal?"

Nelson shook his head. "None. My trust in a manipulative sociopath cost all of us our freedom...and it cost my brother-in-law his life." He closed his eyes for a few moments, obviously trying to control his feelings.

"Why do you owe the Chinese 10 million dollars?" Jake asked.

"The Cliff Version is that Bingwen recruited some heavy-hitter investors. I put the money into what I believed would be a sure thing, an investment that would quadruple within the year. One of my former associates, who's now justifiably in federal prison, was pushing a half dozen investments. He was the best salesman I ever knew. 100% believable. Like many before me, I believed him. When interest rates plummeted and the banks tightened up on loans, all his investment recommendations tanked. What I didn't know, was that the Chinese investors, all Beijing businessmen, were hooked up with 14K. They ordered 14K to murder Bingwen. It was clear that they'd murder me next. So, I rigged my own death."

"But they found two bodies in the plane."

"Both were cadavers."

"How was the plane flown?"

"Like a drone. We controlled the plane from a nearby airport. After we crashed the plane in Lake Wallenpaupack, we drove away. My dental records, actually x-rays of the cadaver, were all planted weeks before in my dentist's office. I was now officially dead."

"That's impressive, Nelson." Jake turned to Chen. "It looked to us like you were about to run away."

Chen nodded. "An OCLP informant in Hong Kong, embedded with 14K, finally found out that I was related to Nelson. That I was Lila's father, and that Lila was married to Nelson. They are days, or minutes, or who knows how long, from abducting me. Just like you were able to discover that Nelson was still alive, so did Beijing. I came here to get Nelson and Lila. We leave tonight."

"Where will you go?"

Chen shrugged. "We'll figure it out."

"I have a question?" Todd said.

"Okay," Nelson said.

"Is there any hope that you can reason with Beijing? Make a deal?"

"No," Chen answered. "We lost their money; we have to pay with our lives."

"What if you returned the 10 million? Would you be forgiven?"

"Maybe?" Chen responded. "But I wouldn't be surprised if they demanded more. Maybe 12 or 15 million. Once they had the money, there's no guarantee that they still wouldn't kill us. It's all about setting an example."

"Now what?" Jake asked.

"We hug goodbye and hope that 14K never catches us," Nelson answered.

"That's the plan? Run and keep running?"

"Nothing else will work. I was greedy and I was duped. I'm sorry." He looked at everyone, his eyes brimming with tears.

Jake walked over to Nelson and hugged him; tears were also dripping down his cheeks. Quietly he whispered, "You're alive. That's the important thing. How can I get in touch with you?"

"I love you, Jake. I'm so sorry that I put you through this. Please, for both our sakes, don't *ever* try to find me again. Trust me, if I figure a way out, you'll be the first person to know." He reached out and took his wife's hand. "It could be a lot worse. I'm alive and I'm with the person who makes me incredibly happy. It's a big world and I'm learning every day how to stay off the radar." He smiled, held Jake in a bear hug, then backed away. "Thank you, all," he said, "for caring about me. I'm fine. Life's not perfect, it never is, but it's a lot better than the alternative."

Jake turned toward Chen. "Who is the other man in your shop? I recognized him when you both left together."

"My boss. He owns the business."

"More than a month ago, in Hermosa Beach, before I wound up in the hospital, he was running after me."

"I didn't know," Chen said, with a confused expression on his face."

Nelson glanced at his watch. "Is it possible he's with 14K?"

Chen nodded.

"We need to leave, now," Nelson said. "He must have followed Jake after he came into your shop."

"There has to be a way out of this," Jake responded.

"Jake! You're not hearing us," Nelson said harshly. "There is no way. Please, always know that I love you. Most importantly, don't waste any more time obsessing how to save me. I'm fine. If you budge an inch out of line, Beijing will find us." He looked around the room. "All of us."

CHAPTER 27

THE NEW NORMAL

• • • •

THE WEEKS AND MONTHS passed.

Jake and Gina got into the rhythm of their new lifestyle. With his full beard and glasses, Jake sometimes looked in the mirror and it took a second for him to recognize himself. No one in the community, except Morrie, had any idea who they really were.

Gina made friends with the women on their block and enjoyed sharing recipes and even learning a little Yiddish. Nightly, she studied for the Series 7 and 63 exams.

Day and night, Jake obsessively read one financial report after another, trying to discover investment leads to improve the bottom line on *West Coast Investment Trust 20*. It was going well. Over 5 million dollars in new investments and a 30 day return of 11%. Already, Jake had twenty clients who loved working with him and who had referred a half dozen of their friends. Morrie was more than satisfied.

Jake was happy that Morrie was happy, but knew that at this rate, it would be years before he'd raise anywhere near 10 million dollars; although he'd amassed more in the last month than he'd earned waiting tables for three years. He was fully aware that Nelson had warned him not to get any more involved, but Nelson's words didn't stop him from scouring the internet trying to discover unique companies. How he would find Nelson was a total mystery. Nevertheless, he continued his obsession with making lots of money fast. There remained the possibility, despite Nelson's warning, that if he could pay off 14K the problem would be solved. He and Gina could come out of hiding.

Yet, living in the Hassidic neighborhood had its positives. The neighbors were friendly, shopping was convenient, and for the first time in years he didn't continually worry about money. Plus, and it was the biggest plus in his life, being with Gina, surpassed everything. He was still head-over-heels in love with her and thought of himself as one of the luckiest men on the planet.

One evening, Jake Googled, *Hong Kong, 14K Triad*. It was an interesting history lesson. Wan Kuok-Koi, aka Broken Tooth, was the leader. After a long, gory history of murder and mayhem, Wan was imprisoned in Macau for 14 years. In December 2012, he was released. Then in 2018, with the blessing of the Cambodian government, he became chairman of The World Hongmen History and Cultural Assn. Wan announced that the organization would establish schools to let foreigners and overseas Chinese nationals study books on topics such as loyalty, filial piety, benevolence, and justice. The association would also be involved in selling watches, tea, and running hotels and casinos. Jake shrugged when he read that Wan was blacklisted by the US Dept. of the Treasury. Of course. Why shouldn't they blacklist a known killer and crook. Occasionally, even the Feds got it right.

What Jake read next totally got his attention. When the Hongmen Association was initiated, it launched a new cryptocurrency, HB (Hongmen Cryptocurrency). Like most everyone, Jake knew a little about cryptocurrency, but he didn't know much. He did know that a lot of people were getting very rich. He stayed up until 4AM educating himself. Simply put, cryptocurrencies were a digital form of currency that could be traded on a cryptocurrency exchange using an online ledger called a blockchain.

Satoshi Nakamoto (a pseudonym) created Bitcoin in 2009. Now there were hundreds of different types of cryptocurrencies of which Bitcoin and Ethereum were the leaders.

The next day, at 1PM when the market closed, Jake wandered into Morrie's office. "Hey Morrie, how are you?" he asked, and took a seat in front of Morrie's desk.

"Very well, God willing. How are you, Jackson?"

"Okay... Morrie, what do you know about cryptocurrency?"

"The basics, and that Bitcoin made a lot of people rich."

"Do you know anybody who's an expert?"

"Why?"

"I need to be up on all the latest investment developments. You never know... Cryptocurrency is an intriguing sector."

"So now it's a sector?" Morrie said, both palms up in the air.

"Morrie, what would you call it?"

"Mishigas... Craziness."

"Making billions of dollars isn't mishigas, Morrie. The amount of money that some people are making is obscene."

Morrie smiled. "Okay. Okay. I'm on your side." He picked up his phone and scrolled through his contacts, "I know someone. A bit strange, somewhat reclusive, but very smart. I haven't seen him for a while." He jotted down his phone number and name and handed Jake the paper. "Jason Krepps. He was here, right on this floor, till about a year ago. Now..." He shrugged. "I have no idea where he is. Just say you work with me, and that I recommended you."

"Thanks, Morrie."

On the way back to his office Jake called Jason.

Jason's message simply stated, "Leave your name and phone number."

Jake explained that he was Jackson Wolfe, worked for Morrie, and was very interested in cryptocurrency.

Two days later, Jake's phone rang. "Hello."

"This is Jason."

"Hi Jason. It's Jackson. Thanks for calling back. Gotta minute?"

"Yes."

Jake explained his interest in cryptocurrency, how he wanted to learn how to invest.

"What do you do with Morrie?"

"I started an investment protocol and I'm in the process of getting new clients. The minimum investment for new clients is in the area of $100,000, give or take. So far, it's doing well for a new portfolio offering."

After a long pause, Jason said, "Jackson, I'd be willing to meet with you."

"Where and when?"

"8 o'clock, tonight. There's a Coffee Bean off the 60 in Diamond Bar. Know Diamond Bar?"

"No."

"You take the 110 to the 60. The Coffee Bean is in Diamond Bar Village."

"Okay. I'll find you. I'm six feet tall, full beard."

"Jackson, please wear civilian clothes. I don't want us to standout. Do you have jeans and a sweater or sweatshirt? Something like that?"

"Of course. I work for Morrie, but I'm not part of the Hassidic community."

"See you tonight." Jason clicked off.

Back home, Gina encouraged Jake to go alone. She was committed to finishing her test preparations and didn't want any distractions.

At 7 PM, Jake put the address in the GPS. 45 minutes later, he parked the Toyota in front of The Coffee Bean, went in and ordered a medium coffee. The place was empty except for him and the barista. A few minutes later, a short, thin man, mid-thirties, clean-shaven, walked in. He saw Jake and walked over to the table. "Jackson?"

"Jason?"

"Yeah, I'll get coffee." Minutes later he was back and staring intently at Jake. Finally, he asked, "Why did you want to meet with me?"

"Morrie recommended you."

"I know that. But why go to all this trouble? There are dozens of other ways to learn about cryptocurrency – U tube, crypto for idiots, who knows? It's easy to buy into an ETF or pick up some Bitcoin or Etherium or whatever. Why me?"

"I need an expert. Someone who can help me past the usual barriers."

"What's the rush?"

Jake wondered how much he should explain, how honest he should be. He went for honesty. "My brother is in financial trouble, made huge mistakes. Got in with the wrong people. Dangerous people. He needs a lot of money."

"So, like I asked, why me? Do I look like I have a lot of money?"

"No. No. I want to get advice on how to get in on the ground floor. Bitcoin and Etherium are established. I was hoping for an opportunity to invest in something in the more formative stages. That's where the money is. I have no idea whether that's your area or not. If not, I still appreciate that you agreed to meet with me."

"Okay, I get it." Jason took a sip of coffee. "You mentioned that you were starting a fund or an investment vehicle with Morrie. How's that going?"

"Doing well. Building relationships slowly. The new investors seem happy with what we've developed." He went on to explain the details of his investment strategy.

"It sounds like an excellent long-term investment."

"Thanks. I hope so."

Jason focused his gaze on Jake, hardly blinking. He asked, "What do you know about cryptocurrency?"

Jake nodded. "Some basics. There are two trading techniques, Fundamental Analysis (FA) where you can determine whether an asset is either over or under valued and Technical Analysis, where a trader predicts future price movements. FA can be used to determine if an asset is worth investing in. TA can be used to determine when to invest."

"Any thoughts on Derivatives?"

"They reflect how cryptocurrencies are performing."

"Thoughts on scalping, swing trading..."

"In scalping, traders profit off small price changes. Swing traders take advantage of how the currency is trending." Jake hesitated, then asked, "Jason, why did you agree to meet with me?"

Jason sighed and took a sip of coffee. "Like you, I need money. I figured that if you work for Morrie, you're legit. If you're starting a new investment strategy, maybe you can be of help to me, and I can be of help to you."

"I hope so, Jason."

Jason nodded. "Okay. You can come over, Jackson. But you can't tell anyone anything. No one! Ever! My location and everything else must be 100% secret." Jason stared at him, unblinking.

"I promise."

"Okay... Follow me."

• • • •

JAKE FOLLOWED JASON'S old Jeep Cherokee for about ten minutes. Jason turned onto a gravel road and parked in front of a huge metal building that looked like an airplane hangar, one that could handle 747 jets. Jake pulled in beside him.

As they stood in front of the large metal front door, Jason held out his hand. "Jackson, I need you to give me your phone."

Jake hesitated, reached into his pocket, and handed it to him.

Jason unlocked the door and Jake followed him in. Jason immediately shut the door and triple locked it. When he turned on the lights, Jake's mouth dropped open.

CHAPTER 28

There were rows of metal shelves, at least 20 feet high, running 90 or 100 feet all the way to the end of the building. On the shelves were whirring boxes, hundreds of them. They filled the area with a sound akin to millions of buzzing bees.

"Every penny I have has gone into creating this," Jason said.

"Your own Blockchain," Jake responded.

"Yes."

"All by yourself?"

"It took over a year. Day and night. I have two assistants."

"What's the plan?"

"A new crypto. Totally secret and protected. The Blockchain is almost done and 100% secure."

"How'd you do this, Jason? It's incredible."

"I've been working on it for years. I started with the theory and design during my second year in college."

"Where'd you go to school?"

"MIT."

"You developed this alone?"

Jason nodded and took a deep breath. "I'm trusting you with everything. My future. All my savings. I hope I'm not making a mistake."

"I won't betray you." For a moment, Jake almost told Jason his real name, but decided against it. If 14K had any inkling that he was associated with Jason, nothing would stop them from doing whatever it took to destroy Jason and take this over. In the true sense of the word, he would never hurt or lie to Jason. Ever.

"Like I said, I need money. My college loans are due, and it costs thousands a month to keep the blockchain going – electricity, new ASICs, cooling fans," he pointed at dozens of large fans on the ceiling and to the back wall, where a half-dozen backup generators sat. "Generators, just in case there's a power outage. Also, I need to pay my assistants."

Jake pointed to the hundreds of boxes on the shelves with wires coming out of them. "What are they, Jason?"

"Those are called Mining ASICs. There are three hundred of them."

"What does that mean?"

"Application Specific Integrated Circuits."

"Like computers?"

"Exactly, but with very high hash rates. So, the processing of the crypto can be faster. The older technology used GPUs, but ASICs are much better, faster, more efficient, cheaper to run."

"How much do you need to finish this?"

Jason hesitated, then said, "around 500K."

"That's a big number.

"Yeah. I've already put in over a million. Then, I need to promote it. That'll be tough. Maybe even more expensive."

"Gabby, my girlfriend, studied economics at Wharton School. If you want, you can meet her. She's whip smart, but I'd have to explain everything to her."

"Girlfriend?"

"We live together and went to Penn together. We both majored in economics. She also works for Morrie. Soon, we're planning on getting married. She's everything to me."

Jason hesitated, then said, "Okay. Let's get together tomorrow evening. At 8."

"Here?"

"Yeah."

• • • •

AT 8:00 PM, JAKE AND Gina, pushed the bell at the entrance to Jason's crypto hanger.

Minutes later, the door opened, and Jason, wearing a washed-out MIT sweatshirt, stood back, and let them in.

"Jason, this is Gabriella...Gabby." Jake said.

"Pleased to meet you," Jason mumbled, standing awkwardly, the whirring of the computers surrounding them.

After a few moments of silence, Jake said, "So, I explained what I could to Gabby. She has some ideas that might be helpful. Please show her what you've built and explain the system? It's so impressive."

Jason walked Jake and Gina up and down the eight rows of ASICs and generators, pointing out how he developed an efficient way for the fans to pull out the large amounts of heat that the computers produced, and how each aisle had filters that needed to be manually washed and cleaned at least every other week. The ASICs had to be protected from dust.

When Jason was done explaining everything, yelling above the constant din, Jake asked, "Is there anywhere we can talk? Where it's quieter."

Jason led them to a ten by twelve office, lined with sound proofing material along the walls and the ceiling. There was an unmade cot in the corner, presumably where Jason slept. They pulled up chairs and sat around a battered wooden table. Jake said, "Maybe you can fill us in on why your cryptocurrency will be better or more saleable than the ones already out on the street."

"Okay," Jason said, staring at a space somewhere over Gina's shoulder, not making eye contact. "What do you know about P2P networking in blockchain technology?" he asked.

Gina and Jake looked at each other and shrugged.

"How about EVM?"

"Nothing," Jake answered.

"Geth? Mist?"

"Nothing," Gina answered.

Jason said, "The basics of cryptocurrency design is that each ASIC is called a node. When each node is connected to another node, a network is created. The P2P Network. Peer to Peer network is the basis for blockchain technology. Each peer is connected to another peer by the internet. No central server is needed. If someone wants to tie into my blockchain, they would be doing it directly to my network. With me so far?"

"Sort of," Jake answered.

"So, by nature, it's safer," Gina said.

"Yes! No governmental or third-party interference. One person to another," Jason answered, more animated. "Now EVM or Ethereum Virtual Machine is a software platform based on blockchain and it defines the rules for validating new blocks.

"Smart contracts are blockchain-based applications that run based on preprogrammed conditions." He looked at Gina. "It prevents fraud or third-party interference."

"I'm with you," Gina said.

Jason continued. "To do all this, most programmers use GETH and MIST. The important fact is that the software that I've developed cuts down on the detailed programming needed to run a blockchain. My 300 ASIC blockchain is the equivalent of 5000 ASICs that are needed for Ethereum and Bitcoin."

"Why is that important?" Jake asked.

"Why?" Jason said in a loud voice, then quickly toned it down, "It's safer and more reliable and much, much cheaper. Without my programming, the building we're in would be 16 times bigger, the size of 4 or 5 football fields. I would have had to invest at least 17 million dollars to get the same effect that I got with 1 million."

"Wow," Jake said.

Jason continued, "Also, it's impossible for anyone to steal information or do anything that would affect the value of each newly minted coin. Plus, I've created my own literal cloud. You can never lose the information, no matter what happens. Because my system is so streamlined it only needs 10 percent of the energy that other platforms need."

"Sounds like a game changer," Gina said.

"Yes! Exactly!" Jason responded.

"Jason, how would the money you need be spent?" Jake asked.

"Add 100 ASICs. Hire another assistant, pay the rent and electric bills, get more backup generators, employ a better, more efficient filtration system. Pay my student loan so the banks don't come after me. I'm a year behind."

"How long will it take to get everything up and running?" Gina asked.

"If I started tomorrow, two to four months." Jason looked at Gina and said, "Jackson mentioned that you might have some ideas how to promote my system. Maybe raise some cash?"

"Jason, you've already done most of the work. It's better, safer, cheaper, no governmental interference, and tamper proof. Plus, given Jake's and my contacts, maybe we can start with the investment community? Then reach out to anyone engaged in international commerce. Here's an example. A graduate student I know recently moved back to Israel. She's involved in a startup in Tel Aviv. There's a good chance she knows other entrepreneurs who might be interested. So many people are sick and tired of having everything they do, every investment, every purchase, every expense, sitting out there for the world to examine. For their government to examine. Most people are not educated enough in the world of Bitcoin and Ethereum. It'll be our job to educate and attract users and point out how your product is so much better."

Jason nodded, his expression not giving away any clue as to what he was thinking.

"Does your crypto have a name?" Jake asked.

"CLEO. Coin Led Energy Organization," he answered, his mind elsewhere.

"I like it," Gina said. "I like it a lot."

"How 'bout we all think about this and then touch base?" Jake said.

Jason nodded, obviously lost in thought. Then he led them to the front door, and without another word, gave them back their phones and let them out.

In the car, Jake asked, "What do ya think?"

"I think Jason's a genius, but he has no clue how to market CLEO. Plus, raising at least half a million dollars will be another challenge. He probably needs closer to a million, or two, what with advertising costs. And realistically, what do either of us know about marketing?"

"Not much... You sounded awfully impressive."

"Well, it's how I would've answered a test question. Putting it into practice is a whole other level of expertise. I'm not sure I really know how to do that comfortably."

Jake nodded.

"What if Jason's not interested?" Gina said.

"Then he's not. But if he is, we should have a real plan in place. Winging it and risking all his hard work and money isn't fair. Everything you said to him was valid, but you're right, we need a professional to execute a top-notch marketing plan. We don't know enough. Maybe talk to Morrie about this?"

"Maybe?" Gina said, her expression somewhat vague.

"What? What are you thinking?"

"There's something to be said about staying under the radar. Talking to Morrie would mean dozens of rules and innumerable governmental and corporate hoops to jump through. Do we really want to subject ourselves and Jason through all that? Plus, they'd get a huge percentage just for giving us their blessing. Right?"

Jake nodded, not knowing where Gina was going with this line of reasoning.

"So, I have an idea. But I need to know. Why are you so interested in doing this, Jake? Financially, we're doing very well. Are you still trying to find a way to save Nelson? Is that what this is all about?"

"No!" Jake said, abruptly. Then added in a softer tone, "of course not. You don't need to worry."

Gina looked hard at Jake, then said, "Okay, I'm taking you at your word." But her expression said otherwise.

CHAPTER 29

"Tanya, hi. It's Gina. Hope I'm not calling too late."

"No, not at all. Nice to hear from you."

"Thanks. Nice talking to you too... Did I understand you correctly when you mentioned that your father's an investment banker?"

"You did. He runs one of the largest investment equity firms in California. Why?"

"Any availability tomorrow to meet with Jake and me? We'll explain everything then. It's important."

"Important or not, it'd be a pleasure. Does 6 PM work? An early dinner."

"Perfect. Why not come to our place? I have a new recipe for brisket, mashed potatoes, and veggies."

"Sounds yummy. Is Todd also invited?"

"Of course. Always."

• • • •

TODD SLID HIS CHAIR back and sighed, "Gina, that was delicious. Just as good as my grandmother makes. It brought me back to when I was a kid."

"I want that recipe, Gina. It was *so* good," Tanya said.

"No problem. Thank you, both. Tomorrow I'll congratulate Sophie, my neighbor, on what a success her meal was."

Jake slid his chair back and patted his stomach. He got up and kissed Gina on the forehead. "You're the best."

Gina smiled. "Okay, team. Now it's down to business. But first, I need your promise that this is all confidential. It can't be discussed. Not one word to anyone. Agreed?"

"Yes," Todd and Tanya said, almost in unison.

Gina spent the next fifteen minutes describing in detail everything that she and Jake knew about Jason's project. What he said. What they saw. And why, in her opinion, it would potentially be a huge money maker.

"When you say money maker," Tanya said. "How much are we talking about?"

Jake pulled out his iPhone and looked at his notes. "Well, let's examine what happened to Bitcoin in the last 10 years. It started out at a nickel a share or coin as they call it. Now it's over six thousand per share. If you invested $10,000 in 2009. It would be worth 1.2 billion dollars."

The four of them sat for a minute in absolute silence.

Jake broke the silence. "Investing in this new, much better, cryptocurrency, if it goes well, might bring us all complete financial independence. We can afford homes in Los Angeles, have college money for our children, and whatever else we want." He smiled at Gina, willing her to not be able to read his mind.

Tanya sighed. "What can I say? Count me in. Should I talk to my father tomorrow morning? It sounds like an amazing opportunity."

"We're waiting for Jason to get back to us. If he's interested, we'll need to raise the money fast. If he's not interested, then we had a good excuse to get together," Jake said.

"I hate to sound so naïve, but how does all this work?" Todd asked. "I mean, how can we, or anybody, invest in this project?"

Tanya spoke up. "By osmosis, in high school, just sitting around our dining room table, I learned a lot. What I know is that if my dad agrees that it's a worthy investment, he'll send out evaluators – stock people, accountants, cryptocurrency specialists, and whoever else is needed. Jason, who's now the 100% owner of CLEO, would have to agree to give up a percentage of his ownership in return for my father's money. In this case, Jason would request somewhere in the one-million-two-million-dollar range. What percentage he'd have to give up, for that kind money, I have no clue."

"What if we invested *our* money with Jason before the investment bankers get involved? Maybe we could own a percentage of the company?" Gina said.

"Ha. I have about a hundred bucks. Will that work?" Jake said with a laugh.

"I'm serious, Jake. I think this is a chance to earn enough money so none of us will ever have to worry about finances again."

"Can we visit Jason? See his operation?" Todd asked.

"Why not," Jake answered. "That would be a logical next step."

"Well, how much money do the four of us have?" Gina asked. "I personally have $25,000." She turned to Jake. "That'll be our share."

"I'd put in $12,500," Tanya said.

"It would tap me out. But if I took my savings, I could put in $12,500 too," Todd said.

"Are you sure, Gina?" Jake asked, his expression appearing somewhat confused.

"Of course, Jake. Are you going anywhere? Are we a couple?"

"I'd never leave you, ever." His eyes welled up. "I love you."

"I love you, too. Okay, so that's settled. $50,000 is a significant amount." Gina looked at Jake. "Maybe that would be enough money for Jason to keep running his operation until we get real funding? Who knows how long that might take?"

"What if we can't get him the funding?" Tanya said. "Trust me, my father is a hard-nosed businessman. My involvement is no guarantee that he'll do it. There's a chance we'd lose all our money."

"That's true. It's also true that risk takers deserve a percentage of CLEO," Gina answered.

Todd sighed. "I'm still in."

"Tanya, if your father isn't interested, we'll reach out to our boss or find other investment firms." Jake glanced at his watch. "It's 10 o'clock. Should I call Jason?"

"And tell him what?" Gina asked.

"The truth. Everything we just talked about. See if he's even interested."

Everyone nodded and Jake punched in Jason's number.

"Hello," Jason answered.

"Hey Jason, it's Jackson."

"Hi Jackson. I was going to call you..." Silence.

"Okay... What're you thinking?"

"I don't like talking on the phone."

"Okay. Wanna meet somewhere in the middle? Wait, let me go online and find a place." Jake opened his computer, and checked out a map of LA. "How 'bout where the 10 meets the 60? On Caesar Chavez?"

"Yeah. That's good. There's a burger place there. Maybe Fat Burger? Not sure if that's it. It's near the off ramp."

"Gina and I will see you in about thirty."

CHAPTER 30

I n the empty parking lot of a boarded-up Best Burgers, Gina and Jake watched as Jason pulled in next to them. They got out of the car and waited as Jason got out of his Cherokee and approached them.

"You want to sit in our car and talk?" Gina asked. "It's kinda chilly out here."

Slowly, Jason nodded. "Yeah. But please turn off your cell phones."

"Okay," Gina said. "Mine's in the car."

Jake took his phone out of his pocket, pushed the off button, and handed it to Jason. Once they were in the car, Jason in the back seat, Gina handed him her phone, which he immediately powered off. He placed both phones on the seat next to him and took a deep breath. "I guess you figured out that I have trouble trusting people. From the time I was a kid, people cheated off me in tests. I never got less than an A and they used me, pretended they were my friend. Even at MIT, people, well one guy, stole my idea during a project. So...like I said before, I'm running out of money. Fast. I'm not sure what to do."

"How fast?" Gina asked.

"In two weeks, I'll have to let my assistants go. For sure, I can't buy any new equipment." He shook his head. "I'm so close, but everything is so damn expensive."

Jake said, "Tonight, just before I called you, we had our best friends over for dinner. I know we promised to not talk to anyone about your project, but we never mentioned your name or where you're located. We talked about your project, obviously no real details, because we don't understand how you created CLEO. Even if we did, we wouldn't. We're not mathematicians or physics majors. I told you that Gabby and I studied economics at Penn, but we're just learning the basics of cryptocurrency. One friend is almost finished his residency-training in psychiatry, and the other friend is a middle-school teacher, whose father is very wealthy. Runs a large equity investment firm. The reason we met with them was to see how much cash we could raise, because we know it might take a while for any investment firm to come up with the kind of money you need to get this project off the ground. We assumed you'll need money to keep going until that happens."

"How much money?" Jason asked.

"$50,000. It's all we have. We'd be risking everything. It's nowhere near what you'll eventually need, but we hope it'll be enough to keep CLEO running."

"What do I have to give you in return?" Jason asked, his expression stoic, not giving anything away.

Jake shrugged. "A percentage of your company. Of course, we'll discuss it. But before that, our friends want to meet you and see your place. Like us, they've promised to not say anything to anyone. We all believe that this is our chance to become financially independent."

Jason sat staring into space.

"Gabby and I thought that going directly to Morrie would be Plan B. There would be too much red tape before any investment firm, like his, would back you. It'll be tough enough getting Tanya's father, that's our friend's father, to come up with a million plus. Before we'd agree to let any company in on the project, you'd have to give it your stamp of approval. No one will do anything without you saying, yes. You're the boss."

Gina smiled at Jason. "My thought is that you continue to do what you do best, create the best cryptocurrency on the planet. We'll," she looked over at Jake, "be with you every step of the way, making sure that the marketing campaign is in place and that legally we'll all be protected. I'll personally review every piece of the puzzle to protect us and our investment."

"Are your friends honest and trustworthy?"

"Todd, the psychiatrist saved my life. I was attacked by the same people who are after my brother and was hospitalized under his care. I'd do anything for him. If he trusts Tanya, that's enough for us."

Jason nodded, "Okay," he said. "Will tomorrow morning, early, work for you and your friends?"

"I'll call them now, on speaker phone. Okay?" Jake asked.

Jason nodded.

Jake called Todd and explained that their friend wanted to meet him and Tanya in person before taking them to the facility.

Jason nodded in agreement.

"Todd, there's a Coffee Bean in Diamond Bar Village. Can you be there at 7AM?"

"I'll cancel my morning appointments," Todd responded. "Tanya's with me. Let me ask her if she can do it." A minute later, Todd got back on speaker phone. "Jake, we'll both be there."

• • • •

BY 7:15, JAKE, GINA, Todd, Tanya, and Jason sat at an outside table at Coffee Bean sipping their coffees and eating pastries. Todd looked at Jason and said, "Thank you for meeting with us. I'm Todd." He dug in his pocket, pulled out a battered wallet, and showed Jason his Driver's License and his California Medical License. "I don't blame you for being wary. It makes sense to know exactly who you're dealing with. Especially with something as special as you've invented."

Jason nodded appreciatively.

Tanya followed suite and showed Jason her driver's license.

Shrugging, Jason pulled his driver's license out and showed everyone.

Jake smiled. "Okay, we got that out of the way. Any questions from anyone?" Thank God, Jason never asked for his or Gina's driver's licenses, he thought.

Jason nodded. "Todd, Tanya, do either of you know much about cryptocurrency? Mining? Setting up a blockchain?"

"I'm a psychiatrist," Todd said. "I don't know anything, really, except how Bitcoin created a slew of millionaires."

Tanya said, "I'm a teacher, screenplay-writer, and I'm in the same boat. I'd love to be independently wealthy so I can devote my time to writing. I can't wait to see *your* creation. My father is the rich one, the man who runs a very successful investment equity firm. I think he'd be excited if I approached him with your idea, but I need to understand it better."

Jason finished his coffee, stood up, and said, "Okay. Please follow me. I'll explain everything when we get there."

• • • •

AN HOUR LATER, THE five of them left the whirring computers and sat around the table in the sound-proofed room. "Any more questions?" Jason asked.

They all shook their heads, no.

"So how do we do this?" Jason asked.

Jake spoke up. "Jason, have you registered your company?"

"I did. It's a corporation."

"Do you have the articles of incorporation?"

Jason stood up, walked across the room, and opened the top drawer in one of the six, metal, four-drawer filing-cabinets against the wall. He took out a sheath of papers and laid them on the table.

"Give me a few minutes," Gina said. She picked up the papers and carefully read the ten pages. When she was done, she nodded. "It looks good, Jason. CLEO was incorporated in California four years ago. That's when you were still in college?"

Jason nodded.

Jake said, "Last night I ran the numbers. I think a 4% stake in CLEO would be fair. You invested a million or so in hardware and operating costs. Plus, if you add all the sweat-equity you've put in, your company is worth, let's say $1,300,000."

Jason shook his head. "I think it's worth a lot more, Jake. I'd be willing to give up 2%."

Todd said, "Jason, what if you don't get the rest of the funding? I mean you deserve to get it, but what if you don't? We'll lose all our money. Honestly, for me it's a stretch investing the $12,500. But I'll do it if the odds are I'll make a good profit. Being a resident psychiatrist means I've been living from hand-to-mouth for many years. Plus, I have a medical school debt of over $200,000. Like you, it's not been easy for me to pay my rent, food, loan, and whatever."

For minutes, they all sat in silence. Jason said, "When will you give me the money?"

"What percentage are we talking about?" Jake asked.

"I'll do 2 and ½," Jason said.

"Do 3% and we'll Venmo you $5,000 each now, that's the most Venmo allows. That's $20,000 in your bank account this afternoon. Within the next 48 hours, we'll give you certified bank checks for the $30,000 balance," Gina said. "I brought a contract, and I'm also a notary. I have all my authenticating materials right here in my bag."

"You're a notary?" Jake said, obviously surprised.

"I moonlighted all last year. It pays pretty good money. I went to peoples' houses for mortgage closings, bank loans, that sort of thing."

"I never knew," Jake said.

Tanya spoke up. "I'll talk to my father this afternoon. I'll go straight to his office from here. Hopefully, we'll know something very soon. All our money depends on it."

Jason hesitated and finally smiled, "Okay, 3%. Where do I sign?"

CHAPTER 31

"Dad, I need to talk to you," Tanya said into her cell phone, glaring at the officious, very attractive, brunette, twentyish woman in the man-cut, black suit sitting at the mahogany receptionist desk. "It's important."

"Hi, Tanya. Where are you?"

"In the reception area. Jules is giving me a hard time."

"We've had some unwanted visitors... Is something wrong?" Ted Roth answered, his voice sounding worried.

"Not life-threatening. But it's imperative." Tanya glanced around the 600 square foot area. As always, she was impressed with the old-world sense of opulence and character that went into the design – 18-foot ceilings, soft leather sofas and club chairs, mahogany wainscotting, beautiful artwork, and the sense that this was the place where successful, rich people came to become even richer.

"You scared me. Sure, I have a few minutes. I'll let Jules know."

The phone rang at the receptionist desk. Jules picked it and nodded. All six feet of her, in stiletto heels, stood up. "Please follow me," she said.

"Stop it!" Tanya barked. "I know where his office is!"

Jules hesitated, nodded, and sat back down.

Tanya entered her father's huge corner office – thick-pile gray carpet, floor-to-ceiling windows with views of the Century City towers, an enormous mahogany desk, plush sofas, a conference table, and a 75" flat screen TV with a live feed of the stock market. Ted immediately stood up from behind his desk and met Tanya as she entered the office. He opened his arms and gave her a big hug, which she returned.

"Sit down, sweetie. Tell me what's up," he said, motioning for them to sit in the club chairs facing each other.

"Dad, this might sound a bit presumptuous, but I think I have an investment you'll find very lucrative and interesting."

"Okay. Tell me about it."

"Are you familiar with cryptocurrency?"

"A little. We haven't gotten involved in that sector. It seemed too unpredictable. I do know, of course, that people who got involved when it first came out have made a ton of money."

"Exactly. The CEO of the company I'm referring to is an MIT graduate who's spent the last four or five years developing his own currency. I just got back from his facility where he's set up hundreds of ASICs to build his own blockchain. He apparently developed an algorithm that is 70% better than Bitcoin or Etherium – much more efficient, uses less electricity, and very user friendly."

"Tanya. What's an ASIC?"

Tanya took out her iPhone and read from the notes she'd taken. It's an acronym for an advanced computer, Application Specific Integrated Circuits. It's used in building the blockchains or mining process in electronic coinage. But it's really a way to keep track of all the buying and selling of the coins." She pointed to the large TV screen on the wall. "Not too different from trading equities."

Ted nodded, listening intently. "Why are you so interested in this? Usually, you're absolutely bored by any type of investment that I've mentioned."

Tanya nodded. "I'm bored and *really* tired of teaching. If I can make a lot of money, I can follow some of the dreams that I have."

Ted opened his arms and gestured all around his office. "I'll give you whatever you want."

"Dad. Back at NYU, you specifically lectured me on how important it was to get a practical degree, like teaching, so I could make a living. Seriously, it was not great advice." She held up her hand. "I know you meant well. I know 100% that it was out of love, but the problem was that I wasn't strong enough to just do what I wanted. I was afraid to really think for myself. This is my chance. Now, I'm strong enough."

"But you were never interested in economics or investing. I would have *loved* for you to major in business and come to work with me."

"Dad, I'm still not interested in business." She took a deep breath. "What if I asked you to invest ten to thirty million dollars to fund my screen play? To take it all the way from the written page to the big screen or these days Netflix or Amazon or HBO or whatever?"

"I..." Ted hesitated, seemingly at a loss for words.

"Exactly," Tanya interrupted. "It would be a real longshot. Probably a money loser. I'd *never* ask you to invest in something that would be so iffy. On the other hand, if I earned my own money, then I could take the risk. It would be all on me. Risking *my* money on *my* dream is what this is all about."

Ted sighed. "Okay, go over this again with me. Why will it be better than Bitcoin? Why will this make so much money?"

"Full disclosure. Todd and I, and two other friends (both graduates of U of P in economics) have already committed $50,000, $12,500 each. Seed money, until we can get an equity investment firm to fund the CEO. He said he needs a million. I don't know, probably more. We have a signed, notarized contract for a percentage of his company."

"How much of a percentage?" Ted asked, his expression all business.

"I can't say. It's privileged information."

"Tanya!"

"Look dad, this is business. You're the first company we've approached. Just check this out ASAP or we'll move on to the next potential investor." Tanya stared hard at her father, no evidence of any weakness.

Ted looked back at his daughter, finally after a long minute, he broke out in a big grin. "You'd have made a hell of a trader," he said, with more than a mote of pride.

"Thanks," Tanya smiled briefly, controlling her desire to break out in hysterical laughter. Her father respected strength and intellect. She was determined to show him both.

"Okay," he said. "I haven't done this in years, but I want to do it now. I'm excited to do it now, with *you*. Please call the CEO. What's his name?"

"I can't say until he gives me permission."

"Okay. Fair enough. See if you can arrange a meeting tomorrow. It would also be helpful if your business associates were there. I've made it a firm policy to know exactly who I'm dealing with. Toxic relationships are almost guaranteed to cost me money. Make sense?"

"It does." Tanya got up, walked over and hugged her dad." I'll check with everyone and get back to you in a few hours. "Is that okay?"

"More than okay. I'm so looking forward to this."

Tanya left the office and Ted punched in Jules' number.

"Yes, Mr. Roth," she answered immediately.

"Be prepared to cancel my appointments for tomorrow. When I have more details, I'll give you the specifics," he said, a huge smile covering his face.

• • • •

THE NEXT DAY AT 4 PM, Jason, Ted Roth, Jake, Gina, Tanya, and Todd sat around the table in Jason's sound-proofed room. For over an hour, Ted had been asking Jason questions – how long until he'd have everything ready to go, why he needed so much more equipment, specific details how CLEO was different and better than other cryptocurrencies, how many others knew about his work, and on and on. As Jason answered every question in detail, Ted typed his answers into a MacBook Pro. "Two more questions, Jason. You mentioned that Bitcoin has 21 million coins. How many will CLEO have?"

"40 million. My thought is that this will allow the initial entry into CLEO trading to be pennies. But the more an individual purchases, the more they can make, both by appreciation of each coin and a fixed trading charge."

"Okay," Ted said, continuing his typing. "What will the charge be and how is it levied?"

"The individual or group purchasing the coin will pay ½ a percent. That number can never be raised or lowered. It's all part of the algorithm."

"So, it can't be influenced by inflation or demand?"

"Correct. But the value of each coin will still be influenced by supply and demand, just like Bitcoin's value is influenced by market forces."

"Got it," Ted said, as he turned to Jake and Gina. "How did you both discover Jason?"

"After tossing around a dozen different ideas on how to make a lot of money quickly, I asked our boss at IBC, Morrie Weisberg," Jake answered. "He suggested that I contact Jason. He knew Jason from IBC, before he left to work on CLEO full time."

"Is Morrie involved in the project?"

"No. He knows nothing about what we're all doing. No one, but the six of us, knows anything. We, Gabriella and I, decided that we didn't want to go through the conventional way of funding a startup. Too many regulations. Too many hoops to jump through. Too many people who'd want a slice of the pie. The government breathing down our throats. We wanted this to be quick and silent. Not a word on the street until everything's ready to go. We don't trust anyone but ourselves. And now we trust you, Mr. Roth, because we trust Tanya."

"Please call me, Ted, everyone," Ted said with a smile. "Tanya, you can still call me, Dad."

Everyone chuckled.

"Let me think about this and consult with my head of strategic planning. I give you my word that absolutely no details will go anywhere except my inner circle. They are all under strict contract to remain silent. If they divulge anything, they are terminated and subject to huge contractual fines. Besides all the legally binding secrecy, you might wonder why you can trust me. It's simple. I love my daughter, and I would never do *anything* to betray her or her friends. Just like I would never betray anyone who invests with me and my company." He cleared his throat. "I will get back to Tanya tomorrow afternoon, at the latest. This is one of the more interesting projects that has crossed my path." He looked at the five hopeful young people sitting around the table, hanging on his every word. "Thank you all, for this opportunity," Ted said, stood up, and left the room.

Back in his sleek Model S, Tesla, Ted backed out of his spot, looked at Todd's weather-beaten motorcycle, Jason's battered Jeep Cherokee, and Jackson's Toyota and sighed. Where did all the years go? He remembered clearly what it was like to be worried about money, not exactly poor, but certainly not financially comfortable. They all seemed like nice kids, very bright, very motivated...very hopeful. That expression of hope and anxiety on their faces touched him more than they would ever suspect. Tears came to his eyes. He saw how much Tanya loved Todd, and how he reciprocated that love. He liked Todd. It took a lot of guts for a man to walk around wearing a yarmulka, especially when he wasn't particularly religious. He wondered what that was all about. His gut feeling was that Todd had principles and was willing to back them up with actions and not just words.

Jackson and Gabriella were also very smart and obviously in love.

Tanya's friends were all impressive people.

Jason was also an amazing young man. On a person-to-person basis he didn't emote all that well. But, as far as developing his crypto project, he really knew his stuff. Every question that he asked him was fielded with knowledge and clarity.

Ted had spoken this morning to a college friend who taught at MIT, and he was kind enough to look up the details on Jason's education. The kid was a genius. MIT gave him a full ride – tuition, housing, and a job doing research in the math department. Also, a large loan for living expenses that Jason hadn't made much of a dent in paying back. Jason was so far ahead of his peers that his first two years of advanced calculus and physics were waived.

The boy was on to something, but he needed a lot of money to make the project successful, a lot more than he was asking for.

CHAPTER 32

J ake carried two large pizzas into the house. After everyone was settled in around the dining room table, sipping beer and munching on pizza, Jake looked over at Todd. "You're the shrink. What do you think? Will Ted go for it?"

Todd shrugged. "I'm not playing poker with him. No tells. Tanya, what do you think? Will he fund the project?"

"Your guess is as good as mine, Todd. I've never seen him at work before."

"He was thorough," Jake said. "I learned a lot just listening to him."

Gina caught Tanya's eye. "I like your dad. There's something about him that engenders trust and respect. He knows what he's doing."

Tanya nodded. "Starting with nothing, he built one of the largest equity investment firms in the country. He's very smart and sure of himself." She looked at Todd. "Maybe now you can see why it was so hard for me to disagree with him."

"I do understand," Todd responded. "It would be hard being his daughter and having an opinion that he didn't agree with... I hope he thinks this is a good deal. Investing $12,500 doesn't seem like much, but in my pathetic, financial world, it's a lot of money. Tanya, if I take the job at UCLA, and I'm certainly leaning toward it, I'll make a decent living, but LA is so godawful expensive. A starter home is a million plus. In Westwood, it's probably twice that."

"We're going to make millions and millions," Jake said, crossing his fingers. "So, you'll buy a house with your share, Todd?"

"I've spent my whole life worrying about money. What a relief it'll be to pay off the 200K and change that I owe the government on my school loans. Money is a constant stress. A house? Now, that would be a real bonus. How about you, Jake?"

"A home and money in the bank." He looked at Gina. "What'll you do?"

"First thing I'll do is pay off all the school loans for myself and my sisters. Second is make sure my family never worries about money again." Gina raised her eyebrows at Tanya. "Your family is so wealthy. Will the money mean anything to you?"

"Ha. It'll mean an awful lot. I've completed two screenplays. They're both in the bottom drawer of my desk. Years ago, I tried pitching them, but no luck. Do you have any idea what it costs to produce a movie? From concept to screen? In the range of 5 to 50-plus million dollars. If I had that kind of money, I'd put my heart and soul into writing and producing the kind of movies that would change the world."

"What's an example?" Todd asked.

"How 'bout our toxic prison system? The United States is one of the few major powers that focuses mainly on punishment – an eye for an eye. Religious fanatics and greedy corporations run this country. One of my screen plays is about a young woman who kills the man who tried to rape her. The man's family hired a Harvard-trained, snake of an attorney. The girl has no money. She had a court appointed, idealistic lawyer, and in the end is convicted. Prison is no picnic. While she tries to survive, her boyfriend, a guy in law school, living in his car because he used all his money to try and save her, is doing everything he can to get her conviction reversed. The screenplay exposes all the corruption in the for-profit-prison system. Whatever it takes to keep the cells filled with paying customers, they do. Forget rehab. Forget getting people ready to reenter society. And justice? That never enters the equation. They just want the money," Tanya said passionately.

"What a powerful plot and concept," Jake said. "I'm impressed."

"Me too," said Gina. "I love it."

"I agree," Todd said, and put his arm around Tanya. "You never told me."

Tanya kissed Todd on the lips and turned to Jake and Gina. "Thanks guys, that means a lot. By tomorrow afternoon, we'll know if my father is in or out... What do we do if he passes? I mean really, he didn't become a multimillionaire by just being nice. No-matter how much he wants to please me, I guarantee he won't risk millions of his investors' money if he doesn't believe in the project."

Jake handed out four more bottles of Stella. "If he passes, Gina and I will compile a list of other potential investors. Within 48 hours we'll be in contact with them. Whatever it takes, let's make this work!" He raised his beer bottle, and everyone joined him in a toast.

• • • •

THE NEXT MORNING, AS Jake sat anxiously in his office at IBC, reading the LA Times, he froze. On the second page was an article describing a bloody gang war between 14K and MS13. Thus far ten people were murdered – eight gang members, a three-year-old child, and her mother.

He walked over to Gina's desk, and just as he was about to tell her about 14K, he froze. Her eyes were red, and tears streamed down her cheeks.

"What's wrong, honey?"

Sobbing, Gina tried to catch her breath. Finally, she blurted out, "Jake, I can't do this anymore. I miss my family. Don't get me wrong. I love our life together. Our neighbors are wonderful. I really like the ladies, sharing recipes, talking about life... They're very good people. I like working for Morrie. The guy's an angel. It's mainly my family. Other than the one short phone call to my dad to let him know that we're in hiding, I haven't spoken to any of them, or my friends, in months. They must all be worried sick. I've got to see them! But I can't! This is terrible. We're trapped in a horrific nightmare." Again, she started to sob.

"I'm sorry. I'm so sorry I got you involved in all this. Maybe, we FedEx a burner to your dad, at the university? At least you can update him, talk to your mom, to your sisters. I'll buy new burners this afternoon. At least we can do that, right?"

Gina stood and embraced Jake, burrowing her face in his shoulder.

Jake's phone rang. It was Todd. "Hey, what's up?" Jake answered.

"Tanya just called. Ted wants us all to meet at his office this evening, 7 PM. Does that work?"

"Sure."

"Can you call, Jason?"

"Of course. Good news or bad news?"

"Tanya doesn't know."

• • • •

AT 7 PM, THE CRYPTO-Five filed into the lush conference room and took seats around the 15 foot long, mahogany table. Ted sat at the head, his poker face in place. "Anyone like some water? Coffee? Tea?" he asked.

All five sat frozen, having no clue what was in store for them. No one uttered a word.

Ted smiled. "Well then, what about champagne and some cheese and crackers?" The door to the conference room opened and a thirtyish man, dressed casually in slacks and a button-down shirt, rolled in a cart. Moments later, he poured the bubbly liquid into six flutes, and passed them around.

After everyone had taken a sip of their drink, Ted said, "There's good news and more good news. I've spoken to my research team, and they are all very excited to be working with you. They think Jason's innovation is brilliant. They also believe that we can make a lot of money if CLEO is marketed quickly and correctly."

"Sir, uh Ted," Jason said hesitantly. "First, thank you very much. So...I need to know what percentage you'll be wanting?"

"Of course, Jason. Number one, we'll be giving you 1 million dollars to finish building the infrastructure. In a case like this, you'll be working with one of our engineering specialists. But, please keep in mind, it's your company. We just want to facilitate your ideas. Number 2, it'll cost a lot more to market CLEO than you imagined. That'll cost 3 million dollars. We're talking about a total of 4 million dollars."

"Why so much?" Jake asked. "How is that money allocated?"

"We have an international footprint, Jackson. What it means is that our equity investment specialists who are in contact with investment firms like IBC, RBC, Sun Capital, Fidelity, Charles Schwab, Mellon, Goldman Sachs and on and on need to be educated regarding CLEO. There will also be a TV push on the stock market channels and financial networks. We'll have brochures, TV spots, radio spots. The main message is simple. Beat Bitcoin at its own game. Takeover the cryptocurrency market. It's a twenty-to-forty-billion-dollar market. We also have a complete staff of lawyers who will protect us against any-and-all attempts to take control of intellectual property or thwart our goals." He looked directly at everyone and said, "We are willing to do this for 40% of CLEO."

Jason's face lost all its color. He just kept shaking his head, looking very much in shock.

Ted was silent for almost a minute. He said, "Jason. Is there something wrong with my evaluation?"

"I won't do this, sir," he said. "I'll have nothing left. All my work...for nothing."

Jake said, "Please, Ted. Would you give us a few minutes?"

Ted nodded. "Take all the time you need." He pointed to a button, under the table, to the right of where he was sitting. "Whenever you're ready, just push the button." He got up and left the room.

CHAPTER 33

When the door closed and Ted was gone, Jake said, "That's a huge percentage."

"That's what I think," Jason said. "I won't do it!"

"I agree, Jason. The way these things work is that this is just the first round of investors," Jake said. "When round two is needed, if it is, there won't be much left to divvy up."

"Just to play devil's advocate," Gina said. "Four million *is* a lot of money. I had no idea it would be that expensive. But advertising and training will cost a lot and –"

Tanya broke in, "I think my dad just threw that number out there, expecting us to negotiate. If we just accept what his initial offering is, then we're giving away too much. He's a negotiator. Always was. Always will be."

"Four million *is* a lot of money, but not for Ted," Todd said. "My sense is that this doesn't qualify as pocket change, but still, it's not an amount that'll break his bank. Equity investment firms deal in hundreds of millions. I think we should make a logical counteroffer and back it up with facts."

"What do you mean?" Jason said.

"Well, you already invested at least a million and –"

Jake intervened, "And sweat equity is worth ten times that. Without your invention, there would be no CLEO. No forty-billion-dollar idea. What are you comfortable with, Jason?"

Jason sighed. "20...maybe 22%. No more."

"Okay, I think we should counter with 15%. See what Ted says," Jake responded. "If he's really that hardline, then we'll go to plan B. I'd love to work with Ted, but we shouldn't give it all away so quickly." He looked around the room. "Are we in agreement?"

Gina said, "Tanya, I really like and respect your dad, but we all signed on to help and protect Jason. And hopefully for all of us to make a lot of money. I agree with Jackson. In six months, if we need another round of financing, Jason might lose control." Gina took a deep breath. "Tanya, if we get tough in here, are you okay with that? I mean tough enough to walk out of the room and start making phone calls tomorrow to other investment firms?"

"Absolutely. Let's go for a fair deal," Tanya responded, her tone firm and strong, a lot like her father's.

"So should I push the button?" Jake stood up and walked over to Ted's chair.

Everyone nodded. No hesitation.

Five minutes later, Ted returned, calm and smiling. "Okay, everyone. What do ya say?"

Jake leaned forward in his chair, a serious expression on his face. "Ted, we all like and trust you. We know that you have years of experience and are very successful. Just like you most likely did research on Jason, we did the same with you and your company. All A plus ratings. Our hope is that you like us and believe in CLEO as much as we like you and trust you. For us, CLEO is a once in a lifetime chance to make an enormous amount of money. Your offer of 40%, in our opinion, is too high. We agree that four million dollars is a lot of money, but the chance to make billions is also very high." Jake took a sip of champagne and cleared his throat.

"Jason is a genius." He looked over at him and smiled. Jason smiled back. "His algorithm is beyond anything that has ever been developed. On your tour of his facility, you saw all that he accomplished. Everything that he did, he did alone. That amount of work, his genius, and his dedication is worth a lot. Jason's sweat equity is worth tens of millions. I correct that statement. Thousands of millions." Jake pointed to Todd, Tanya, Gina, and himself. "We have invested enough money for Jason to continue his work until we get financing. We're hopeful that you'll be in the trenches with us, but we're not desperate. We also hope that you won't take offense at our counteroffer."

"What is it," Ted asked, the smile long gone and the poker face back.

"15% and our commitment to do everything in our power to work with you and make this the most successful investment you ever made."

Ted nodded. His gaze lingering on Tanya a little longer than on anyone else. "Gentlemen, Ladies, I'll be back in ten minutes." He got up and left the room.

"Wow, Jackson. That was impressive," Gina said. "You sure you weren't hiding out in the back of my entrepreneur's class last year?"

Jake smiled. "Just selling a lot of veal piccata and Caesar salad, light on the dressing."

"Thanks, Jackson," Jason said. "You were amazing."

"So are you, Jason," Todd said. "What you've created is the real deal and none of us should ever forget that." He pointed to Tanya. "Your father loves you so much. Did you notice the way he looked at you? He wants this to work, and my sense is that he'll do almost anything to get that to happen. He'll come down... There's no way he'll pass on the deal. For him it's a Grand Slam. He gets to make a fortune *and* work with his beautiful, brilliant daughter. No reasonable man would pass up that kind of chance. I wouldn't...if I'm ever lucky enough to have a daughter like you."

Tanya blushed. "Thank you."

"Let me make a prediction," Todd added. "He'll come down to 30% and pronounce that this is his last and final offer. Last night, I did a lot of research on startups. The average first round of angel investors usually agrees to a 20% share in a company. I don't think Ted will go down that low. He's too savvy and four million is no chump change."

"So, how do you think it'll go?" Jake asked.

"I think when he says 30% or maybe even 35%, we'll all look at each other and shake our heads. You'll thank him, and we'll all smile politely. Then, we'll get up to leave. Ted will stop us, I think. At that moment, Jason will look at Ted, hesitate, and then say, Ted, I'll do it for 20%. Ted will hesitate. and then say, alright, you got me. I'll do it for 25%. This time it really is my last and final. Jason will hesitate and respond. Either yes or no. That's up to him."

"Todd, if you're right, 25% will be a fair deal. In fact, if it goes the way you're predicting, I'm not going anywhere without my favorite shrink and newly minted market analyst," Jake said.

Todd chuckled.

Jake looked at Jason. "What do you think, Jason?"

"I won't do it for more than 22%," he said, no hint of a smile, just an anxious man whose future lay in the hands of others. "With your 3% that leaves me with 75%. If this doesn't work, let's shop around."

Todd said, "Okay, Jason. We're all behind you. I suggest you counter at 17%. That number gives a little more wiggle room."

"Are we all in agreement?" Jake asked. "22% or nothing."

Everyone nodded.

Jake picked up the bottle of champagne and refilled everyone's flute. They all touched glasses just as Ted came back in the room.

Ted sat down and said, "30%. That's my last and final." He had on his game face. No messing around.

As a unit all five investors made motions to stand up. Jake said, "Ted, we just can't. Thank you very much. I'm sorry we wasted your valuable time. Hopefully soon, you'll read about us in the Wall Street Journal."

As they pushed their chairs back Ted said, "Wait. Let's discuss this a little more."

Slowly, they all eased back in their chairs.

Jason said, "There's not much more to discuss, Ted. 17% is my final offer. Last and final, sir."

Ted stared hard at Jason, who shrugged his shoulders, seemingly apologetic that he couldn't go higher. Finally, Ted sighed. It looked like this was a sigh he had perfected over the years. "Gentlemen. Ladies. I'll do 25%. This is really it. It'll break my heart if you don't accept, but I just can't go any lower."

Jason took a sip of champagne and a deep breath. For a full minute, he sat as if paralyzed. Then, he cleared his throat and said, "I need 22% or we'll talk to other investors. I'm sorry, sir." It looked like he was about to cry. Nothing about his expression or feelings was false. He'd make the world's worst poker player.

Ted stared hard at Jason, then at everyone else, again spending a few extra beats looking at Tanya. Finally, he stuck out his hand, inches away from Jason. "Jason, you have a deal."

The Crypto-five all stood and clapped.

Ted walked around the table and shook everyone's hand. When he reached Tanya, he kissed her on the forehead.

With a big smile, he said, "Thank you all for your trust. I will do everything to keep it. My goal is that within three to six months, we'll be live. CLEO will be launched, and the world will embrace it."

The room reverberated with more applause.

CHAPTER 34

Jake and Gina devoted their days to researching companies for *West Coast Investment Trust 20*. Using the algorithm that they developed in college, factoring relevant current events, they made short-term and long-term forecasts. In the few months since they initiated the fund, they had accrued over 25 million dollars in investment money and were on a first name basis with over thirty-five enthusiastic investors.

A week after Ted agreed to take CLEO public, during their regular weekly meeting with Morrie, Jake asked him, "Are you happy with our progress?"

"Happy? I'm ecstatic. You are both brilliant, and the way your fund is going is nothing less than a miracle. Why? Do you have a problem with me? With what I'm paying you?" He looked a little frantic. "I'm increasing your salaries effective immediately! 20%! Is that okay?" He looked genuinely troubled.

Jake and Gina looked at each other and Jake said, "No, that's not what we wanted to ask you."

"It doesn't matter. You've both earned the increase. It's done. I'm notifying accounting immediately."

Gina smiled, "Thank you, Morrie. That's more than generous. You're wonderful."

Morrie beamed.

"Thank you, very much," Jake said. "More money will certainly be helpful, but it doesn't solve our problem. We're hoping that you might have a suggestion to help us. As you well know, Gabriella and Jackson are figments of our imagination. We can't fly. Can't buy real estate. Can't get married. Gina can't take her Series 7 and 63. Future social security benefits won't happen." Jake took a deep breath. "We need to find a way to become authentic people without the government or *anyone* knowing what we're doing. It needs to be like we always existed. The Chinese government has its tentacles into every aspect of the web. We've avoided all social media in fear that we can be tracked through friends and family. If we apply for name changes using regular governmental channels, the Chinese will know. *Any* suggestions? We're desperate."

Morrie looked thoughtful. He picked up his phone, went through his contacts, and shook his head. "I don't know anyone. I can ask around... Should I do that?"

Jake held up his hand in a stop gesture. "No! It's too dangerous. But thank you."

On the way back to their office, Todd called. "Hey Todd, how are you?"

"Very well. Just checking in. Tanya took a leave of absence from the school district and is working full-time with Ted's team helping Jason. Ted just released $250,000, and Jason ordered a batch of new equipment. That's one big thing. The other is that I accepted the assistant professor position at UCLA. I gave notice on my townhouse in Redondo, and Tanya and I are looking for an apartment in Westwood. We're thinking of getting married."

"Congratulations. You two make a great couple. We love you both," Jake said, trying to sound upbeat and supportive.

"What's up, buddy? Something amiss?"

"Why? Why do you ask?"

"I don't know. Just the psychiatrist in me. You sound a little off your game. Maybe I'm wrong?"

"Nah, you're right. Gina's really upset about being isolated from her family. Last week we sent a burner to her dad, at the university, and spoke to him. He was great, like he always is. But it's not enough. Her family is the best. I was close to her mom and dad and her sisters. They're remarkable. The fact that I gave all that up, including Gina, to write my novel was nuts. What was I thinking?"

Todd laughed. "That's a story we'll examine later, over a couple of beers." He laughed again. "Well, maybe more than a few."

Jake laughed with him.

Todd said, in a serious tone, "The identity problem needs to be addressed...and solved soon. There must be a way."

"If you can think of one, please tell me."

"Hang on, I'm thinking."

"You have an idea?"

"Maybe? Let me make a phone call. I'll call you back."

• • • •

THAT EVENING, AS JAKE and Gina sat at the dinner table finishing up a lasagna that Jake had picked up from Whole Foods, Todd called.

"Hey, Todd," Jake said, wiping his mouth. "We were just finishing dinner. I'm putting you on speaker. Any miracles come to mind?"

"I'm sorry. No miracles. In fact, just the opposite. I have a friend who teaches IT at UCLA. I thought maybe he'd have some contacts, but no luck. You and Gina are really in a bind. I'll keep working on it."

"Thanks, buddy. We'll see you soon."

. . . .

THE NEXT EVENING TODD called again. "Jake, a friend just emailed me a news blurb. Hahnemann Hospital, one of the major medical training centers in Philly, went bankrupt and closed its doors. My friend's looking for a new residency program. He also mentioned that Hahnemann moved all their records to a storage facility."

"Hahnemann closed? I was born there."

"Maybe that's even better. I'm not sure."

"What do you mean?"

"Maybe it's just a fantasy, but doesn't it seem reasonable that hacking into a defunct database located in a storage facility would be easier than getting into one that's being used by a functioning hospital or medical school?"

"I see where you're going. You mean in terms of changing identities?"

"Maybe? I just saw a movie where a family had to go into the Witness Protection Program. If the government can redo records, why can't someone who's computer savvy accomplish the same thing? The less people that are involved, the safer you and Gina will be."

"I guess."

"If the government uses computer hackers, why can't anyone?"

"You're right. Thanks, Todd."

That evening, Jake sat and stared out the window into the darkness. There had to be a way to fix this problem. He remembered something he researched while writing his novel. The bottom line of identity change came down to one thing, a birth certificate. It was the foundation of building a legitimate identity.

He picked up his phone, went to contacts, and called Larry Girard.

Larry picked up on the second ring. "Jerry? Is that you?"

"Yeah. Everything good?"

"No complaints."

"Glad to hear that. Larry, the reason I called is that I have a problem and hope you can meet with me. It would be better if I explained it in person. If you can help, I'll pay you."

"What kind of problem?"

"I'll tell you in person."

"Okay. When?"

"The sooner the better."

"I can take a long lunch tomorrow."

"Where do you work?"

"Santa Monica."

"How about we meet at the Cheesecake Factory? It's at the end of the promenade in the Santa Monica Place Mall. Does 1PM work?"

"That's fine. Very convenient."

"Lunch is on me. It's a long story. Look for a guy with a full beard."

CHAPTER 35

Jake parked a few blocks from Ciao Ristorante.

It was the first time since he was attacked by the Hong Kong Triad that he'd ventured back to Santa Monica. As he walked down Fifth Street, he saw his reflection in a store window. He truly didn't recognize himself. The combination of his beard, jeans, a black leather bomber jacket, and a woolen watch cap, gave him a sixties-throwback-hippy-look. Maybe a guy who specialized in writing poetry? Or who worked with the French Resistance? He chuckled to himself, remembering Gina's flirtatious comment when they first met. God was she funny.

For a moment, Jake's failed writing-past tied his gut in a knot. Would he ever write again? Would life ever go back to anywhere near normal? He sighed. No-matter what happened, being with Gina more than made up for it. He couldn't imagine ever again living without her. Also, it didn't hurt that they had over $38,000 in their savings account and were debt free.

What should he tell Larry? How much could he trust him?

He entered the Cheesecake Factory ten minutes early and was seated at a table facing out toward the Third Street Promenade. The restaurant was half-filled and had a contemporary vibe – modern wood and steel tables, an open kitchen with a large grill and big ovens where you could see the pizza cooking, indoor plants that looked like tall sprouts of grass, and dozens of slowly circulating ceiling fans.

When he saw Larry come in the door, he rose and waived him over.

They shook hands and Larry sat down. He smiled, "In a million years I wouldn't have recognized you, Jerry."

Jake sighed. "Sadly, that was the plan. I can't have anyone recognize me. It would be too dangerous. Even you. I can't tell you my real name or exactly what's happening. If I'm vague, please don't take offense. As the cliché goes, 'What you don't know can't hurt you.'"

Larry nodded.

The waiter came over and they ordered two small pizzas, salads, and two draft beers.

Minutes later, sipping the beers, Jake handed Larry an envelope.

"Inside the envelope is $500, two names, and approximate dates of birth. I'll explain what we need. Whether you help or not, the money is still yours."

Larry took a large swallow of beer.

"I need two new identities. One for me and one for my girlfriend. Something on the order of what happens when the FBI puts a person in the Witness Protection Program."

"Jerry, or whatever your name is, I'll call you Jerry. Did you break the law? Are you or your girlfriend criminals?"

"No! I've never broken the law. The group trying to find us is an international Hong Kong triad called 14K. They're after a relative of mine and thought that they could find him through me. You saw what I looked like when we met. They almost killed me. That was why I hid out in the hospital. You know, acted so weird and wouldn't talk. The names in the envelope are random picks. They have no connection to who we really are."

"So, if I understand you correctly, you're asking me to hack a government database and create two new identities. Right?"

"Not really. What I have in mind is dicey, and I'm sure challenging, but I think much safer."

"Okay, what exactly do you want?"

"Hahnemann Hospital, a medical school and teaching hospital in Philadelphia, just went out of business. They closed their doors and transferred all their patients to other facilities. From what I heard; patient records are being stored somewhere in the city, in a warehouse. There must be thousands and thousands of birth certificates that were recorded and stored over the last hundred years. I'm not sure when they started putting them on computer files, but I'm guessing for at least the last thirty or so years. So, what I need are authentic birth certificates for myself and my girlfriend."

"I'm still a bit confused. Can you clarify this?"

"I need proof, written into the database, that we were born and exist. So, if a governmental agency needs validation, it'll be right there in black and white. Given the fact that Hahnemann no longer exists, I'm assuming it'll be easier to get into their database. With our names on file, I'll be able to apply to the Pennsylvania Bureau of Records, or whatever it's called, and request certified birth certificates. Plus, when you're in the database, you can request social security numbers. Even though we don't have the exact numbers, we can then apply for valid social security cards. Apparently, that's the way it's done. Social Security numbers are assigned when you're born. That's it. Can you, do it? Will you?"

Larry sighed. "The main problem, Jerry, is that I don't want to risk getting in trouble. Finally, after all the hell I went through medically, my life has dramatically improved."

"Okay, I get it. How about you go home and see how hard it would be, and if you can do it safely? Either way, the $500 is yours. If you can add us to the database, I'll pay you $5000 in cash? Is that fair?"

"More than fair. I'll call you tonight or tomorrow and let you know what I decide."

• • • •

AT 11 PM LARRY CALLED. Jake picked up on the first ring. "Larry, hi."

"Jerry, hope I'm not calling too late."

"Not at all. And please forgive me for pushing you so hard. I don't want anything bad to happen to you. I was being selfish."

"It's done."

"What?"

"It took almost no time."

"You're kidding me."

"You can apply anytime you want to the Pennsylvania Department of Records in Harrisburg and request birth certificates. It's a done deal."

"Meet me at the same place, same time tomorrow, so I can give you what we agreed on. Larry, I can't tell you how relieved and appreciative I am."

"Forget it, Jerry. It was nothing."

"Larry. You saved our lives. That's *not* nothing. Please! Let me do what's right. Meet me at the same time, same place. But this time lunch is on you! Now that's fair!"

Larry laughed. "Okay. Okay."

• • • •

IT TOOK THREE WEEKS for the official Pennsylvania birth certificates and six weeks for the replacement social security cards to arrive. One week later, Gabriella and Jackson Wolfe, using their new cards, took their driving tests and were issued California licenses from the DMV. That same week, Gabriella sat for her Series 7 and 63 exams. Fifteen days later, she was notified that she passed and was now qualified to sell stocks and bonds in the state of California. When that happened, Morrie immediately raised her salary. If you combined their salaries, plus the percentage from *West Coast Investment Trust 20,* Jackson and Gabby were now earning *over* $400,000 a year!

From that day forward, Jake and Gina buried their given names. When they told Morrie, he pulled out a bottle of sherry from his desk drawer, filled three glasses, and recited Kaddish, the prayer for the dead. Afterward, he embraced them both, and wished them long and happy lives in their official new identities. Their new names were written in stone. Even in the privacy of their own home, with no one around, they called each other Jackson and Gabby.

Over the next month, they made hundreds of cold calls promoting *West Coast Investment Trust 20.* They traveled to San Diego, Newport Beach, Santa Barbara, Ventura County, San Francisco, and spoke to dozens and dozens of financial advisors all over the state.

By the end of June, they had seventy-five *West Coast Investment Trust 20* investors. According to Morrie, they had done the impossible. They were managing a fund worth over 37 million dollars. He called them magicians, geniuses, God's Hassidic disciples. But we're not Hassidic, Gina said. Morrie smiled. God works his wonders in many ways.

Gabby shipped her Prius, that had been "hidden" in Ted's parking structure, back to her parents in Philly. She was afraid that selling the car would have raised a red flag for the Chinese. She bought herself a new, white, Honda Accord Hybrid. The pink slip showed that it was solely owned by Gabriella Wolfe.

Jackson Wolfe returned the leased Toyota and took an Uber to the BMW dealer close to their home in West Hollywood. After test driving four vehicles, he bought a one-year-old, 3 series, BMW convertible with just 4,000 miles on it. It looked brand new and came with a three-year warranty. Whatever happened to his thrashed Alfa would remain a mystery for the ages.

Saturday nights, Todd and Tanya met with Jackson and Gabby for beers and pizza. Never once did Jackson ever share what *his* real dream was – that CLEO would make a fortune and he'd miraculously find a way to extricate Nelson from 14K.

On June 30th Todd finished his residency, and on July 1st he was officially hired as an assistant professor on the psychiatric faculty at UCLA. He and Tanya rented a two-bedroom apartment in Westwood Village. Every morning, Todd walked to his new office at the hospital and Tanya had an easy ten-minute drive to Century City where her dad had his offices.

On the surface everything was going well. Gabby spoke to her sisters, mother, and father on a regular basis. All of them used burner phones by the dozens and were extremely careful to follow a strict protocol – no more than two calls per phone. Never use real names, disclose addresses, or give any clues as to who they really were.

In their spare time, Gabby and Jackson joined Tanya as she shadowed Ted's cryptocurrency experts. Every aspect of the launch was examined in minute detail. Nothing was taken for granted.

Finally, after months of preparation, CLEO was scheduled to go public on Monday morning.

CHAPTER 36

"**G**abby you ready?" Jackson called from downstairs. It was 5:30 AM. The stock market opened in an hour.

Gabby hurried down the stairs, dressed in a silk, long sleeve blouse, and perfectly matching skirt.

"You look beautiful," he said, just as she leaned close and gave him a kiss on the lips.

"Thanks, Jackson. Now, we find out if we're millionaires or just *comfortable*."

Jackson laughed, but his stomach was in a knot.

"You, okay?" she asked.

"Yeah, why?"

"It looks like you just swallowed a sour pickle."

"I'm fine. Just excited."

At 6 AM, Jackson, Gabby, Todd, and Tanya joined Ted and another man at his Century City conference room. Ted personally poured everyone a cup of fresh coffee, and offered croissants, bagels, scones, and fresh fruit from a silver serving plate.

Jason was back at his crypto-facility, along with Ted's computer specialists, all on-hand to handle any trading issues. There was a Zoom hook-up from Jason's quiet room to Ted's conference room with an airplay to a 75-inch TV screen at the end of the room.

After they settled into their seats, Ted said, "First I want to introduce, Zion. He's one of our foremost experts on crypto. As the day progresses, he'll most likely be able to answer any questions." Zion was a heavy-set Caucasian, scruffy beard, looked like he was an Israeli or from somewhere in the Middle East. He glanced up from his computer, smiled, then immediately focused back down on the screen.

"Okay then. I think most of you are attending your first IPO, Initial Public Offering. Most of the time, companies like mine allow the public to buy stock shares in advance and we distribute detailed documents describing exactly what it is you're buying – the upfront and backside charges, the warnings of buying a particular stock or bond, how you can lose your money etcetera, a description of the sector and on and on. In this case, we," he made a motion signaling the people sitting at the table, "are the only IPO investors, besides Jason of course. For me, it's a totally new way to sell and promote an IPO product. You just log on to CLEO's site, Robinhood, or Coinbase, then electronically buy and sell what you want. When Bitcoin came out, the initial cost was less than a penny. That first day it went up to 8 cents. An eight hundred percent rise in value." Ted sipped his coffee and pointed to the TV screen.

"At this exact moment," he looked at his watch, "10 minutes before the start of trading. A CLEO coin is worth one dollar. The days of less than a penny are long gone. As the day progresses, we'll all watch as the value of CLEO progresses, up or down. Of course, we all hope it goes way up. But like with any investment, that can't be predicted.

"We did everything possible to make this IPO an event that excites and promotes crypto investors to put their money into CLEO. We promoted this IPO as an opportunity to *not* miss out, like many did with Bitcoin, as well as letting everyone know how superior CLEO is to any existing cryptocurrency. When I say everyone, I mean it. This was a world-wide push.

"Computer experts like, Zion, have exponentially expanded Jason's initial ability to buy and sell coins. If someone's interested, we want them to experience a professional and glitch-proof interaction. At this moment, we have half-a-dozen experts on site with Jason. If anything goes wrong, they will fix it AS-AP. They're also in constant communication with Coinbase and Robinhood."

Ted looked at his watch, then pushed a key on the computer in front of him and created a split-screen – half the TV screen showed the standard stock market visual, the other half focused on CLEO's trading value. The three people standing on the dais at the market were counting down from ten. The bell sounded, and the market was open for business.

Jake sat frozen at the table. CLEO was fixed at $0.80 per coin. That meant that the initial $25,000 investment that Gabby made was now down to $20,000, a $5000 decrease in value. "Excuse me, Zion," he said. "How come the value is down 20% from the initial investment? How was that valuation determined? It seems so random."

"Good question," Zion answered, in a heavy Israeli accent. "It's a complicated algorithm that includes the value of hardware, mathematical extrapolation of cryptocurrency values, supply and demand of this type of currency, and things of this nature."

"What does it really mean?"

Ted chimed in. "We'll know what it all means in minutes, then hours. The value will vary as we learn in real time what value the street places on CLEO. The value that we placed on it will soon be meaningless."

As they watched the TV screen, the value of a coin rose to $0.83.

Two minutes later it was up to $0.90. By 6:45 AM, $1.00. The investment was now back to what they'd initially put into it.

By 7:00 AM, it hit $1.50.

Three minutes later, $1.70.

Gabby grabbed Jackson's hand. Her teeth were clenched, and her eyes were focused 100% on the screen.

By 8:00 AM, CLEO hit $2.20. By Jake's calculation, their $25,000 dollar investment was now up to $55,000. He refilled everyone's coffee cup and took a big bite of his bagel smeared with cream cheese.

Ted picked up his phone and said something. Moments later he left the room.

Todd said, "We've already doubled our money."

By then, it had risen to $3.30.

"Jesus," Tanya exclaimed. "Now it's *over* three times what we put in. An investment of $25,000 is worth $82,000. This is crazy."

The four friends sat in awed silence as CLEO skyrocketed. At 12:01 PM it was up to $13.00.

Todd said, "Hey, Zion. If we wanted to sell some coins and turn it into cash, how do we do it?"

Zion looked up from his computer. "According to the underwriters, there is no lag time. That means you are free to sell whenever you want. The best way to do that is to get online with Coinbase. It's headquartered in San Francisco. Unlike the stock exchange, they're open 24/7 and charge about 2.5%. So, for example, if you sold $100,000 worth of CLEO, you'd pay them $2500. Coinbase has been around for many years and, in my opinion, is the most reliable and safest way to do cryptocurrency exchanges."

Now, CLEO was up to $15.70. $12,500 was worth $196,000 minus the $5000 rate of exchange, leaving a total worth of $191,000.

"Zion, do you have a moment to help me do that?"

"Of course."

Todd stood up, looked at his friends and shrugged. "If it didn't go up one more cent, I'd still be a happy man. He walked around the table and sat down next to Zion. It was 12:25 PM and CLEO was now up to $30. That brought his initial investment of $12,500 up to almost $400,000.

Tanya got up and sat beside Todd. "How much will you sell, honey?"

"All. I can pay off my loan and have a few hundred thousand for a down payment on real estate."

"How 'bout if I sell three-quarters of mine? Hedging a bit, in case it keeps going up. Then I can spend more time writing, and we can go in together on a condo or a house. A $600,000 down payment is amazing. Normally, it would take years to accumulate that." She hesitated, then said, "If I sold it all, we'd have $800,000. $600,000 down on a house, and $200,000 in the bank sounds even better. I was never much of a gambler."

Todd kissed Tanya and smiled. "I want to take the money before I wake up and our beautiful carriage has shrunken back into a poppy seed."

Zion said, "I put all your info into the Coinbase website. At this exact second, both investments are worth $850,000 minus charges. Together, you'd net about $830,000. Is that what you want? Shall I execute the trade?"

Tanya and Todd said, "Do it!"

At the other end of the table, Gabby had already gone online with Coinbase. "Jackson, I think we should cash out. An $800,000 windfall is crazy wonderful. Wait! Now it's $830,000. It will take years to accumulate this kind of money."

Jackson sat paralyzed. Finally, he said, "What if it skyrockets again tomorrow?"

"I never thought CLEO would go up this fast. Jackson, we'd be set. Financially safe."

"Gabby, is this a professional or an emotional decision?"

"Both. What's wrong, honey? You seem so sad."

"I'm fine. Sell before we're back to square one. I trust you. You're brilliant and logical. As you know, at times my judgement is really flawed. I think this is one of those times." He took Gabby's hand. "Push the sell, now!"

She did. The initial investment of $25,000 was transformed into $860,000.

Smiling, she looked over at Jackson and gasped.

Jackson's head was in his hands. Tears were rolling down his cheeks soaking his shirt.

CHAPTER 37

At 1 PM, just as the market closed, Ted walked back in the room. He thanked Zion, made a motion for him to leave, and then sat down. When Zion was gone, he said, "I've never, in all my years, seen anything like this. This was crazy. Beyond crazy. People everywhere in the world are acting like CLEO will never stop going up. Maybe they're right. Maybe not. May I ask what you all did."

"We sold everything, Dad," Tanya said. "It just seemed too good to be true." The smile on her face told it all. She was ecstatic.

"Same with us," Gabby said. "In my experience and what I learned in graduate school, when something is too good to be true, it's not."

Jackson got up from the table and filled his coffee cup. "Anybody want some?" he asked, his expression back to neutral.

No one took him up on it.

"I'm in shock," Todd said. "I've spent my whole life worrying about money. To make this much so fast is shocking. Overwhelming. I'm still trying to catch my breath. I just logged on to my online bank site, and the money is *actually* sitting right in my account. *It happened.*" Todd started chuckling, then laughing, and soon he was hysterical. Laughing so hard that tears ran down his cheeks. Then Tanya joined him in laughter, as did Gabby, and Ted. Jackson forced a smile, trying hard to join everyone in one of the most amazing experiences of their lives.

When they calmed down, Gabby asked, "Ted, what did you do? I'm dying to know. And, truth be known, scared that we really blew it."

"No fears. I sold 80%. That's a profit of over 51 million dollars. I agree with Gabby. If something is too good to be true, be very, very careful. My investors will be more than satisfied."

"What did Jason do?" Jackson asked. His expression was back to normal, except his eyes. They had a haunted faraway look.

"Full disclosure," Ted answered. "Before I sold, I called Jason and told him exactly what I was doing. I don't know what he decided." Ted walked over to the coffee urn and filled up his cup. He walked back to the table and sat down. "Also, we," he motioned to the four of them, "never discussed an aspect of my business that most people don't know. You all brought this opportunity to me. Often, I have an agreement with the broker to get a finder's fee. Because this was your first foray into this type of investment, you didn't know that." He reached into his jacket pocket and took out four envelopes. Ceremoniously, he stood up, walked around the table, and handed each of the puzzled young adults an envelope. "Please," he said. "Do me the honor of opening them."

In each envelope was a check for $275,000.

"That's the equivalent of 2% of the profit," Ted said. "Again, I want to thank all of you for your trust."

The four of them stood, faced Ted, and clapped. Tanya ran over to her father, wrapped her arms around his neck and gave him the same kind of squeeze she used to give him when she was three years old. At this moment in time, he was once again her superhero.

• • • •

WHEN GABBY AND JACKSON walked in the front door of their home, Gabby pointed to the sofa in the living room. "Please sit down," she said. "We need to talk."

"Later, please," Jackson said, almost in a whisper. "I just want to take a nap. I didn't sleep well last night."

Gabby glanced at her watch. "It's 4 o'clock. Let's have dinner at 6. I'll make pasta and a salad. Then we'll talk, okay?"

"Okay," he said in a monotone, and trudged up the stairs to their bedroom.

At 7 PM, after all the dishes were washed, each holding a glass of wine, they sat down in the living room. Jackson sat frozen on the sofa, facing Gabby who sat on a side chair.

All through dinner Jackson hardly said a word. Gabby didn't push him but tried her best to start a conversation. Jackson wouldn't engage. Couldn't engage. His expression reminded her of pictures she'd seen of concentration camp survivors, haunted and terribly depressed.

"Jackson, please tell me what's going on. We just made over a million dollars, and you look exactly like you looked when Nelson died. Well, when we thought he died."

Jake just looked at her and shrugged, a helpless gesture that brought tears to her eyes.

"You are the most articulate man I ever met. It's why you can write novels, have your characters fill the pages with their thoughts, come up with dozens of scenarios. Pitch an investment scenario that has Morrie in awe of you. Please, honey, don't wall me out. Don't create an impossible situation like you did before we broke up. You say you love me. Talk to me."

"I do love you. More than anything. I never want to live without you. I can't live without you."

"I love you too. Whatever's wrong, we'll deal with it. I would do anything to help you." She got up and sat next to Jackson, then reached over and held both his hands.

"I know you would, and I'd do anything to help *you*. But there's nothing you or anyone can do. It's hopeless..." He turned to Gabby and tears filled his eyes. "I had this fantasy that CLEO would skyrocket." Jackson shook his head and covered his face with his hands.

"It did skyrocket, Jackson. We have enough money to buy a home. It would have taken forever to save this kind of money. Over a million dollars! Please explain what you're referring to."

"I wanted to help Nelson. CLEO needed to go high enough so we'd have ten million dollars, enough to repay 14K. Get him out of their clutches."

"Oh, honey," Gabby said, putting her arm across his shoulders and smoothing his hair. "You're a good man, but that was a fantasy."

"What if tomorrow it goes up tenfold? Then there would be enough."

"What if it doesn't? Are you upset that we sold too quickly? Even Ted sold 80%. He's very savvy. Right?"

"I know. I don't trust myself anymore. My judgement is flawed. How can I even be involved in running *West Coast Investment Trust 20?*" He swiped the tears away from his eyes with the back of his hand. "If anyone knew the screwed-up decisions I've made, they'd put all their money in ETFs or better yet, under a mattress."

Gabby took out her phone, checked an app, and said, "You know, that unlike stocks and bonds in the U.S., cryptocurrency is traded 24/7. Wanna guess what it is now?"

"150, right?" He shut his eyes, waiting for the worst.

"No. $12.05. Down more than 3 clicks from where we sold."

"See," Jackson pointed out. "I'd have held on for dear life and watched as it circled down the drain into the sewer. Thank God, you have common sense."

"Doesn't a million dollars cheer you up even a little?"

"Not really. Either way, what I wanted the money for didn't happen. It wasn't even close." Jackson stood up. "Don't be angry with me, Gabby. I just want to go to sleep. I'll feel better in the morning."

Helplessly, Gabby watched Jackson slowly stagger away.

The next two weeks, Jackson functioned as if everything was fine, but Gabby knew he wasn't close to being fine. He remained closed off and refused to discuss anything of consequence. Even bringing up how to invest their new-found wealth fell on deaf ears. Never once did CLEO rise above 8. One day it even fell to 5.

Gabby called Jason to check on how he was doing. Jason was upbeat and very excited. He reported that on the day of the IPO, after he spoke to Ted, he also sold 80% of his ownership in CLEO. It made him a very, very wealthy man. He was currently in multiple discussions with other cryptocurrency entre-preneurs. They were intent on purchasing the rights to his algorithm. So, what now? Gabby asked him. Not sure, Jason answered, but I have another idea that I've been working on. It'll take a bit to develop. Gabby congratulated him and told him to keep in touch. Jason thanked her and said he never could have ac-complished this without all their support.

When Gabby told Jackson, he just shook his head in shame. "If you hadn't taken charge and sold everything, we'd have nothing."

"We still would have quadrupled our money," Gabby said.

"Please don't patronize me," Jackson responded in an angry tone, and stalked upstairs to the bedroom. It was 4 PM. He stayed up there all evening and didn't come down for dinner.

The next morning, Gabby called Todd.

CHAPTER 38

G abby sat at the kitchen table; her hands wrapped around a cup of tea that had long ago gone cold. She glanced anxiously at the front door. When the bell rang, she jumped up and opened the door.

Todd stepped inside and hugged Gabby. "Sorry things aren't going well, Gabby."

She shrugged. "Like a drink – wine, coffee, tea, water?"

"No thanks. I'm fine." He followed her into the living room, and they sat down. "So, tell me what's going on?"

"I'm overwhelmed. Ever since CLEO's IPO, Jackson's been withdrawn. He was counting on making a profit of 10 million dollars to help Nelson get out of the clutches of 14K. No matter what I say, he reverts to blaming himself. Earning a windfall million dollars seems to mean nothing to him. He says that he wouldn't have sold CLEO when the rest of us did, in the hopes that it would keep rising exponentially. He keeps repeating that he's incompetent to run the fund we started. That if people knew the way he behaved, they'd be better off putting their money under a mattress."

"Is he sleeping?"

"He spends a lot of time in the bedroom, even during the day. He just lies there in the dark. At night, around 4 AM, I hear him wandering around the house."

"Eating?"

"He must have lost at least ten pounds. When we sit down for a meal, he moves the food around his plate but hardly touches it."

"Sex?"

"Nothing." Gabby laughs harshly. "He has absolutely no interest in me."

"Are you afraid he'll hurt himself?"

Gabby shook her head. "I don't think so."

"Is he tired?"

"He complains constantly of being exhausted."

"Has he shown any interest in writing, working out, or doing anything that's fun? Reading? Watching TV?"

"As far as I can tell, he does almost nothing but stare into space."

Todd nodded and sighed. "Is it okay if I talk to him?"

"Of course, but I don't think he'll agree to talk to you." She pointed upstairs.

Todd stood up and headed for the stairs. "I'll do my best."

"Make a right at the top of the landing. Our room is at the end of the hall."

Todd went upstairs and stood in front of the closed bedroom door. He knocked. No response. He knocked again. Still nothing. He opened the door and stepped into the dark room. "Jackson, you awake?" he asked, his voice barely above a whisper. "It's Todd."

"I'm sleeping, Todd. I don't want to talk." Jackson's voice was raspy.

"Yeah, I figured that. You mind if I turn on a light?"

No answer. Todd flipped on the wall switch.

Jackson lay under the covers, the blanket over his head.

"Jesus, Jackson. You look like a lump."

No answer.

"C'mon, Jackson. Stop hiding."

"Todd, I'm not in the mood. Just go."

"I'm not going anywhere until we talk."

"Fuck you, Todd. I'm not talking. Go shrink somebody else."

"Gabby called me. Told me what was going on."

"She exaggerates."

"She's worried about you and rightly so."

No answer.

"Jackson, you're my friend. If truth be known, probably my only friend. Please crawl out from under the covers and talk to me. I believe I can help you. Your problem is one that I deal with all the time."

"Sorry, Todd. There is no help. Thanks for coming, but please leave."

"If after I say my piece, and you still want me to leave, I will. Okay? I saved your ass up on Nine North and you trusted me. Trust me again. The worst that happens is that you're right and no one can help you, even me."

Jackson reluctantly pulled down the covers and sat up on the side of the bed. He was still dressed in jeans and a sweatshirt.

Todd shook his head and frowned.

"What's with the look?"

"Fully dressed under the covers at 7 PM. No problem?"

"You know, Todd, you're an asshole," Jackson said wryly.

"That, my friend, is food for another discussion."

"Fine. So, what do you have to say?"

"Gabby described what you've been doing and not doing over the last few weeks. Ready? Here goes... Constant fatigue. Up at 4 AM unable to sleep. That's called early morning awakening. Emotional withdrawal. Weight loss – about ten pounds. Loss of interest in almost everything. No interest in sex – I don't blame you on that one, Gabby is really unattractive –"

"Fuck you, Todd."

"Fuck you back, Jackson. I'll continue. Self-incrimination. Loss of confidence. Depression. What you have has a name, buddy. It's called a Major Depression."

"So now you finally have a reason to put me on drugs?"

"It's possible, but unlikely. Gabby also said that you're very upset because you didn't raise the ten million dollars that you imagine Nelson needs to buy back his freedom. You were counting on CLEO going through the roof and saving your brother. I'm condensing a bit. Anything I have wrong?"

"Fuck you, Todd," Jackson said, and sighed deeply.

"Is that a yes, or a no?"

Jackson massaged his scalp, got up, and walked around the room. He stretched and sat back down on the side of the bed. "All right. Everything you said is true. Happy?"

"Ecstatic. You made my day. I have a theory. Want to hear it?"

"Do I have a choice?"

"Not really. Every person I've treated with the symptoms that you has had one thing in common, unidentified rage. Not just simple anger. Plus, and this is important. They don't know that they're angry."

"What are you talking about?"

"You're furious with Nelson."

"That's bullshit!" Jackson yelled. "Nelson was a terrific brother. When our parents died, he was everything to me. Mother, father, friend... He paid for Penn. Cash money out of his own pocket. Without him, I'm not sure I would have survived. For sure, I wouldn't have gone to an Ivy League college."

"That's why it gets complicated. Not only are you furious with him; you also love him."

"You got one thing right, I do love him." Tears filled Jackson's eyes.

"How 'bout the fact that he took investors' money and got in bed with one of the most nefarious gangs on the planet?"

"He didn't know that he was getting involved with them," Jackson retorted, glaring at Todd.

"What about due diligence? Shouldn't that have been part of his research? Look at all Ted did before he took CLEO public. No stone unturned. Right? He obviously loves Tanya, but he did his own research. Made his own, professional decision."

"Fuck you, Todd. Nelson made a mistake. Anybody can make a mistake."

"This wasn't just a mistake. I was there with you when Nelson admitted that he was greedy. His greed got his brother-in-law killed. Almost got you killed."

"That's unfair. He didn't know... Nelson didn't know," Jackson said in a whisper.

"The problem, Jackson, is that on some level he did know. He just wanted the money. He wanted to be rich."

"What's wrong with that?" He pointed to Todd and himself. "We wanted to be rich, too."

"Of course, we did. But we told the truth and did our due diligence. Did you lie to Jason?"

"No."

"We were careful. Used a known professional to help us. We did absolutely *nothing* that would hurt anyone. Do you lie to the people who invest in your fund?"

"Nelson didn't know what he was doing! He didn't know," Jackson repeated, taking deep breaths, trying to catch his breath.

Todd just listened patiently.

"Why the fuck didn't he know?" Jackson mumbled, more to himself than to Todd. "He should have known! He should have! He wasn't stupid. Why the hell wasn't he more careful? If he just looked a little below the surface, it was clear that the whole scheme was shady."

Todd nodded in agreement.

"He ruined his life, and...mine." Jackson pointed to his beard. "Now, I've got to spend the rest of my life as Jackson Wolfe. Jake Bennett died. He's gone."

Jake sat on the side of his bed and lowered his head. "Please Todd, I just can't talk anymore. Maybe in a few days. Can you give me that?"

"Of course. Tell you what. How 'bout we meet at UCLA in two days?" He looked at his iPhone. "Late lunch on Friday at 2? I'll text you where to meet."

"Okay. Thanks, Todd," Jake said, his face in his hands.

Todd walked downstairs. Gabby was waiting at the bottom of the steps.

"What's wrong with him, Todd?"

"He blames himself for not helping Nelson."

"What's going to happen?"

"We're meeting on Friday at UCLA. I think that it would be best if he took a few days off and not distract himself with work. Let him be immersed with his thoughts and feelings."

"He won't hurt himself, will he?"

"No. It's nothing like that. He just needs time to reflect."

CHAPTER 39

That evening, Gabby convinced Jackson to take a few days off. They agreed that she'd tell Morrie that he had the flu and didn't want to infect anyone.

Thursday morning, at 9 AM, three hours after Gabby left for work, Jackson got in his BMW, put down the top, and headed toward the beach in Santa Monica. He parked, walked down the California Incline, out to the concrete walkway and bike path. It ran south for miles, all the way to Venice, and north toward Malibu.

It was cloudy, the waves choppy, and a stiff sea breeze rustled his hair. He zippered up his sweatshirt, put his hands in his jeans, and headed north.

He thought about what Todd had said about him having a Major Depression. That all his symptoms were explainable. That he was furious with Nelson.

How could that be? It made no sense. After all that Nelson did, how was it possible that he was angry at him? Todd had to be wrong in his thinking. He was a smart guy, but what he said made no sense.

Jackson walked for about a mile and decided to get a coffee at Back to the Beach, an outdoor restaurant with all the tables on the sand.

When the waitress seated him, he looked through the menu, and on a whim ordered blueberry pancakes and a plate of fruit. He was hungry for the first time in weeks.

As he sipped his coffee, ate his breakfast, and stared at the gray ocean, he remembered an incident in Hong Kong. He was waiting for Nelson at a restaurant on Hong Kong Island. He waited for over an hour, tried calling Nelson, but it went right to voice mail. Finally, he ordered dinner, ate it, and went back to the hotel. That night, Nelson didn't come home. At 10 AM, Nelson came back to the hotel, acting like nothing happened.

"Where the hell were you?" Jackson asked.

"I was out for the night. What's the big deal?"

"I waited for over an hour at the restaurant. Why didn't you at least call?"

Nelson shrugged. "I forgot all about it. Sorry." He washed up and changed his clothes. "Got a business meeting. I'll let you know my status around 5." Then he left.

And that was it. He called at 5. Said he had more meetings and would see him in the morning.

Jake waved to the waitress, a college-age girl, and she came over. "More coffee," he barked.

The waitress looked shocked.

As she walked away, Jake said, "Please come back. Why did you look at me that way?"

She shook her head and didn't say anything.

"Please, tell me. It's important."

"Look, I need this job. Really need it." Her eyes were wide, and she looked like she was on the verge of crying.

Jake reached in his pocket and took out three twenties. "This is for breakfast and a tip. I need you to *please* tell me why you looked at me that way. I'm not angry at you. I'm just confused."

The waitress took a deep breath. "It's not what you said. It was your tone. You barked at me like I was a dog. A low life. I don't want to have to put up with that."

"And you shouldn't..." Jake closed his eyes for a second and sighed. "Please accept my sincere apology. I'm going through a rough patch, and I took it out on you. You're an excellent waitress. My meal was served promptly, and it was piping hot. Believe me, I've been treating a lot of people poorly. Maybe with your help, I'll do better."

The girl smiled and patted his arm. "Thank you, sir. I hope so. When I first came over to take your order, I wondered if you were okay. You looked so sad. I'll bring you a fresh cup of coffee."

Jackson smiled and looked at her nametag. "You're a perceptive person, Lola. Thank you, again."

Jackson sat and stared at the beach, the ocean, and all the people passing by, for another hour.

When he left the restaurant, the thought crossed his mind that maybe Todd was right. Where was all this anger coming from?

• • • •

ON THURSDAY MORNING, Jackson returned to the beach and rented a bicycle. He rode for almost two hours. On Washington Blvd. in Venice, he found a bar steps from the sand, and enjoyed a beer and a chicken and cheese quesadilla.

When the waitress handed him a bill, he said, "Thank you for your excellent service," and gave her a large tip.

• • • •

FRIDAY AT 3 PM, HE met Todd at the outdoor restaurant next to the Ronald Reagan Medical Center.

They ordered salads and crispy French bread. As they ate, Jackson shared what happened over the last two days.

"What do you make of it?" Todd asked.

"You were right. I was angry. I never talk to people the way I talked to that young waitress. I was an asshole. I'm still not exactly sure where it's coming from."

Todd sipped his water, not saying anything.

"You said I was angry at Nelson."

Todd nodded.

What Nelson did was selfish," Jackson mumbled.

"It was," Todd answered softly. "But, and it's a big but, being selfish doesn't negate all the good he did for you."

"But how can I hate him and love him at the same time? I remember a term we learned in Psych 101 or whatever, ambivalence. I understand the concept, but it makes no sense. It's like I'm schizo."

"You're not. Ambivalence is perfectly normal and healthy. Love and hate exist in a parallel universe. It's the way the mind works," Todd shrugged. "The nature of the human beast."

Jackson looked at Todd, "You make this all sound so simple. Is it really that simple?"

"When you're dealing with a person who's basically healthy, it is pretty clear cut."

"You're saying I'm basically healthy?" Jackson said wryly.

"You're a basically healthy asshole."

Jackson chuckled, reached across the table and took Todd's hand in both of his. "Thank you."

"My pleasure."

"So, I'll be alright now?"

"Probably some ups and downs. Just remember that it's okay to hate someone you love."

"It's that simple?"

"Well, like I said, you're basically healthy. If you had an underlying bipolar disorder or a personality disorder, it would have been a whole different ballgame."

"Todd, you're really good at what you do. I'm beyond lucky that you're my friend."

"Thanks. I'm also beyond lucky to have you as *my* friend. For me to accumulate the million dollars that's sitting in the bank would have taken half a lifetime. How'd you do that? It was like magic."

Jackson sighed. "Just like you're good at helping people with depression and anxiety, etcetera, I'm good at figuring out how to invest and make money. I just never knew how good. Plus, discovering Jason, who's a true genius, was more luck than skill. And don't forget Gabby, who did major research and got Tanya in on the deal. Without her, who knows if Ted would've signed on or even talked to us?"

"Alright, Jackson, setting your humility, decency, and sense of fairness aside, let's just agree that we're both wonderful. Yeah?" Todd chuckled.

CHAPTER 40

When he got home, Jackson put his arms around Gabby and kissed her on the lips. "I love you. I'm sorry I was so impossible to deal with."

"Why? If you can, please explain it to me. The last three weeks were a nightmare."

"It was a nightmare for both of us. The good news is that for the first time in weeks my appetite is back. I'm eating up a storm. How 'bout we make omelets, toast bagels, and brew coffee?"

Gabby looked at her watch. It's only 5 o'clock. Then she smiled. "Okay. I'll make the omelets. You make the coffee and bagels. Then you'll tell me everything! Agreed?"

"Of course," Jackson answered and hugged her again.

When Jackson finished eating, and he ate everything including the uneaten parts of Gabby's bagel and omelet, Gabby looked at him and said, "So? What in God's name happened, honey? Start at the beginning."

"You know that I blamed myself for not being able to save Nelson. When we only made a measly million dollars on CLEO instead of ten million, I felt hopeless and like a failure. Logically, I knew that I was being unreasonable, but I just wanted to sleep, to hide, to crawl under the covers. I had enough energy to go to work and pretend that everything was fine, but not a moment passed that I didn't feel washed out and exhausted.

"Todd diagnosed me with a Major Depression. He listed every symptom that makes up the diagnosis, and I hit the jackpot. I had them all. He also pointed out that not only did I love Nelson, but I hated him. Really hated him. Nelson lied and almost got me killed. We had to change our identities. Can't see your family. And on and on. But, because Nelson was so good to me – paid for Penn, was a good brother, a parent surrogate, blah, blah – I couldn't accept my anger. I...I took it out on myself. The last two days, just being alone, thinking, going to the beach, was helpful. I was mean to a nice little waitress at Back to the Beach. When I pleaded with her to tell me what I did, she said that I barked at her like she was a dog. It validated that Todd was right, about me having pent-up anger."

Gabby teared up.

Jackson got up and embraced her. "I don't know what I'd do without you. Even in the depths, there was never a doubt about how much I love you."

As Jackson sat back down at the table, Gabby said, "As you were talking, what came to mind was that time when we broke up. You were so insufferably stubborn. You refused to get a decent job and at the same time write. I never suggested that you not be a writer, but for you it was all or nothing. No compromise."

Jackson stared intently at Gabby and slowly nodded.

"Wasn't that around the same time when Nelson pretended to die?"

"Yes."

"Is it related?"

"You mean Nelson's death and my behavior?"

Gabby nodded, affirmatively.

"I just got goosebumps. Maybe you're on to something?"

"What are you thinking?"

"A year ago, the way I acted was crazy. Rejecting you, your family, my degree in economics...and for what – to work as a waiter while I obsessively focused on a longshot at publishing a novel. I knew when you confronted me and said that I could work *and* write that you were right. Why couldn't I agree to a perfectly reasonable compromise? You accepted my desire to write and simply needed me to accept that you wanted a home, kids, decent cars, all the things that any healthy person would want." Jackson choked up. "All the things that I also want. And it gets even crazier. In all the time we were apart there was never *anyone* else that I wanted to spend my life with. It was always you, from the second we met. So, your question is an excellent one. Why did I do what I did?" Jackson shrugged. "Why do you think?"

"The truth?"

"Yes."

"I've never said this before. Nelson was a nice guy, but somewhat of a bully."

"A bully?"

"If you didn't do what he wanted, he got distant and rejecting. Were you aware of that?"

"No... Maybe? I knew something was off, but I didn't spend time thinking about it."

"Jackson, he was manipulative."

"Hmm. When I was a senior in high school, we had a major argument about me having a curfew. I was almost 18 years old, and he demanded that I be back in the house by midnight. I told him to go fuck himself. He said, and I quote, if I kept fighting with him about it, he'd ask me to leave, to live on my own. To keep the peace, I agreed. But it didn't really matter because often Nelson never even came home at night. He was dating a lot.

"There was no compromise. It was his way or war. This is so weird. I'm sure Todd would have a field day with this factoid. My last novel is entitled, CAIN'S BROTHER. It's a story about the conflict between two brothers. Good versus evil."

Gabby took Jackson's hand in hers. "Do us both a favor and talk some more to Todd. What you just told me is *really* interesting."

• • • •

A FEW DAYS LATER, AT Nate and Al's deli, in Beverly Hills, Jackson and Todd enjoyed a late lunch of roast beef sandwiches. Jackson told Todd everything that he'd shared with Gabby.

"How do you feel, buddy?" Todd asked.

"Back to normal, thanks to you. Energetic. Sleeping well. Able to concentrate again. Driving Gabby a little crazy with the return of my libido," Jackson said with a laugh, and Todd joined him. "But I'm intrigued by this whole process. I mean, let's face it, even the title of my book is right out of Freud's playbook. CAIN'S BROTHER. Don't you think?"

Todd nodded. "You're on to something. Was Nelson always pushy?"

"I think so. After our parents died, for a while we were both in a state of shock. Then he clearly took over the parenting role. Somehow, he forgot that I was a senior in high school and treated me like I was thirteen. When I blew up and demanded that he back off, he was a little better. But as I think about it, I remember that I was always tiptoeing around him. Watching what I said, omitting anything that I thought might provoke him."

"What happened after his so-called *death*?"

"Whatever Gabby suggested, I refused. No matter how reasonable the request."

"Hmm. You acted the same way Nelson did. Your way or the highway."

"Honestly, Todd. I was nuts. Who in their right mind would walk away from someone like Gabby? She loved me and was willing to bend way more than fifty percent. I was a stubborn idiot."

"What about this theory? How 'bout instead of losing Nelson, you became him? It solved the problem. If you are him, then he never died."

"Todd, I knew he died? I wasn't in denial or anything like that."

"Think of it this way. The conscious part of your mind only accepted the loving feelings toward Nelson. The other part of your mind, the unconscious part, became Nelson. Nobody, including Gabby, was going to tell you what to do. Period. Also, your unconscious was a prime force in writing CAIN'S BROTHER. Two brothers who spent their lives battling each other. A combination of love and hate."

Jackson sat with a stunned expression on his face.

"What are you thinking?"

"It's so interesting. Since I've been back with Gabby and working in economics, the field that I actually got my degree in, I haven't written a word. Well, a lot of prospectus-writing and economic clarifications, but no fiction. It never crossed my mind to get back to that. It blows my mind.

"Todd. I've had a complete psychoanalysis in the last week." He laughed. "Why does it take some people hundreds of hours on the couch? Years of teasing all this out."

"That's a good question. I think it's because you and Gabby are such a perfect match. I sense zero ambivalence when it comes to her. If she was unavailable, I don't think any of this would matter. You'd be unhappy and searching to recreate what you once had with her. You're soulmates. Accepting that your feelings toward Nelson are a combination of love and hate is a lot easier when your life is going so well. You've achieved love, a great career, and a lot of money. By most standards you're a successful man."

"Plus, I got lucky and met you."

Todd laughed. "Well, that goes without saying."

Jackson laughed too. "Okay, buddy. Now it's my turn."

"What do you mean?"

"You helped me. Let me help you."

Todd looked a little baffled.

"You and Tanya have over a million dollars in the bank. What's the plan?"

"Not totally sure. Like I said, I want to pay off my school loans. That's about $205,000. And we've been looking at real estate. According to Ted's financial expert, we're pre-approved for a house worth $1,600,000. That's if we put $800,000 down."

"Fabulous," Jackson said. "How much is your monthly payment on the school loan?"

"About $450 a month."

"You know that Gabby and I developed an investment portfolio. If you really want to preserve and grow your wealth, *do not pay off your school loan!* As of this week, we have over 40 million dollars that we manage. If you invest $250,000 in a mixture of low beta and high beta investments, that means both low and high risk," Jake took out his phone calculator and punched in numbers, "You'd make an average somewhere between $800 and $2000 a month. That would net you between $600 and $1750 a month after paying off the monthly amount of the school loan. If the fund goes as well as it is now, you could possibly walk away with an extra $18,000 a year, give or take. If you then take the standard deduction, which is $10,000, the money will just about be tax free."

Todd looked a little shocked.

"So, I know that you want to be debt free. But this is an alternative way to pay off your debt and grow your wealth. Student loans are by nature very low in terms of percentages charged. Investing in equities, if they're chosen correctly, can over the long haul make you and Tanya wealthier. Do you know how much interest you're paying on your school loan?"

"Yeah. I just got all the details, 2.5%."

"See what I mean? If you can earn four or five times that, why not?"

"But the market isn't a sure thing."

"True. But with your new job, $450 a month won't be that big a deal. Better that the quarter of a million remains under *your* control. How many years would it take for you to accumulate $250,000?"

"A long time." Todd took out his phone calculator and punched in some numbers. "Maybe five years? Probably more."

"A quarter of a million dollars is a lot of money. Wouldn't it be better to take somewhat of a risk, and I'll make sure you understand the risk, before you pay off a low interest student loan?"

"What kind of risk are you talking about, Jackson?"

"First, whatever you decide to do, it'll all be through IBC, a first-class organization." Jackson then went into detail explaining all the choices that Todd had, and how he could concentrate on his career while the investments worked for him.

"Jackson, where do you and Gabby have your money?"

"At this minute, like you, everything is in the bank earning just about nothing. But now that I'm feeling better, it won't be long until we do what I'm recommending that you do. I'm going to email you and Tanya the prospectus. Read it over. Talk to Ted."

Jackson's phone rang. It was Gabby. "One second, Todd. It's Gabby."

"Honey, when will you be home?"

"Why? What's wrong?" Jackson caught his breath.

"Mordecai Toland is here."

"Who?"

"He and his wife own the house where we're living. He wants to talk to both of us."

CHAPTER 41

When Jackson walked in the house, Gabby and a heavy-set man with a full beard, a yarmulka, and a black suit were sitting in the living room, each holding a coffee cup. The man immediately stood up and smiled when he saw Jackson.

"I'm Mordecai Toland," he said, and held out his hand.

Jackson shook it. "Hi, Mordecai. I'm Jackson. It's a pleasure to meet you. Your generosity in letting us stay in your home was more than we could have hoped."

"It was a mitzvah, Jackson. And thank you for paying the rent in such a prompt manner and also paying for the first few months, which was a welcome surprise."

"It was our pleasure."

"Honey, would you like some coffee, tea or something to drink?" Gabby offered.

"No thanks. I just finished lunch. To what do we owe this visit, Mordecai?" he asked, motioning for Mordecai to sit down, as he took a seat next to Gabby on the sofa.

"I was just telling Gabby that I was offered a new job, Chairman of the Department of Jewish Studies at NYU. We have family back in New York and have decided to accept the offer."

"Congratulations! What an honor."

"Thank you. So, to get to the point, I'm here to tell you that we're putting the house up for sale. Also, I want to propose an offer. I did some research and spoke to a realtor friend. Believe it or not, our house is worth $1,100,000. A house, just around the corner, very similar to this house, just went on the market, also for $1,100,000. If you take into consideration realtor fees, which come to $55,000, our net would be $1,045,000. So, my proposal is that if you want to purchase the house, we'll charge $1,045,000. You save realtor fees. We eliminate the stress of listing it. Are you interested?"

Jackson and Gabby looked at each other. Gabby said, "Would you give us a few minutes? Make yourself comfortable. We'll go upstairs and make a decision."

"Of course. Please, take your time."

. . . .

JACKSON AND GABBY SAT down on the bed in the master. "Wow," Jackson said. "What do you want to do?"

"I want to buy the house."

"Really?"

"I love it here. The house is comfortable, open, airy, convenient to shopping and work, to the Farmers' Market. It's so bright we almost never need to turn on the lights during the day. I like the neighbors, the ladies especially. Most importantly, it feels safe living here. There are a half-dozen women I can call on to help with anything I need...like babysitting," she said with a mischievous grin.

"What?" Jackson exclaimed.

The mischievous grin never left Gabby's face.

"Are you telling me that you're pregnant?"

"I just tested myself. We're having a little baby, Wolfe."

Jackson's eyes went wide with surprise. Seconds later tears rolled down his cheeks. "That's wonderful. Beyond wonderful," he choked out, and embraced Gabby. "I'm the luckiest man alive."

"And I'm the luckiest woman. Do you like it here, too?"

"I've been too busy being crazy to think about it, but as I reflect on our life, I've enjoyed it, a lot. Everyone's been nice. Morrie's a gem. The house is great. It's bright, sunny, quiet, three bedrooms. I'd be proud to own this house. But what about you being a shiksa, in the midst of a community of Jewish women?"

"From my experience, Judaism is a religion that doesn't proselytize and is accepting of other points of view. Like I said, the women I've met are wonderful. Smart, sensitive, giving. They've embraced me. My being Italian seems like no big deal to them."

"Okay, let's buy it. But one other thing." He knelt in front of Gabby and said, "Will you marry me?"

"A very tricky question. Let me think about it," Gabby said seriously, scrunching up her forehead. She waited five beats and apologetically said, "I've always wanted to marry a French Resistance fighter. I just don't know."

"How 'bout an investment broker and former waiter? I know a lot about pasta and can pour wine really well."

"Interesting... A good wine pourer is my second choice. Should I go for being realistic or wait around for my first choice?"

"Tough call," Jackson said with a cocky smile.

Gabby teared up. "I'm trapped, no way out. You're the only man I'd want to spend the rest of my life with. I love you."

"I love you too." Jackson stood up and took Gabby in his arms.

They sat back down on the bed. "So, what do we offer, Mordecai?" Gabby asked.

"How 'bout we offer $1,010,000?"

Gabby thought for a moment. "How 'bout I open a bottle of wine, get some cheese and crackers, and we offer $1,000,000? All cash."

"All cash. Hmm. How much do we have in the bank?"

Gabby punched in the banking app on her phone. "$1,300,000 and change."

"That much?"

"On top of the CLEO miracle, we've stashed away over $50,000. We'll also have enough to handle most of the taxes."

"That's amazing. What if Mordecai won't budge?"

"I vote we pay what he wants. I really do love the house."

"I have an idea. Let me present our offer, okay?" Jackson asked.

"Of course. I've heard that wine pourers make excellent businesspeople."

Smiling, they kissed again and walked downstairs.

Mordecai was standing, looking out the window. He turned when he saw Gabby and Jackson and smiled. "Please sit," Jackson said. "We have a counter-offer."

"Of course." Mordecai sat down and looked up expectantly.

"Give me a minute," Gabby said. "Do you drink wine and do you like cheese and crackers?"

Mordecai patted his stomach. "I do."

Minutes later, they were sipping Justin cabernet.

"Delicious," Mordecai said, putting another slice of cheder on a cracker.

"Like Rabbi Avrum Goldstein told us, 'Sometimes, God works in mysterious ways,' Jackson said, and put down his glass of wine on the coffee table. "My brother died recently..." Jackson's eyes teared up and he took a few deep breaths.

"I'm sorry," Mordecai responded.

"Thank you, Mordecai. It was a difficult time, but with Gabby's help I'm doing better. So, when we first moved here, we had nothing. You were so kind to let us live here until we got on our feet. We owe you and your wife a lot. Again, thank you."

Mordecai nodded his head in acknowledgement.

"My brother wasn't a rich man, but his estate left everything to me. What we'd like to offer is $1,000,000. All cash. We accept the house as is. No need to fix anything. We'll waive all the inspections. Close escrow whenever you want. As soon as the papers can be drawn up and signed."

Mordecai nodded thoughtfully. "If you can go up to 1,020,000, we have a deal."

Jackson looked at Gabby and then at Mordecai. "How about we split the difference? $1,010,000. If you want, you can use your realtor friend? Let's also split what he charges for his time. We can even do this tonight if you want. Only one other request. The terms of our deal remain confidential."

Smiling, Mordecai stood up, and shook Jackson and Gabby's hands. "I accept. How about we get together tomorrow at 11AM? I'll bring my wife, the realtor, and all the paperwork. Please check with your bank about wire transfers." Mordecai picked up his glass of wine, finished it, and with a smile on his face, said goodbye and left.

After Mordecai was gone, Gabby said, "Jackson, I was surprised that you brought up Nelson's death. Was that a ploy to get Mordecai to come down in price?" She was obviously confused.

"No! That would be low and manipulative. What happened was that it struck me how after I spoke with Todd, I needed to accept the fact that Nelson is out of my life. If I attempt to find him, not only am I risking his life and his family's life, but I'm risking our lives. All three of us." He patted Gabby on her tummy. "Loving Nelson means letting him go. Saying Kaddish for him. Saying goodbye, forever. He made a bad decision. He seemed happy until I tracked him down and placed him in jeopardy. Also, would it really be helpful to give 14K, 10 million dollars? Who's to say that they wouldn't take the money and then kill us? Trusting vicious sociopaths is stupid. From now on, I'm not going to be stupid. I love my brother but fixing what he did is outside of my power."

CHAPTER 42

O
ne week later, laughing and kissing, Jackson carried Gabby across the threshold of their home. They had just left the notary's office. The papers were signed, and the money transferred. They were now official homeowners.

"Okay, you take it easy. I'll get dinner ready," Jackson said, glancing lovingly at Gabby. "Todd and Tanya will be here in about an hour."

"This pregnant gig is really working," Gabby said with a laugh.

"You're right. I'll even open and pour the wine."

"I knew it! Marrying an expert wine pourer was a brilliant move. Too bad little junior Wolfe will only let me have a few sips."

Laughing, they prepared spaghetti bolognaise and a big salad.

When the doorbell rang, Gabby and Jackson opened it. Todd and Tanya stepped in the house and Todd lugged in a big box and put it on the dining room table. "What's this, Tanya?" Gabby asked.

"To celebrate your new home. May you enjoy love, safety, and good friends."

Jackson opened the box. Inside was a Sonos speaker system.

"The sound is spectacular. After dinner I'll help you set it up and we can all dance. Unless you don't like it..." Todd said, looking expectantly at his friends.

"We love it!" They both said and embraced them.

"I've never really seen your home, except for the living room," Tanya said. "Please take us on a tour."

• • • •

AS THEY FINISHED THE meal, Jackson looked at Todd, and said, "What's wrong? You look a little under the weather."

"We got a sharp dose of reality this afternoon. Prices in Hermosa Beach and Redondo Beach are insane. We didn't even bother looking in Manhattan Beach because it's even more pricey. A tiny two-bedroom cottage, six or seven blocks from the beach, east of PCH, needing a lot of fixing-up, is *over* $1,500,000. A house like yours, with three bedrooms and around 2500 square feet is well over $2,500,000. And, there would be a bidding war for it."

Tanya chimed in, "And believe me, it wouldn't be anywhere near as lovely and charming as your house. I love your home! You two are so lucky. For $2,500,000, you get a fixer that needs a lot of work. We'd be mortgaged over our eyeballs."

Gabby looked pensive. She said, "If you two would consider moving to this area, there's a house around the corner. It just went up for sale."

"What's it listed for?" Todd asked.

"$1,050,000."

"You've got to be kidding me. We could buy it for cash." He grabbed Tanya's hand. "You could spend full time writing. We can easily live on what I make."

"That's what we did," Jackson said. "We paid cash. Didn't want a mortgage. We'll think about investing, like you and I talked about, after we're settled in a bit. The plan is for Gabby to work parttime when um..."

"We're pregnant," Gabby blurted out. "Just found out."

"Oh my God, congratulations," Tanya got up from the table and hugged Gabby. Todd pumped Jackson's hand. "Congratulations, buddy. What great news."

"That's why we need a decent size house," Tanya said. "Who knows when, but one day we'll be in the same place that you both are." She looked at Todd. "Are you committed to living at the beach, honey?"

"Not anymore. I like it here." He looked around. "I like your home, the area, the way that I feel when I see your neighbors. It brings back memories of living with Bernie and Rivka." He laughed. "Living here, I'll never have to explain again why I wear a yarmulka. It's also a lot closer to work than the beach. How 'bout you, Tan? Do you like it here?"

"It reminds me of living in The Village or Soho. A slice of New York City, but not too far from Beverly Hills, UCLA, and even the beach." She reached out and took Gabby's and Jackson's hand. "Being so close to you both would be wonderful."

"Do you want to see the house that's for sale?" Gabby asked.

Both Todd and Tanya nodded.

"Let me call Morrie. He knows everyone."

An hour later, the four of them walked down the street and headed around the corner. "How did you arrange this so quickly?" Tanya asked in awe.

"I mentioned to Morrie that the buyers, our best friends, can pay cash. Plus, they're able to close escrow tomorrow or whenever the seller wants."

Both Tanya and Todd laughed, nervously.

A tall Hassidic man met them outside the house. "Shalom," he said. "I'm Levi."

Gabby introduced them all. "Thank you so much for doing this at such short notice, Levi," she said.

Levi shrugged. "It's my pleasure. I asked the owners to step out for an hour so you can have a chance to get a better feeling for the house. You can't tell because it's dark, but during the day the house has a wonderful sunny exposure. The owners are both in their eighties and have lived here for thirty years. They are moving in with their daughter in Palo Alto."

After wandering through the house for half an hour, Todd said to Tanya, "It's bashert."

"Huh?"

"My grandmother said it many times. In Yiddish it means, destiny. The house needs updating. Kitchen appliances, bathrooms are dated, but...I really like it. How 'bout you?"

"I love it. I want this house, Todd. Let's buy it."

"Gabby," he called from across the living room. She walked over to where they were standing, in front of the stone fireplace. Todd whispered, "I'm going to make them an offer they can't refuse."

CHAPTER 43

S EVEN YEARS LATER

. . . .

GABBY WALKED PAST THE open bedroom door and smiled. Her six-year-old son was saying, "Daddy, tell us the genius story. 'Kay?" The room was dark, lit only by vague, ghost-like shadows from the small night light.

"Yes, yes, Daddy. Tell us that one," Gina echoed. Gina was four and for this special moment in time, she *always* agreed with her big brother, Nelson. They lay next to each other, Gina holding Nelson's hand. The story was scary, and Nelson would protect her.

"Shouldn't we ask our guests? Maybe they want a different story?" Jackson asked with a smile. He was still lean, athletic, and sported a carefully trimmed beard. He turned to Bernie and Becky, Todd and Tanya's two children, also lying next to each other on the second twin bed. They were each a few months younger than his two, and all four were inseparable. For that matter, both families were inseparable. "That's my favorite story in the whole world," Becky blurted out. "Please tell it, Uncle Jackson."

"How 'bout you, Bernie? What do you think?" Jackson asked.

"Yes! I love that story, Uncle Jackson."

Tears of joy filled Gabby's eyes. Who could have predicted, when she and Jackson harmlessly flirted so many years ago in class, that life would have turned out the way that it did?

"Okay, here we go. Everyone ready?"

"Yes!" all four children responded.

"Hold on to your magic blankets! Once upon a time, in a far-off magical land, there were four best friends – Nelso, Gino, Berno, and Becko."

"Are you sure they aren't us?" Becky blurted out.

"They are all the same ages that you are, but I'd have to say, no. This happened in La-La-Land. This is Los Angeles. But you have a good point. They are *very* similar." Jackson grinned.

Becky smiled and settled back against her pillow. Uncle Jackson couldn't fool her.

'So, back to our story. These four friends were all very special, so special that teachers and even professors from colleges like Berkeley, UCLA and–"

"That's where my daddy works," Bernie said. "He's a sicatrist."

"You're right. He's a wonderful psychiatrist and helps people who are sad or upset. UCLA is one of the best colleges in the country. He's a professor and teaches all the young doctors who want to be psychiatrists. Meanwhile, back to our story. Even teachers would have called the four friends, geniuses. But no one, not even their mommies and daddies, knew how really smart they were, because they *always* kept it a secret."

"What's a jeenis again, Uncle Jackson?" Becky asked.

"A genius is a very, very smart person."

Becky nodded to herself and snuggled closer to Bernie. "My mommy's a jeenis, too. She writes things that become movies."

"She is. I love what she writes," Jackson said. "Back to the four friends. They had invented something that no one in the entire world had ever invented. It was a special little box, the size of a peanut."

"That's really small, Daddy," Gina exclaimed.

"I know. In fact, it was so small that each child had one of the little boxes on a chain around his or her neck. And this is *really* important. They had a secret signal that only they knew. If one of them yelled, N G Double B, they all immediately squeezed the peanut box. It stood for, Nelso, Gino, Berno and Becko."

Nelson whispered, "And if they squeezed the box, they become invisible?"

"Exactly. You might wonder how four children invented something so amazing. Well, the answer is that they are all math geniuses. They figured it out by using special formulas and mixing a magic potion made from salt, orange juice, puppy fur, egg yolks, and peanut butter. They'd mix it all up and squeeze it into the little boxes."

"They could use Puffy's fur," Gina said.

When she heard her name, the 6-pound ball of white fluff, lying on the end of the bed, barked. Everyone laughed.

"So," Jackson continued. "One day, they were walking home from school when a medium-size truck pulled right beside them. Four ginormous men jumped out, grabbed each child and threw them in the truck. As the door closed, Becko yelled, N G, Double B! And there was a loud POOF. Can you guess what happened?"

Bernie said, "They became invisible!"

"That's right. And we'll find out tomorrow night what happened to those mean men when our heroes became invisible. The bad creeps had no idea what was in store for them."

"Uncle Jackson will we be here tomorrow night?" Becko asked.

"Of course. Remember your mom and dad are on vacation?"

"I remember."

"Yep. They went to Palm Springs for their anniversary. Boys you go to Nelson's room and get in bed. No fooling around. Okay?"

"Daddy. Can Mommy come in and give us kisses?" Gina asked.

"Of course."

"Maybe we'll be invisible, and she won't see us, Uncle Jackson," Bernie said, laughing.

"Anything's possible. Now scoot."

"Daddy, can mommy give us a kiss too?" Nelson asked.

"Of course. If I tried to stop her, she'd probably beat me up."

Everyone laughed, and the boys sprinted off to Nelson's room.

Jackson walked out in the hallway and into the master bedroom. Last month they bought new furniture, had new carpets installed, and added a 65-inch TV. Both he and Gabby still loved the house and the area. It had worked out better than either of them expected. Three years ago, he and Gabby signed an equal partnership contract with Morrie. They took over half a floor in the building and hired four associates. Their investment portfolio was verging on four-hundred-million dollars and the minimum initial investment was set at $250,000.

Pizza night had evolved into every other Sunday evening. It included Todd and Tanya's family, the Cohens from next door, also secular Jews, and Morrie's family. It was a raucous, kid-centric evening that had been going on for years. The expectation was that it would continue forever.

"Hey, Hon, where are you?" Jackson called.

Gabby came out of the bathroom, her eyes still red from crying.

"What's wrong?" he asked, suddenly on high alert.

She came over and hugged him. "Nothing. It scares me that everything is so good." She sniffled. "I heard you reading to the kids. You are amazing."

"It was just a bedtime story, honey."

"It's a story that they will never forget. A story that they'll tell their chil-dren."

"Well, I could tell them about the time I hid out in a psychiatric hospital from mass killers...but that's way too far-fetched. No one would ever believe it. Right?"

Gabby snuggled closer, wondering not for the first time if big Nelson would ever emerge from hiding. She left her husband's embrace and went to kiss all the children.

Whatever happened, they would deal with it.

Don't miss out!

Visit the website below and you can sign up to receive emails whenever ART SMUKLER publishes a new book. There's no charge and no obligation.

https://books2read.com/r/B-A-ADCU-JUDCC

BOOKS 2 READ

Connecting independent readers to independent writers.

Also by ART SMUKLER

The Real Story, A Mystery
NINE NORTH

Watch for more at artsmuklermd.com.

About the Author

Art Smukler is a board-certified psychiatrist, specializing in intensive psychotherapy. As a UCLA professor, he ran an award-winning conference and received the coveted "Golden Ear" award. He's published in psychiatric journals and won the Award for Excellence in creative writing at The Santa Barbara Writers Conference. Now a full-time author, he applies his comprehensive understanding of the human psyche to the motivations of his fictional characters. This is his fifth novel.

Read more at https://artsmuklermd.com.

Made in the USA
Las Vegas, NV
16 November 2022

59668249R00125